THE OTHER TWIN

ALSO BY SHALINI BOLAND

The Ex
The Birthday Party
The Honeymoon
The School Reunion
The Silent Bride
The Daughter-in-Law
A Perfect Stranger
The Family Holiday
The Couple Upstairs
My Little Girl
The Wife
One of Us Is Lying
The Other Daughter
The Marriage Betrayal
The Girl from the Sea
The Best Friend
The Perfect Family
The Silent Sister
The Millionaire's Wife
The Child Next Door
The Secret Mother
Marchwood Vampire Series
Outside Series
A Shirtful of Frogs

THE OTHER TWIN

SHALINI BOLAND

Published by Thomas & Mercer, Seattle

www.apub.com

Amazon, the Amazon logo, and Thomas & Mercer are trademarks of Amazon.com, Inc., or its affiliates.

EU Product Safety Contact:
Amazon Media EU S.à r.l.
38, avenue John F. Kennedy, L-1855 Luxembourg
amazonpublishing-gpsr@amazon.com

ISBN-13: 9781662529542
eISBN: 9781662529559

Cover design by The Brewster Project
Cover image: © Serg Zastavkin / Shutterstock; © Yevhenii / Adobe

Printed in the United States of America

*To my Friday Ladies who have been there through
it all*

Prologue

Her skin is waxy, her lips tinged blue. She's beautiful, lying on the concrete, so still in the darkness, eyes closed, hair splayed out to the side like a dark sunburst, blood pooling around her head. Shadows from the streetlamp and the shimmer of recent rain make the whole image surreal, like a movie set after the director has yelled cut and the extras have gone home.

I tiptoe around her, careful not to step in the blood, my hands steady, almost detached from the rest of me. I get low, nearly kneeling, lean over, and position my camera so that I can capture her face. So I can get a good image of the main event — the gunshot wound that has ruined her forehead.

My shoes make small, nervous squeaks against the wet pavement. Otherwise, it's quiet except for the distant hum of a car engine and the snap and whirr of my Polaroid camera.

I've been trying without the flash, hoping the streetlight will capture the subtlety, but it's too dim, the shadows swallowing all the colour. So I switch on the flash and the world jumps into hyper-reality, every pore and freckle and blood droplet seared into each photo.

Still, I'm critical. I think I'm too close. I take a few steps back and move around to the side. Flash, whirr, flash, whirr, the sounds rhythmic as a heartbeat. I feel a thrill, something dangerous and electric, coursing from my palms up my arms into my chest.

I've never done anything like this before. It's like acting. Like art. It's a different feeling. I like it. I'm focused on the details. The way her make-up has started to run, the flecks of mascara beneath her eyes. The longer I stay, the more I want to correct her pose, to shift her arm or drape her hair more elegantly, to remove the stray leaf stuck to her wrist that breaks the composition.

I think that should probably do it, but I take a couple more to be on the safe side. Better to have too many than too few, right?

I'm weirdly proud of the work, the way an amateur chef is proud of a well-executed soufflé, and I can't stop myself from shuffling through the photos, choosing favourites already. There are some good ones here, at least two that could win a photography contest, if only there were a category for this kind of thing.

I nod, satisfied.

Today has been a good day.

Chapter One

JADE

The north wind whistles down Blake Street, slicing through my thin denim jacket and setting my teeth on edge. I pull it tighter around my body. No time to stop and do it up properly, I'm late for my shift at The Oak, the grotty pub where I've worked for the past four years. It was meant to be a stopgap, but the months and years have somehow run away from me, and now I'm twenty-eight with no life plan aside from earning enough to pay the rent with a smidge left over for something other than bills or beans on toast.

I live on the outskirts of Southampton in a rundown, depressing suburb that's low on kerb appeal and high in crime. The Oak is only a fifteen-minute brisk walk from home, but I still always manage to be late. I think living so close by gives me a false sense of security. Mags won't be happy. She's threatened to sack me so many times, but never follows through because I'm good with the customers. It takes a certain type of person to cajole pissheads out the door at closing time and deflect lecherous creeps without sparking their anger. I guess I'm talented that way – lucky me.

Hurrying past familiar rows of bland terraced houses and flats, I intermittently check the dense, flowing traffic for a gap to cross, but the cars, buses, bikes and vans are whizzing by too fast and, annoyingly, there's no pedestrian crossing on this stretch of road, despite Mum's letters to the council about it.

Mum works at the same pub as me. She got me the job when I was unemployed, sweet-talked Mags into throwing a few shifts my way. I thought it would be too much – living and working with my mother – but it's actually panned out okay as Mags tries to stagger our shifts. That way, while Mum's at work, I get the flat to myself, and vice versa, like an unglamorous timeshare. Although we still see more of each other than we'd each like.

As it's a one-bedroom flat, I sleep on the sofa bed in the lounge, which is hardly ideal, but I guess I've become used to it over the years, and at least it's cheap. As a kid, we shared the bedroom, but I opted for the lounge once I reached fourteen. Mum isn't thrilled that I'm still at home, 'cluttering up the place', but she hasn't kicked me out – yet. I think she secretly savours the company, although you wouldn't know it to hear her moan about everything I'm doing wrong with my life. About how I should have worked harder at school, or how I should be more proactive and get a better job. Like she's one to talk!

The only thing less ideal than my home life is my relationship. Zac, my delivery-driver boyfriend, clocks insane hours – longer than mine, actually, but I don't let him know that. We like to engage in a lot of one-upmanship about whose life is the crappiest. He thinks I have it easy because I don't have impossible schedules and I don't have to deal with traffic, but at least he's not on his feet for hours, plus he's never had to mop out a men's bathroom after a football match.

Zac and I have been together for almost two years now. I wouldn't say he's 'the one', but we do okay. And he does bring me snacks from the petrol station when I'm feeling tired, which in my world is basically love.

I cling to the hope that we might be able to move out of our parents' homes one day soon and rent our own place, although I can't help but wonder if living together would ruin us. I'm worried he'd get on my nerves. I just have to weigh up whether he annoys me more than Mum does. If I'm being brutally honest, I'd prefer to live alone. I can't think of anything more luxurious than having my own apartment and being able to come home from work and shut the door on the world. To have peace and quiet whenever I want it, or to play my music loud without Mum telling me to turn it down. Earbuds just aren't the same as blasting it out through the speaker.

Power-walking the last stretch, I hope I can beat the rain. The clouds overhead are the colour of dull tin, smothering what little there was of the hopeful blue that promised more than it delivered. I can still feel the damp chill in my hair, which I twisted up into a messy bun after my shower in the hope it might dry by the time I get to work. No such luck.

The Oak comes into view on the opposite side of the road. It sits at the end of a drab parade of retail outlets – a newsagent's, dry cleaner's, fish and chip shop, a Tesco Express petrol station, a barber's, and a charity shop with a plastic skeleton in the window wearing a Santa hat, even though it's June. The only shop that's never changed is the one that sells doll's-house furniture. I never see any customers in there. Probably a money-laundering front.

Quickly checking the time on my phone, I see it's already five past five. So I'm officially late. I'm really going to have to cross this bloody road somehow. The traffic is now crawling – not quite gridlocked, but close enough that cars nudge forward in juddery increments. There's a line of buses, and the vinegary smell of chips hangs over the street like a greasy fog. I plant myself on the kerb and try my usual tactic – pick a driver, stare into their soul, and hope their innate British politeness will force them to let me cross. It works about one in twenty times – maybe today I'll get lucky.

That's when I spot the Range Rover. It's shiny, black, and obnoxiously expensive, the kind of car that glistens even on an overcast day. It creeps forward, indicator ticking, then slows to turn in to the Tesco petrol station opposite. I'm about to seize my moment and dart behind it, when something makes me pause. Maybe it's the way the windows are rolled down despite the cold, or the low bass of a song I don't recognise. But the car draws my attention, and that's when I see her – the passenger.

Mum. She's in the front seat, laughing with the man in the driver's seat. He looks like the worst kind of corporate cliché – navy suit, high-collared shirt, sunglasses despite the dark clouds. I can practically smell his expensive aftershave wafting across the street.

Mum, *my mum*, is sitting six inches away from this man, her face lit up in a way I don't think I've ever seen. I don't even recognise her at first, not really. Her hair is different – darker, glossier, ironed into careful waves, instead of her usual straw-blonde with grey roots. Has she splurged on extensions? *Is she wearing a wig?* She can't afford either. Unless her mystery man bankrolled it. There's a pop of pink on her cheeks, a new lipstick on plump lips, and a patterned scarf I've never seen before draped around her neck. Suddenly, Mum looks less like the woman who falls asleep in front of *Antiques Roadshow* with a microwaved curry, and more like a model for a Marks & Spencer ad.

Has she somehow got herself a new boyfriend? She told me she was going to Lidl after her shift. Mum always insists she isn't interested in romance. She says she likes being single. Why would she lie about that? My dad was out of the picture before I was born, and she hasn't had a relationship since – well, not one that I've ever known. And where the hell did she get the time to do all that primping? I only saw her this morning before she left for work. Unless she didn't go to work.

I stand here, invisible, as the Range Rover glides on to the petrol station forecourt. I'm rooted to the spot, watching as Mum leans across, her hand on the man's arm, both of them doubled over at some private joke. It's so surreal I half think I'm hallucinating it. Me, late for work while my mother's on a date – on an actual date – with a man who probably owns more cufflinks than the number of pints I'll pull tonight.

I take a step back and watch, heart thudding. They don't see me. Mum is close to the man, gesturing at something on his phone. From this distance, she looks . . . happy. Like, properly happy. I haven't seen that expression on her face – ever.

I twitch forward, thinking I'll catch Mum's eye, force her to see me, but she's lost in the man and whatever he's saying. I don't know whether to feel angry, or betrayed, or what? Mostly I just feel left out, like there's been a party and I wasn't invited.

Realising I've missed my chance to cross, I fling out a hand to try to stop the navy VW Golf that was a few cars behind the Range Rover, hoping the driver will take pity and let me through, but he flies past. I chance stepping off the pavement, but that earns me a blaring honk from a white van. I step back, flip the driver the middle finger, and glance over at the Range Rover, which, to my dismay, rather than stopping for fuel, is using the petrol station to do a slick U-turn.

I wave frantically, trying to get Mum's attention, but she's still locked in conversation with the driver, laughing. An Audi lets them out, and Mum waves a thank-you to the driver before they head off down the road, leaving me slack-jawed on the pavement I realise another white van has stopped near me, flashing its headlights to let me go.

I scowl. Typical that *now* someone lets me go. As I cross, the driver revs his engine and inches forward, trying to spook me. He and his passenger think they're being hilarious. Normally, I'd either flirt back or tell them to piss off, but I'm too distracted this evening. My gaze storms along the road, searching for the retreating taillights of the Range Rover, and I almost walk straight into the newsagent's sandwich board. It's started to spit with rain, and I duck my head, quickening my pace.

What's Mum up to with that rich stranger? Maybe I should call her, right now, and ask her what the hell is going on, and why she's keeping secrets. Instead, I reach the side door of the pub, swipe my warped staff key through the security lock, and shoulder my way inside.

Chapter Two

BELLA

Reece slides his arm around my waist, pulling me in close. I'm not expecting it, but the warmth of his palm on my lower back calms the low-level tremor that's been running through me all day, the anxiety under the general hum of party preparations. He presses his lips just beneath my ear to that oddly sensitive spot on the curve of my jawline. 'Great job, babe, everyone's loving it,' he murmurs.

It's so distinctly intimate that I automatically brace myself, worried about being seen by someone – one of the waitstaff, a junior agent, my parents – but we're momentarily alone in the far corner of the Skiff Hotel's garden.

'Thanks,' I say, though my voice comes out in a breath, barely audible. I tilt my face up and plant a light kiss on his mouth. The kind that's just short of dismissive. I reach for my glass of champagne that I set down on a low wall, the stem slick with condensation. I sigh. 'Don't know why, but this year's party's been like, off-the-scale stressful to organise. Maybe it's the numbers, or maybe it's just . . . everything.'

Reece, ever unflappable, shrugs as if this is a known, natural state of affairs. 'Because you've got so much going on, Bells. You do more than anyone else I know. Every year, the guest list gets bigger. You're always pushing for more. But I guess it's what I love about you.' He smiles, and I wonder if he's being supportive or if he's just relieved that I'm the one micro-managing every detail, so he's free to float and charm. I stop myself from going down that track. It's not fair to Reece. It's not his place to organise this. It's mine. Reece has a career in insurance sales, and he works hard. But I'm always the one to manage our social affairs, so it would be nice if he offered to help out every once in a while.

Our annual summer party started out as a works do for the staff, but over the years it's grown into quite the local event. My parents always drilled into me that the property game is all about making connections. So, the more guests, the better. Today is a chance for the staff to booze and schmooze with real-estate royalty, and hopefully even make a deal or two.

Out on the lawn, the Skiff's garden is a soft chaos of bunting and glassware and laughter, the air tinged with the briny tang that always wafts up from Lymington Quay, just visible through the hedge. Most of my staff are young and fresh out of school or uni, dressed in their best. My parents are here too, not quite fully disappeared into retirement, deep in conversations with old colleagues. I also invited a lot of my friends, most of whom are well connected, with careers in travel, tech or art, or the various maritime businesses that thrive here; and of course Reece, my boyfriend of three and a half years, is here, his jawline and haircut as perfect as our surroundings.

Reece and I met through mutual friends at a house party. I say 'house party', when what I mean is 'stately-home party'. A New Year's Eve bash thrown annually by my school friend Madeleine and her husband, Monty. Reece did all the running while I played hard to get, but I let myself be caught in the end, and we've been an item ever since.

Today's event would be nice anywhere else, but here, in the epicentre of New Forest real estate, people treat these functions with the gravity of a royal wedding. The Skiff's garden has always been neutral territory, a space apart from the high-stakes rivalry of the high-street agencies. When Dad ran Newbury's, the summer bash was his way of declaring dominance, and the other firms sent in their spies disguised as 'well-wishers'. Everyone in Lymington pretends not to gossip, but the town runs on it as reliably as the ferry schedule.

I try to ignore the impostor feeling that sweeps over me, the sense that I'm a child pantomiming adulthood in a borrowed dress. I can feel my family's expectations lurking beneath my skin, as if my DNA itself has been animated by the scent of crab canapés and the thrum of distant jazz. It doesn't help that Mum has already texted three times today, each message a thinly veiled directive: *Don't forget the gluten-free puffs for Simone. Did you remember to book the garden heaters for the evening? You'll be amazing – just relax and enjoy it, darling x*

I wonder if everyone in their late twenties feels this permanent churn, the sickening mixture of luck and dread, as if at any second the dazzle of any momentary success will turn on you. I know how lucky I am. If I weren't me, I'd probably hate myself.

A few tables over, I spot my new sales junior, Freya, deep in conversation with her boyfriend, who's already sweating through his too-tight shirt, snagging more than his fair share of mini burgers from one of the trays as it passes by. On the other side of the terrace, my school friend Tori is holding court over a crowd of the more laid-back set, the ones who claim they only do property in the summers between yoga retreats and sculpture residences. I watch as Tori scans the crowd, eyes darting, and for a moment, she catches mine and grins. She flashes the old sign, index finger to temple, then flicked outward – everyone's crazy. I smile, calmed by her reliable good humour, and raise my glass in a silent toast. The glass is lighter than I expected. I glance down and realise I've nearly finished it already.

The garden is loud – all these people I'm supposed to know, each one a potential client, a possible old enemy, or a distant cousin I've long since lost track of. You'd think I was the socialite of the year, but the truth is, I don't ever have time to see friends and family on a regular basis. My work consumes everything. Since I took over the property business from my parents three years ago, I haven't had a moment for fun or relaxation. So, although Tori and I were as close as sisters once, and although I know every single person here, I don't think any of them are truly my friends. Not anymore.

It's only been two hours, but already the heat of the day is giving way to the evening's chill. I see Reece has sloped off to talk to one of Dad's golfing friends, who is somehow both three feet taller and three feet wider than everyone else, booming out what sounds like a joke at someone's expense.

I duck away for a refill, queuing at the bar like everyone else. I'm halfway through rehearsing a small-talk script in my head when my phone vibrates, a silent buzz in my pocket. I know by the pulse pattern that it's my work account, not personal. For a second, I consider leaving it – just ten more minutes of being present, the way all the mindfulness podcasts recommend – but the twitch in my fingers is too strong. I pull out the phone and glance at the notification. The email is from an address I don't recognise.

I open it, expecting a contract query or an apology from one of yesterday's no-shows. But it's not. The words send a familiar flare of worry down the insides of my arms. There's a moment of vertigo, as if the world has tipped slightly off its axis. I feel like I'm watching myself from above, an actor at my own party, waiting for the next cue. But the truth is, I'm not sure how I'm going to fix this.

I delete the message. It's a stupid thing to do because ignoring it won't make the situation disappear. But I need a reprieve from my anxiety. Out of sight, out of mind. I try to will myself back into the party, into the festive noise and the flush of Reece's praise. I'm not letting this ruin the night. I am in charge here. I am the grown-up.

I toss my thick, chestnut hair and shake out my shoulders. I make a circuit of the garden, checking every table, pausing to greet a few members of staff and to introduce myself to a couple of the new hires' partners. I force myself to make eye contact and laugh in the right places, to compliment the bold choice of trousers or the vintage brooch. I make a mental note to praise the catering on the cheese straws, which are genuinely the best I've ever tasted.

In the lulls between greetings, the email replays itself in my mind, the way a bad song gets stuck in your head. Eventually, the sun dips below the hedge, and the garden is suddenly twinkling with fairy lights. There's a louder hum of music now, and a more raucous buzz of chatter and laughter as the alcohol kicks in and inhibitions are lowered. I feel my mind settling, a little, in the twilight. For a while, I believe my own performance. The party is a success, Newbury New Forest Property Group is thriving, everyone's loving it. Nobody's worried.

But as I drift past half-empty glasses and bits of bunting that have blown on to the grass, I can't shake the feeling that things are about to change. And not for the better.

Chapter Three

JADE

It's just past midnight when I finally reach home, a squat block of flats on the corner of Crouch Street, its once-cream render now cracked and peeling like a bad case of sunburn. I've lived here with Mum ever since I can remember, except for that one disastrous year when I was twenty-two and decided to flat-share with my two best friends from school. The place was awful, with mould on the walls and no hot water, but my so-called friends were even worse and left me with debts that I'm still trying to pay back, six years later. The interest keeps mounting up, so I'm not sure I'll ever be debt-free. That experience has made me quite wary of new people. If best friends can treat me like that, then what will strangers do? Anyway, coming back to Mum's felt like stepping back into a safe harbour. Although she wasn't quite so ecstatic to give up her lounge sofa again.

I trudge up the three front steps and slot my key into the lock, giving it the usual jiggle to ease it open. The lobby welcomes me in with its familiar scent of stale potatoes and air freshener, but I'm used to it now. I cross the worn carpet towards Mum's front door. The flat is at the back of the building, which is actually really good because we don't get any traffic noise.

The pub was busy tonight, which didn't give me much time to think about seeing Mum in that Range Rover earlier. I was so late for work that I couldn't text her until my break. But the message is still showing as unread, so either she's avoiding answering, or she hasn't seen it yet.

I let myself into the flat, shrug off my denim jacket, and hang it on one of the pegs in the cramped hallway. Next, I enjoy the bliss of kicking off my shoes. Always the best part of getting home after being on my feet for seven hours.

I pad into the lounge and sink on to the grey Ikea sofa that sags in the middle. I think this might be one of those nights when I don't bother to convert it into a bed. I might just lie down where I am and pull the duvet over me. My back will probably regret it tomorrow, but the thought of wrestling the sofa into bed mode is beyond me right now. Mum's a stickler for me converting it back into a sofa during the day. She threatened to turf me out if I don't. Says she doesn't want to feel like she's living in a squat. But the last thing I'm in the mood for when I come off a late shift is making up a bed.

I stab the TV remote and wince as it blares out the canned laughter of a comedy show. I quickly fumble to turn down the volume. I don't need the plot, but it's comforting to have the flicker and murmur running in the background.

'That you, Jade?' A sandpapery voice drifts from the bedroom.

Damn. My jaw clenches. 'Yeah, sorry.'

A few seconds later, I hear the bedroom door open and she shuffles into the living room, bleary-eyed in an oversized T-shirt, running a hand through grey-blonde hair. *The brunette hair must have been a wig then.* 'Told you to keep the noise down when you come in, Jade. You know I'm a light sleeper.'

'I said *sorry*.'

'Sorry's no good to me now I'm awake.' She shakes her head and yawns, her jaw clicking. 'Do you want a cuppa?'

'Please.'

Mum sighs and heads over to the kitchenette, filling up the kettle and flicking the switch.

I should probably be the one making tea, seeing as I woke her up, but now I've sat down, my limbs have gone soft. There's an upside to waking her, though, because it means I can ask what she was doing earlier this evening.

'How was work?' she asks, taking a couple of mugs from the little wooden mug tree on the countertop.

'Hectic. Any toast going?'

Mum purses her lips but takes a couple of slices from the bread bin and slots them into the toaster. Next, she takes the milk carton from the fridge, and tuts. 'Forgot to get more milk today.'

'Too busy driving around with your fancy man,' I mutter under my breath.

Mum gives me a sharp-eyed look. 'What's that?'

'Nothing.'

She scowls and shakes the near-empty milk carton as though that's going to magically increase the amount. 'Well, there's enough for tea, but none for my muesli tomorrow, which is annoying.'

I don't respond. Mum always narrates every thought she has in her head. Drives me mad. The kettle clicks off with a hiss, and she sloshes hot water into the mugs.

'Saw you earlier,' I say nonchalantly, watching her reaction.

'Saw me where?'

'Driving down Blake Street in a Range Rover.'

'Ha, ha, I wish.' The toast pops, and she turns away to take it out and start buttering. 'Jam?'

'Yes, please. But, seriously, Mum, what were you doing in that car? And who was the bloke with you? Oh, and why were you wearing a brown *wig*?'

Mum is still turned away from me, but I see her shoulders stiffen. 'Stop talking rubbish,' she snaps. 'I'm not awake enough to cope with your warped sense of humour.'

'I'm not joking.' I straighten up, sensing that she's hiding something. 'I saw you.'

'Well, I've been home all evening binge-watching *Real Housewives*, so you obviously dreamt it.' She brings over my tea and toast. 'There you go, your highness.'

'Thanks.' I grab a slice of warm, buttery toast and cram in a mouthful. It hits the spot, and I relax back against the cushions, still chewing.

'If you really want to thank me, you can nip out first thing tomorrow morning and fetch some more milk.'

'Hmm.' I swirl my tea and blow on it. 'If you've got a new boyfriend, you can tell me,' I add. 'I think it's great. Especially if he's loaded. And you should go brunette permanently. It suits you.'

Mum returns to the kitchenette to retrieve her mug. *Jade*, you're doing my head in with this boyfriend nonsense. I'm taking my tea back to bed.'

'Don't be like that,' I reply, trying to sound sympathetic and failing. 'I'm confused about why you were wearing a wig, though.'

'For the last time, Jade, I was here all evening, I don't own a wig, I'm not going brunette, and I definitely don't have a *boyfriend*.' Her voice cracks.

'All right, calm down. I guess it must have been someone who looked like you. But honestly, she was your absolute double.'

Mum's lips tighten. 'Good night, Jade.' She leaves the lounge and heads back to the bedroom, closing her door with an angry clunk.

I take another bite of toast and chew thoughtfully, crumbs spilling down my top. Mum was definitely acting shady. Not sure what's going on there, but I'm going to get to the bottom of it.

Chapter Four

BELLA

My alarm goes off at 6.30, sharp and offensive. In the confused shock of waking, all I want to do is curl around the warmth of sleep. But I inhale deeply, make a grab for my phone, and send it skittering over the edge of the bedside table. When I finally wrangle it back, Reece stirs beside me, groans, and buries his head under the pillow.

I make the sensible decision to get ready before getting sucked into my messages, so I replace my phone on the bedside table, drag myself out of bed and start the routine. Shower. Hair wash. Full skincare: double cleanse, toner, SPF moisturiser. Make-up: foundation, a touch of bronzer, brows shaped into something resembling confidence. Blow-dry hair into soft, controlled waves. Olive skirt suit, white silk blouse, nothing ostentatious but with the kind of subtle tailoring that cost enough to make me wince. Gold knot earrings, slim watch, matching ring and bracelet. The act of dressing is comforting, a private ritual that soothes my jangling nerves. By the time I spritz on my Kayali vanilla perfume, I almost believe I have things under control.

I finally check my phone. Good – no notifications beyond the daily deluge of work emails and one text from Mum, a meme of a cute dog in a raincoat, along with an accidental string of emojis. No word from Dad, but he never texts in the morning. I start to reply with a thumbs-up and a heart, then erase them and write: *Cute! You and Dad should get a puppy!!!!* Too many exclamations, but it will do.

Twenty minutes later, I'm in the office brewing fresh coffee for the early-bird staff. Our junior negotiator, Ben, is already at his desk. He glances up and gives me a grin that's too big for this hour. 'Boss!' he shouts. 'Crushed it last week. The party was epic. Heard Reece did a speech? Sorry I missed it. Was it cringe?'

I force a laugh. 'Thanks, Ben. It wasn't too bad – just the right amount of cringe.' Although Reece doesn't work for the company, he made a short speech to introduce me to the stage. Once I was up there, I gabbled something semi-inspirational and hopefully thanked all the right people. I guess Reece may have gone a bit overboard in his introduction, but it was sweet of him to acknowl-edge all the hard work I put into the event, so it hurts a little to hear that people thought it was naff.

Ben is still talking animatedly about a potential client who ghosted him and the creative voicemails he left in retaliation. I nod at the right moments, but my thoughts keep spiralling back to the email from last week, and then on to the presentation looming, the reason I spent last night tossing and sweating under the duvet, imagining every way it could go wrong.

'Hey, boss! You need a hand with the brochures for the Flinders Hill apartment?'

I flinch at Ben's sudden proximity, and knock my coffee over. The spill is immediate and catastrophic – a dark wave across the corner of my laptop, pooling into the keyboard and dripping on to my skirt. Ben rushes off and returns wielding a fistful of paper towels, grinning like this is the highlight of his day. I want to snap, to tell him to leave it, but instead I mumble thanks and start dabbing at the mess, as if to erase both the stain and my embarrassment. After my careful routine earlier, I'll now have to go home and change.

Between us, we clean up the mess. I thank him and hurry home. Reece has already left for work, leaving an unmade bed and toast crumbs in his wake. I change into a not-so-nice dark beige trouser suit, but it's okay. I look professional, and that's the aim.

Back in the office, I try to focus on the queries piling up in my inbox, but the simple act of checking items off my list suddenly feels insurmountable. My mind keeps skipping ahead to the meeting, the presentation slides, the potential for mistakes. Even as I go over it for the fifth time, triple-checking every statistic, every graph, every word, I know that I'll go over it all again five minutes before I'm due to present. I do not trust myself to remember anything when the pressure is on.

The morning dissolves in a blur of frantic activity and the hyper-focus that only deadlines can produce. I field calls, answer emails, and run damage control for a client whose buyer is threatening to pull out of a sale. Still, beneath the surface, there's a tremor in my hands and a flutter in my stomach that no amount of herbal tea or yoga breathing can steady.

The day drags and then suddenly speeds up as I count down the minutes to my meeting. I nip into the back office to touch up my make-up, spritz on some more perfume, and take a deep breath. Staring myself down in the bathroom mirror, I repeat the mantra I've been using since uni: 'You deserve to be here. You know what you're doing. You are the boss.' I try to believe it.

The investors' meeting is being held in the lounge bar of the Swan Hotel at the other end of the High Street. The room retains a faint, lingering smell of roast dinners, which does nothing to ease the faint nausea in my gut. There are three of them, all dressed smartly in suits. We make brief small talk before I launch into my presentation, clicking through each slide with what I hope is measured assurance, my voice steady even as my heart ricochets off my ribcage. The questions are tough, but anticipated; the interruptions sharp but not unexpected. At one point, I catch the lead investor, a woman named Harriet Brewer, watching me with a half-smile, chin propped on her knuckles, and I wonder if she's thinking how professional I am or if she can see through the shell to the real mess underneath.

The presentation – including questions – stretches to almost an hour. At the conclusion, there's a moment of silence, then a few nods and smiles. 'Impressive,' Harriet says aloud, and the air changes, relaxes. 'We'll be in touch.' I thank them, collect my things, and leave before my voice can betray me.

I come out of the meeting hardly believing it went so well. My heart thumps with a thrill I'm not used to because it seemed like they might actually be interested in partnering up. My mind races with ideas of what might be, and I'm tingling with nervous excitement.

I walk home along the High Street in a daze, barely registering the coastal breeze or the traffic. Instead, savouring the pink-gold sunset, the faint smell of salt and vinegar from the chippy on the corner, the kaleidoscope of voices and laughter spilling from the pubs and the open doors of corner shops.

My building is a dignified old Georgian block, four storeys and perfectly proportioned, with white-painted sashes and the kind of symmetrical beauty that makes you believe in order. I let myself in and climb to the third floor, rather than waiting for the lift, then fumble the keys at the door, adrenaline still leaching from my system.

Inside, I drop my bag, kick off my shoes, and make a beeline for the kettle. Tea, at times like this, is more ritual than beverage, the act of boiling the water and letting the teabag steep is its own kind of meditation. I sit on the window seat, mug cradled against my chest, and watch the world below. Lymington is a tourist town, as well as a working town. Families push prams over the cobbles; teenagers in identical hoodies share a vape, passing it between them; an ancient woman in a tartan jacket walks a pug in a polka-dot dog coat.

I let my head fall back against the window and squeeze my eyes shut, trying to savour today's success. I remember the first time I ever closed a sale, the taste of pure terror when I realised how much was riding on one signature. My dad hugged me, uncharacteristically soft, and told me, 'Congratulations. It never gets easier, by the way.' He was absolutely right. But today it feels like I've been shown a beacon of hope.

The buzzer goes, and I'm brought back to the present.

A few minutes later, Reece appears in the doorway, still in his work suit, all charm and cologne, holding a paper bag. 'You okay, babe? How did it go?'

Although Reece and I have been together for three and a half years, we still have our own places, and neither of us has brought up the subject of moving in together. I'm glad about it. I may be nearly thirty, but I have no desire to settle down, get married, and have kids. Not for a long time yet, if ever. Hopefully, Reece feels the same. Sometimes he comes here, sometimes I go to his – but I don't love his cold, overly contemporary apartment – and sometimes we don't see each other for days. It works.

Tonight he's bought dinner – something expensive and diffi-cult to pronounce, from the fancy deli by the quay – and he hands over the bag with a flourish. 'Well? How was it?'

I nod slowly, not wanting to sound too enthusiastic in case I jinx it. 'Yeah, it was fine. I think they might be interested.'

He whoops and spins me around, nearly sending the groceries flying.

'It's not definite!' I cry, laughing at his over-the-top antics and setting down the takeaway on the coffee table.

We pour champagne (saved for just such occasions), and in the brightly lit room, we toast. Reece gets tipsy almost immediately, and his jokes become worse as the night draws on, but his enthusiasm is infectious. For a while, the tension that's been wound around my shoulders for weeks, knotted up in between my ribs, loosens its grip, and I'm swept away in the relief of not having failed, in the giddy afterglow of not having been found out.

Still, underneath it all, there's a pulse of fear that never quite quiets. I sit on the sofa next to him, feet tucked beneath my thighs, and think about how I'm going to break the news to Mum and Dad that a third party might be investing in the company. Someone else with skin in the game. Someone who will inevitably want a say in how things are run. It's not that it's bad news; it's just not what they would expect. I worry about their reaction to me possibly giving away a part of the business that they built up from scratch.

Will Mum do her careful frown, the one she polishes for moments of disappointment? Will Dad pretend that he trusts my judgement, even as he interrogates every flaw in my plan? Maybe it's paranoia, but I can already hear the critique in their voices. The urge to impress them is so strong it's embarrassing; I'm nearly thirty and still desperate for approval. But, more than that, I'm worried about whether Dad will get stressed out by the news. And I can't afford for that to happen.

The reason I took over the company in the first place was that, four years ago, he nearly died. It was a Thursday in September when Mum called to say the ambulance was on its way. He'd collapsed in the hallway on the way out to a meeting, clutching the doorframe. Triple bypass, months of rehab, the works. It should have been a wake-up call for him, but in typical Dad fashion, he spent his first week home from the hospital fielding calls from clients, ignoring the literal 'no stress' mandate from his doctor. That was when Mum put her foot down and said they were retiring, no arguments.

I already knew the business inside out, and so it felt like a no-brainer for me to take over, with their guidance for the first year. I wanted to prove to them – and to myself – that I was savvy enough to keep the machine running.

But the truth is, I'm not. Or, if I am, I'm doing it by the skin of my teeth. I don't want to give them a reason to worry – or worse, to step back in and try to fix it. The idea of Dad getting sucked back into the business – grey-faced and wired on adrenaline, winding himself up for a second heart attack – makes me feel physically ill.

Mum has purposely been keeping him distracted over the past few years, with relaxing holidays and other stress-free projects and hobbies such as fishing and cooking – anything to keep his blood pressure low. So if this news triggers his stress again, how will I ever forgive myself?

I remember a time – years ago, before the heart attack – when Dad took me to a client meeting in a hotel bar. I was supposed to just listen and learn, but halfway through, the client turned to me and asked what I thought. I froze. Dad jumped in and said, 'Bells will give it to you straight. That's why we keep her around.' I remember the way he said it, half proud and half joking, but there was a glimmer in his eye like he actually meant it.

Maybe that's what I'm banking on, now – that some version of that glimmer still exists, and that when I tell them the truth, they'll at least respect me for giving it to them straight.

Reece doesn't get my nervousness, not really. He thinks I'm overthinking everything, that I need to 'lean in' and be the confident powerhouse that social media keeps telling women to be. I want to tell him that his faith in me is a double-edged sword. That every time he says I'm killing it, I hear the echo of my own doubts. But instead, I just refill our glasses. Maybe he's right, and maybe not. All I know is that I'm terrified of letting everyone down – my parents, my staff, even Ben, who would probably just high-five me if I crashed the company into a wall. I try to remember it's my life, that I own the decisions and the mistakes, but it never quite sticks.

The rest of the night is a fast-forward of small joys and creeping dread – a thriller we've both seen, but enjoy again, the lazy sprawl of Reece's legs across mine as he falls asleep on the sofa. I sit awake, scrolling mindlessly through news and memes, but underneath it all, I'm already replaying the presentation, cataloguing every error, every unguarded moment, every word I wish I'd said, and didn't say. I wonder if anyone ever learns to stop doing this, or if it just becomes background noise, an endless audit of your own life.

Why do I always find it difficult to be happy? Maybe because I spend too much time second-guessing myself. Maybe because I let every sideways look or slightly delayed response get to me, cracking my resolve. Perhaps I'll learn one day to brush it off, or maybe I'm just wired this way. I try to reassure myself that all that matters is I'm trying my best to make the right decisions for the company, for my parents' legacy, and for myself. But I can't calm my heartbeat or adopt the casual ease that Reece seems to ooze. Maybe one day soon, once this deal goes through, things will settle. I hope so.

Chapter Five

JADE

Zac loads the shopping bags into the boot of his silver Ford Focus, while I stand on the sun-warmed pavement, scrolling through my Instagram feed to distract me from the guilt of today's spending spree. I'm in so much debt that it makes no difference at this point. That's what I tell myself anyway. Perversely, because I owe so much, it feels like it doesn't make a difference to add on a bit more. Whereas, beforehand, when I was in the black, I watched my pennies more carefully. There must be some psychology behind that.

'I'm knackered,' Zac grumbles. 'Didn't realise we'd be going round so many shops. Thought we were just supposed to be going out for lunch.' He slams the boot shut and runs a hand through his short brown curls.

We've got a rare day off together, and I'd suggested grabbing a bite to eat in town, but somehow I got carried away by the summer sales. 'You want me to look good, don't you?' I retort, thinking about how hot I looked in the summer dress and strappy sandals from H&M. I can't wait to wear them somewhere nice. 'Maybe we could go to the beach on our next day off together. Or you could take me to that new cocktail bar in town.' I tilt my head and give him what I hope is a winning smile.

'Yeah, I guess we could go to Bournemouth,' he replies, sliding into the driver's seat as I get into the passenger side. 'Maybe SOBO Beach or over to Sandbanks,' he adds. 'Pricey though. You'll have to chip in for petrol.'

I curl my lip, annoyed that he won't be able to treat me. It won't be any fun if we have to watch every penny. And he'll only moan if I don't offer to pay for a few rounds. Not like when we first met and he couldn't do enough for me. Always treating me and buying me little presents – crap presents, but at least he made an effort. These days, he does nothing but moan. Brings me down, if I'm honest. I pull my seat belt across and click it into place.

Zac starts the engine, then leans forward and points. 'Hey, over there. Isn't that your mum? Thought you said she was working this afternoon.'

I glance up from my phone, squinting through the glare to see a familiar face on the opposite side of the road. A woman coming out of an accountant's office, dressed in jeans, a navy striped top and an expensive-looking blazer. It *is* Mum, and she's wearing the brunette wig again! This time she's alone. No handsome man by her side.

I stare at her face. There's absolutely no doubt about it. It's her. Same features, same expression, same way of walking. This is ridiculous. I'm going to have to confront her.

'Jade,' Zac prompts, 'I said, is that your mum? Did she dye her hair or something?'

I bite my lip. 'What the hell?' I mutter. 'She's supposed to be at work.'

'*Jade* . . .'

'Shh,' I snap. 'I heard you the first time. That's definitely my mum, right?' I glance at Zac's bemused expression.

'Yeah.' He nods. 'But she looks . . . rich.'

I watch as she points a set of keys at a high-spec red Mini Clubman. The lights flash and the alarm chirps.

Zac gives a low whistle. 'Nice car.'

Adrenaline pulses through me, and I undo my seat belt. 'I'm going over there. She can't deny it if I'm standing right in front of her.' I fling open the car door.

'Deny what?' His brow knits. 'What's going on? Jade!'

As I step out of Zac's car, Mum slides into hers and, before I can move, she's pulling away from the kerb, driving off. I swear and slip back into my seat.

'Follow her,' I pant.

'What?' He turns to look at me.

'Go!' I nod in the direction of the rapidly receding Mini.

'Oh, right.' Zac rams the Ford into gear, and we surge out on to the road as he guns the engine, speeding to catch up with her.

'Hang back a bit,' I say. 'We don't want her to spot us.'

'Why not? Surely that's the whole point – you want to speak to her, right?'

'I want to see where she's going.' I crane my neck, peering through the windscreen. 'Just keep her in sight.'

Zac glances at the dashboard. 'Haven't got much petrol,' he warns. 'We might have to stop.'

I huff. 'What are you talking about? We can't stop.'

'It's not my fault,' Zac retorts. 'If I'd known we'd be in a high-speed car chase, I'd have gone to the garage for a full service.'

I can't help snort-laughing at that, remembering it was his dry humour that attracted me in the first place.

He grins back, and I shake my head, adding, 'We'll just have to hope she's not going too far.'

'All right, but if we run dry, we'll be stranded.'

I glance at my phone. 'I could call her? Ask what she's doing.'

He nods. 'Good idea.'

I try her number, but it's no good. 'Voicemail,' I say glumly.

We cruise out of town, traffic humming around us, the outskirts of Southampton unspooling past our windows. My phone lies useless in my lap – voicemail every time I call.

Zac drifts along in the left lane of the dual carriageway so he won't spook her. He peppers me with questions as I stare ahead at the red blur of the Mini, wondering about her destination.

I realise it's actually good to have someone to talk to about it, rather than keeping my worries bottled up. I tried asking Mum on a couple more occasions. But, just like that first night, she shut me down each time. So I fill Zac in.

'So she was in a Range Rover with some bloke you've never seen before?' Zac clarifies.

'Yep, and she denied it. But you saw her just now. It's definitely her, right? I'm not going mad.'

'Hundred per cent,' he says. 'Do you think she's leading some kind of double life? Like, with another family? Maybe that guy was her husband.'

I huff out an incredulous breath. 'No way. If that was true, why would she choose to live in a grotty flat and work shifts in the pub?'

'Maybe it's someone who looks like her,' Zac muses 'She's getting on the motorway. Not sure we've got enough in the tank for that.'

'We'll be fine.' I glance at the petrol gauge. 'It's not even in the red yet.'

Zac shakes his head, but follows her down the slip road anyway. 'Okay, I'm invested now.' He merges the car into the fast-flowing traffic. 'Could she have a sister?'

I considered this possibility back when I first saw this version of Mum a few weeks ago, but I dismissed it. No one could look that similar, not even a sister. I shake my head. 'Mum's an only child. Although . . .'

'What?' Zac prompts, moving into the middle lane.

'You know she was brought up in care, right? Lots of different homes and foster families.'

'I didn't know that.'

'She doesn't really talk about it, even to me. So, maybe she was split up from any siblings she might have had. Maybe she doesn't even know!'

'Yeah, but the social workers would have told her if she had a sister, surely?' Zac indicates and shifts to the outside lane. 'Well, whoever she is, she's going over the speed limit. Must be doing ninety.'

'I just can't believe it's a sibling. I mean, you saw her, she's the spit of Mum. She doesn't look similar, she looks exactly the same.'

'Could be a twin,' Zac says.

I try to calm my breathing. This whole thing is making me feel weird. Either Mum's been lying to me, or she has an unknown sister, both of which are strange. I realise that I could have an aunt! A *rich* aunt.

After ten minutes on the M27, she leaves the motorway at Cadnam and heads south, deeper into the New Forest, towards Lyndhurst. Fifteen minutes later, with the fuel gauge blinking, we drive into Lymington, a swanky coastal town on the edge of the New Forest. The Mini heads down to the marina.

'Looks like she's parking.' I state the obvious as she drives into a public car park and reverses expertly into a narrow space.

'Just as well, 'cause we're out of petrol,' Zac replies as the engine splutters and dies. We manage to coast into a nearby parking space. 'Lucky we made it,' he adds. 'Gonna have to walk to a garage to get some fuel though. Think I've got a can in the boot, otherwise I'll have to buy one. Hope it's not too expensive.'

I'm barely listening. All my concentration is focused on my mother, or the woman who's her double. She exits the car and heads down to the bustling dock, designer handbag over her shoulder. 'I'm going to catch up with her.' I release my seat belt and open the car door.

'Hang on, I'll come with you,' Zac says. 'Just let me grab a ticket.'

'Catch me up.' I clamber out of the car.

The sun is low and liquefied, molten orange bleeding into the marina, but my gaze is fixed on Mum, phone pressed to her ear as she waves to someone on a sleek yacht moored at the quay. The sort of vessel that looks more at home off Cannes than our wind-lashed spit of English coastline, all shining hull and tinted glass, the name *Mimi* painted on its side in curly blue italics.

Some guy, rangy and tanned, is leaning over the yacht's rail in a navy polo and chinos. He looks vaguely familiar. It takes me a second to realise – it's the Range Rover guy from the other week, waving at Mum like they're old friends. Or more. Something sharp and cold needles its way into my gut. I pull out my phone and pretend to check texts, but really I'm toggling to the camera and zooming in.

My view is blocked as more people are trickling on to the yacht, all of them dressed the same way – linen, cashmere, deck shoes, a uniform that signals easy money. The soundtrack is synthy house music and tipsy shrieking, overlaid with the salty tang of the harbour.

I increase my pace, irritated by a dawdling family taking up the whole of the walkway. I skirt around them and see someone else has joined the man on deck. A young woman around my age, laughing and waving, her gold bracelet glinting in the evening sun. Her nose is aquiline, her jawline sharp, identical to my own, and when she looks up, the resemblance hits me so hard I stop breathing for a full five seconds. She's me. Not literally me, obviously. But my double. Same shoulders, same dimples, same . . . *everything*.

That can't be right. I blink and stare, hardly able to believe my eyes. Am I hallucinating? Have I somehow found myself in an alternate universe where there are rich versions of me and Mum? That girl . . . she's the spitting image of me, only slimmer and more glamorous. Like an upmarket version with posh clothes and expensive hair. Could she be my sister? Or – I can hardly believe it – a *twin*?

My mouth goes dry. My heart is racing so fast I'm dizzy. The yacht's crew pass round canapés and glasses of champagne as guests chatter beneath fluttering bunting. I should storm aboard, demand answers. Instead, I sink on to a nearby bench, hands shaking. How could Mum keep such a secret? Am I losing my mind – or have I just discovered a hidden life of hers that I never imagined?

That woman boarding the yacht . . . can she really be my mother? She drives a brand-new car for goodness' sake! No. Mum must have a sister. I need to know who they are and what's going on. I keep my gaze trained on the yacht as Mum's double joins the Range Rover man and my double, and they hug. The three of them could be a family. Maybe they are.

I press my palms to my temples. How could Mum have kept such a huge secret from me? Does she even know about them? Whatever the truth is, I need to find out.

Chapter Six

'We'll get in trouble,' Penni whines, shifting from foot to foot beside her sister, who's already heaving herself up and over the rickety back fence. 'Mike said we're not allowed in the woods without a grown-up.'

'Don't be silly. We won't get caught,' Nicola reassures. 'Come on.' Their foster dad is at work, and their foster mum, Janet, is having a nap upstairs. It's the perfect time for them to have a bit of fun. They won't be long, just twenty minutes or so. Janet always naps for at least an hour, so she won't even know they're gone.

'Okay, but just for ten minutes.' Penni relents, as Nicola knew she would.

She reaches down to give her sister a hand up. They trot through the tall grass and into the woods behind the small house, their laughter mingling with the rustle of leaves. The air is crisp, and fallen leaves crunch beneath their feet as they make their way to their favourite oak tree, its branches sprawling like a giant's arms. With practised ease, they scramble up the sturdy trunk, branches swaying gently under their weight. High above the ground, they settle on to their usual perch, legs swinging in the air. Nicola tilts her face up to the sun that filters through the canopy above, imagining she's in a magical world where there's no one else but the two of them, except maybe a unicorn and some friendly fairies. But definitely no adults. She grins at her sister, fascinated by the dappled shadows flickering across Penni's cheek.

Penni clears her throat. 'Gracie Nugent asked if we want to go round to her house after school one day next week.'

Nicola doesn't even pause to think about it. 'No,' she replies abruptly.

'Why not?' Penni persists, which isn't like her. Usually, she defers to her sister.

'Because she's a show-off,' Nicola says, her voice sharp.

'No she isn't. She's nice.'

That stings more than Nicola wants to admit. Sends a sliver of something twisting in her belly. Jealousy, probably. For as long as she can remember, it's always been just the two of them, clinging to each other and the precarious world they share. They've been abandoned more times than they can count. Their real parents didn't want them, and they've drifted through four different foster homes over the past ten years. This latest one isn't too bad. They've been here just over a year. Mike and Janet are fine. Not great, but fine. They prefer Penni, that's for certain, but the worst thing about living here is that their new school decided to put them in different classes. Penni loves her teacher, Miss Curtis, and has made a few friends, but Nicola hates her teacher, Mrs Appleby, and hasn't made any friends at all, apart from Sonia, who's mean.

'Well, I don't want to go to Gracie's house,' Nicola says, folding her arms and scowling.

'Okay,' Penni replies.

Relief blooms in Nicola's chest for half a moment until her sister's next words, not mean or spitefully meant, but wounding just the same: 'I can go on my own.'

Heat floods Nicola's face, and a tightness pulls at her throat. 'Fine!' she snaps. 'Go! I don't care.'

'You should come too,' Penni coaxes, placing a hand on her sister's arm. Her voice is soft, just like it always is. 'It'll be fun. She's got a trampoline.'

But Nicola won't be soothed or cajoled. She doesn't want either of them to go to Gracie's no doubt perfect house with a matching set of perfect parents. She's terrified that Penni will prefer Gracie to her. It's already bad enough hearing all about her after school. What will happen if they become best friends? Where will that leave Nicola? On her own, that's where.

'It won't be fun and I hate trampolines!' Nicola cries, shoving her sister's hand away in frustration.

Penni's eyes widen in surprise as she loses her balance and slips forward. She slides off the branch with a startled cry, crashing through the branches before landing with a sickening thud on a jagged tree stump below.

Nicola screams, horrified at the sight of her sister lying on her side in a crumpled heap on the forest floor, hair tangled with dirt and leaves. Fear races through her veins as she frantically clambers down, her heart pounding, hands gripping the rough bark, eyes wide and wild, her mind spinning in terrified circles.

'Penni!' she cries, crouching beside her sister. She doesn't know what to do, can't think straight. 'Penni, are you all right?'

Her sister's eyes flutter open, and then close, but she doesn't reply.

What should Nicola do? She's petrified about getting into trouble, but she can't do nothing. She has to get help. Please let Penni be okay. Please.

Chapter Seven

BELLA

Rarely have I felt less like a person who belongs at a yacht party than I do right now, but no one else seems to notice. I'm not sure whose birthday it is, exactly – a vague friend-of-the-family situation. I want to say someone called Miranda or Miriam? Maybe one of Mum's old business acquaintances, or a pal from the golf club. All I know is that we're bobbing in the dock, three decks of strangers wearing pastels and enough sunscreen to make everyone's skin gleam, even beneath the goosebumps. The boat is so big that it's disorienting – a kind of floating hotel with function rooms, a half-hearted dance floor, little alcoves crowded with people, and above it all, the gentle sway you only notice when you try to walk in a straight line after too many glasses.

Reece couldn't make it and I tried to cry off too, but Mum wouldn't take no for an answer. She wanted to show me off to all her friends. It didn't help that she was late – a meeting with her pensions advisor, or something – so Dad and I had to keep each other company for half an hour while smiling at people we've never met before. But now that Mum's here, she's already disappeared into a knot of Pilates acquaintances.

Dad is in the engine room with the only other two men present who give off the vibe of people who could plausibly operate a mechanical device, and I'm left on the upper deck with a clutch of partygoers I vaguely recognise from school, all of whom seem to have become more physically attractive and successful since I last saw them. School reunion, but with sea legs.

I keep checking my phone, waiting for the notification to tell me that Harriet – who's supposed to be letting me know about the possible business investment – has finally replied. I've established an elaborate superstition in my head that if I let the battery drop below 50 per cent, I'll somehow jinx the whole deal, so I'm obsessively rationing every swipe and scroll, glancing at the percentage in the top corner like it's a countdown to destruction. There is, of course, no message from Harriet.

My hands are shaking in a way that I blame on the wind, but when I try picking up a canapé, it wobbles on the napkin. I want to tell my parents about the investment – how close it is, how it could actually change everything – but the prospect of opening myself up to their scrutiny, or their disappointment, makes me want to leap overboard. I think I'll wait until it's a done deal. No point mentioning anything if it all ends up falling through. My stomach twists. If it does fall through, that will be even worse than a confrontation with my parents.

The party is now in full swing, and I wonder how long I have to stick around here. Will anyone notice if I just slope off? Some joker has put on 'Come On Eileen' at a punishing volume, and a group of women in nautical stripes and blinding white trainers are dancing and clapping along, as if the song is some kind of naval anthem. I drift to the rail to get away from them, staring down to where the dock is quickly becoming crowded with overlapping shadows and the occasional burst of laughter. My phone buzzes, and for a moment my heart judders, but it's just a pointless notification about the weather. I look at it anyway. 'Unseasonably cold', it states, which feels like deliberate trolling.

Out of nowhere, my old school friend Tori leans in next to me. She now works in media marketing – or marketing media, it changes each time we meet – and she's already noticeably tipsy, her blonde hair blowing horizontally as she tries to light a cigarette.

'Bells, I swear to God I saw you down on the dock earlier.' She squints at me over the tiny flicker of her lighter.

'Hi, Tori.' I lean in to kiss her cheek and get a mouthful of hair instead. 'Didn't know you were going to be here. Glad you are though.'

'You too. Bloody weather.' She rolls her eyes. 'So, like I said, I saw you on the dock.'

'Well, yeah. I had to walk across the dock to get on to the boat.'

'No, but it was weird,' she says. 'You looked odd.'

I nudge her with my shoulder. 'Thanks a lot!'

'Hang on, stand there, so I can light my ciggie. This weather.'

I move to block the wind. 'I looked *odd*?' I frown. 'Odd how?'

'I don't know, Bells. You were just standing there like a lemon. Like you were worried about something.'

'I'm always worried about something.' I give a self-depre-cating laugh.

She shakes her head. 'No, but your hair was different, and your clothes . . .' She trails off, studying my hair, as if trying to match it with what she saw on the dock.

'Sounds like it was probably someone else.'

'Could have sworn,' she mutters, and offers me a drag of her cigarette, which I take, even though I've never liked the taste.

I nod towards her glass of champagne. 'How many of those had you had when you saw "me", Tori?'

'Um, a few.' She grins. 'Ignore me, I'm actually pissed as a newt, in case you couldn't tell.'

My phone pings again, and I jerk it out of my pocket, but it's not from Harriet. I try to ignore how my hands are definitely shaking now, cigarette or not.

'So, what's new with you? How's the property game?' she asks. 'Whatever happened to those flats you were flipping?' She pouts and tilts her head. 'Can't believe you've turned into such a little business tycoon.'

I swallow down acid and brush off her question with a flick of my wrist. Thankfully, Tori's attention is already wandering back to the cluster of bodies near the bow, where another chorus is kicking off. She asks if I want another drink, and I say, 'Sure.' While she's gone, I gaze out over the water again, expecting to be steadier, but instead my legs feel soft and my head is full of static.

Tori is gone for longer than it takes to get another drink, but then I spy her in the midst of a group of forty-somethings, bellowing out the chorus to the Human League's *Don't You Want Me*.

I retreat to a quieter part of the rail and look down at the dock, and, for a moment, I think I see myself. Just for a second, standing hunched at the water's edge. But when I blink, it's just a coil of rope and a trick of the light, nothing more. I need to get a grip.

I stand there with the dregs of my drink, listening to the party echo above and behind me. I get another weather alert, of all things, and then, finally, a message from Harriet. But it's agonisingly brief: *Can you talk?*

My stomach drops, giddy and terrified at the same time. I look for somewhere quieter, but the whole yacht seems to be awash with noise. I duck down the nearest staircase and find myself in a corridor lined with family photos and nautical kitsch. I call Harriet, and she picks up on the second ring.

'Hi,' I say, going for breezy, but coming off as strangled.

'Bella?'

'Hi, yes, this is Bella.'

'Great. Thanks for calling me back.'

'Hi, Harriet. Can you hear me? Sorry, it's a bit noisy here.'

'Yes, I can hear you fine.' Her voice is professional but friendly. 'I wanted to tell you myself.'

My heart races. A passing waiter nearly collides with me, and I have to curb the urge to snap at him.

'We were very impressed with your presentation, but after further scrutiny . . . I'm sorry, but we're going to have to pass on this occasion.'

'Pass?' My stomach drops.

'We're grateful to you for giving us the opportunity, though, and we'd like to wish you all the best for the future.'

I lean back against the wall, utterly deflated. 'Can I just ask how you came to that decision?'

Harriet sighs, and there's a silence as though she's weighing up what to say. But then she inhales briskly. 'We decided to go in a different direction, that's all.'

I'm not stupid. I understand that's code for *we don't want to get into it*. 'Okay,' I reply. 'Well, thanks for letting me know.'

'You're welcome, Bella. Take care.'

'And you.'

The line disconnects.

I stare at the phone for a long moment, and then glance around. It's only when I see my reflection in a gilt-edged, full-length mirror – hair all wind-messed, expression blank – that I realise I'm still clutching Tori's cigarette, burnt out between my fingers.

I stub it in one of the handily placed ashtrays, pocket the phone, and try to steady my breathing. I can't believe I was worrying about how to break the news to my parents that I was going to be bringing in investors to the company. When the alternative is so, so much worse.

Back on deck, the party is peaking. Everyone is up, arms around each other, swaying and singing off-key, a brief interruption of the usual British reserve. I try to slot myself back into it, but there is an invisible wall now, some membrane between me and everyone else, and I have no idea how to cross it. I know I should give up and go home, but the thought of returning to my empty apartment is too depressing to contemplate after tonight's disappointment. And I'm not in the mood for Reece's optimistic spin on everything.

Along with the heavy feeling of dread, Tori's earlier observation about seeing me looking 'odd' has somehow got under my skin, even though I know it's probably just a combination of her having drunk too much, along with her overactive imagination. I shake it off and decide to find her. Maybe I can salvage the night and try to have a bit of fun.

The rest of the evening passes in a blur of shouted conversation and awkward dancing, with Tori occasionally staring at me with a look I can't quite decode. At some point, I accidentally spill prosecco on someone's boat shoes and apologise so profusely that it becomes a running joke for the rest of the event. I smile and nod and laugh, even though my mind is in a dark pit. I wish I could rewind time. I wish I hadn't been so ambitious. All I wanted to do was make my parents proud. I thought branching out into the property development market was such a smart move. Clearly not.

Chapter Eight

JADE

'Sure you don't want me to come in with you?' Zac asks as I fumble with my seat belt.

I want to accept his offer – his support might calm my racing heart – but I also need space. 'No. I need some time alone. To think.' My pulse thumps like a jackhammer.

He leans over to kiss me, and it feels tender for a change. Like he actually might care about me. 'Don't forget your bags are in the boot.'

I frown, blink, then remember the shopping spree we went on hours ago. It already feels like another lifetime. The thrill of new clothes, new everything, seems laughable now. 'Oh. Thanks,' I say automatically, my mind skittering elsewhere.

'Call me later, if you like,' he offers. 'Might go down the King's Head with Jed and Callum, if you're up for it? Jed's got a new girlfriend. Apparently she works for Nike. Might score us some freebies.'

Part of me wants to go – any excuse to stay distracted – but I shake my head. 'Not tonight. Have a good one.' I force a smile he doesn't return.

'Okay.' He watches me climb out, disappointment in his eyes. I grab my bags from the boot and make my way across the pavement and up the steps towards the apartment building. Glancing over my shoulder, I see him give a forlorn wave and drive away. I want to be alone to process what I saw today, but now that he's gone, I feel a little untethered.

Back in Lymington, I chickened out of confronting my doppelganger. Told myself I need to speak to Mum alone first. To discover what's going on here. If that woman isn't my mother, then who is she? And why has Mum never mentioned her? I might not have spoken to the two women, but I did take a few sneaky photos to prove to myself that I wasn't hallucinating, and to show Mum the evidence, so that she can't give me the brush-off again.

After Zac and I traipsed half a mile to get petrol, all I could think about on the journey home was that I might have a twin. A *twin*. I repeated the word in my head so many times that it started to feel made up. Zac tried talking to me, but I shushed him, needing silence. But thinking only tangled my thoughts further. It was weird enough seeing that posh version of Mum, but to see my own face on someone else was surreal.

Outside the entrance to our block, my arms are laden with bags, and I pause, trying to work out how to get the door key from my bag.

'Jade Morgan?' A man's voice, deep and authoritative, calls from down the street.

Shit. I freeze momentarily, and my heart starts to pound, but I'm quick-witted enough not to turn around. To keep my face turned away so I can pretend I'm not who they're looking for. *Stay calm, stay calm.* If I can just get to my key.

Just when I think I'm going to have to drop all my shopping bags, I glance up to see one of the neighbours heading through the lobby towards me, his gait too slow for my liking. *Come on! Come on!*

'Jade Morgan . . . we need a word.' The voice is closer now, and I hear heavy footsteps along the pavement behind me.

The neighbour opens the door and holds it for me.

'Thanks so much,' I stutter and almost shove past him into the lobby in my haste to get inside, sweat coating my upper lip and beading down my back.

He nods curtly and continues on his way as I hurry across the lobby to Mum's front door, praying none of the other neighbours come along to open the entrance doors before I can get safely into the flat.

I dump my haul on the grey, scuffed mat while I fish out my keys with trembling fingers and finally open our door, my heart a battering ram against my chest. I chance a glance over my shoulder, through the glass doors, to see two huge men in dark jackets striding up the steps outside the block. With a silent prayer, I slam the flat door shut, thanking God for such a narrow escape.

I can't believe the bloody bailiffs have managed to track me down. Thankfully, I've kept Mum in ignorance of my debts so far, but it won't be long until she finds out just how much trouble I'm in. I'll have to warn her never to open our front door. *Damn.* As if my day hasn't been stressful enough without this.

The flat is silent and still. I exhale shakily and stand in the hallway for a moment, letting the quiet press in on me. I'm not a sensitive person, but right now I have this big balloon of anxiety in my chest that I can't shake. I don't like it at all. It's not like me to get flustered.

My phone shows no reply from Mum. I stuff my purchases behind the sofa for now. There's a chest of drawers in the hallway that's already bursting with clothes I don't wear. I should stick a load of them on Vinted, but I doubt they'd fetch more than the postage. I don't know why I keep buying stuff. It's like a fever comes over me. A euphoric buzz that I don't get from anything else. But, right now, I feel the opposite of that – I'm grubby and tired, my mind spinning, pulse still racing from everything that's happened.

Mum's not here, I can tell from the atmosphere, but I check her bedroom anyway – empty. I'm glad. I need some time to calm down before speaking to her. My stomach gurgles, but I'm not at all hungry. I drift over to the kitchenette, pour myself a tall glass of water and gulp it down, hoping it will calm me. It doesn't.

I head to the little bathroom, strip off my clothes, and step into the shower. One good thing about this flat is that the water's always hot and the pressure's decent, something I'm grateful for now, as the sharp jets get rid of today's grime and stress. I squirt on the Bath & Body Works shower gel that I treated myself to today. But its rich cherry scent taunts me – I shouldn't have bought it. I shouldn't have bought *anything* today, not with my debts piling up around my ears. I kid myself that I'll take it all back and get a refund, but I know I won't. I usually prefer to block that part of my life out, but it's getting harder to do that. My spending habit is out of control, and the consequences aren't going to be pretty. Not with the bailiffs on my back. Although, even if they did gain access to the flat, there's nothing much here for them anyway. The TV's old, the furniture's crap. Maybe I should have let them in, saved myself the panic. I shudder as I picture their burly figures. No way am I letting them in.

I turn off the shower and stand in the steam, hair dripping in the warm silence. As I reach for the cardboard-like towel and wrap it around my body, I hear the front door open. My stomach clenches in fear, and then I relax. It will be Mum. But, right now, I don't know if seeing her is worse than seeing the bailiffs. What will she say when I question her? What if she refuses to tell me the truth? What if she doesn't know anything about the two women?

Well, if that's the case, then I'll go back to Lymington. Try to find out who owns that yacht. Look out for the Mini. I took a note of the number plate, so maybe that will help me trace the owner.

Suddenly fired up again, I towel-dry myself and pull on my black and pink knockoff Victoria's Secret dressing gown. I usually take time to apply body lotion after my shower, but I'm too impatient.

There's a knock on the bathroom door. 'Jade, can you let me in? I'm bursting here.'

I take a breath and open the door.

'Thanks, love.' She slides past and ushers me out. 'Thought I was going to wet myself on the way home. My pelvic floor's shot.'

I leave the bathroom and head to the kitchen to make us both a cup of tea. I need something sweet to settle my nerves, and I also need to put her in a good mood before I start interrogating her again. I'm trying to blank out the debt collectors from my mind. I can't cope with that shit right now. I have more important things to deal with.

A couple of minutes later, Mum comes into the lounge, eyeing the two mugs on the coffee table along with a packet of Rich Tea biscuits. 'Ooh, tea, you read my mind.'

I'm seated at one end of the sofa; she comes and plonks herself on the other.

'Good day?' I ask through gritted teeth.

She blows on her tea. 'Not bad. Glad I'm not working tonight, there's a match on so it'll be carnage later. How was your lunch with Zac? Surprised to see you back. Thought you'd be living it up in town on your evening off.'

I sip my tea and take a breath. 'I had a bit of a shock, actually.'

Mum puts her tea down and glances sideways at me. I catch her gaze, but she doesn't hold it. 'Oh yes?' she says warily.

'Yes,' I reply, unsure how to phrase what I want to say.

'Well?' Mum asks.

'Well,' I repeat, cradling my warm mug. 'I saw you, or someone who looks just like you, in town today.'

Mum picks up her tea again and takes a small sip. 'Wasn't me. I've been here – shopping, washing, cleaning, followed by a shift at the pub . . . all the glamorous stuff.'

I study her face intently, looking for any signs of a lie. 'Me and Zac, we both saw you coming out of an accountant's office.'

'Very nice, I'm sure.' Mum finally gives me some eye contact. 'But, as you well know, Jade, I don't earn enough money to have an "accountant".'

'So, you're saying it wasn't you?'

'Course it wasn't me. I was at work!' she snaps. 'Call Mags if you don't believe me.'

'Mum, I know you're hiding something. Anyway, I have photos.' I lift my phone off the coffee table and bring up the picture I snapped outside the accountant's, and the others I took at Lymington Quay. I shift around in my seat so I'm looking straight at her as I flash my screen in front of her face. But she pushes it away, refusing to look, her face suddenly drawn and pale.

She gets to her feet, mug still clenched in her hand. 'Glad you had a good day, but I'm exhausted. Gonna have an early night.'

My chest tightens. 'No. Wait.' I stand, heart pounding. 'You're not running off again. You're not going anywhere till you tell me what you know. Anyway, I haven't finished telling you everything.'

Mum's face flushes the deepest crimson. 'You can tell me tomorrow.' Her lips tighten, and she starts walking away.

But I keep talking. 'Zac and I tailed the woman who looks like you. She was driving a brand-new Mini,' I gabble, shadowing my mother as she leaves the lounge. 'She drove to Lymington. Got on a bloody great yacht – it was a party, I think. And there was another younger woman on board.'

Mum opens her bedroom door, still ignoring me.

'This woman,' I continue, my voice rising, 'she looked exactly like *me*! And when I say exactly, I mean, apart from our hair colour, she was identical.'

Mum freezes in the doorway mid-stride, her back to me, but she doesn't respond.

'Aren't you going to say anything?' I demand. 'Who are they? You must know who they are, or you wouldn't be trying to get away from me right now.'

Mum's shoulders drop and she turns around slowly, her face taut, her eyes bright with emotion. 'I didn't want you to find out,' she whispers.

'Find out what?' I ask, my heart pounding.

'I wanted it to stay just you and me,' she continues, her hands twisting in front of her. 'I should never have moved down here. I'm such a fool.'

My voice hardens. 'Mum, just tell me who they are. Have you got a sister? Have I got a . . . twin?'

She sways, jaw clenched. 'I think I'm going to need something stronger than tea. Fetch that bottle of vodka from the cupboard.'

We return to the living room, and she sits while I bring a couple of glasses, the vodka, and a can of Diet Coke over to the sofa.

Mum pours herself a generous measure of the vodka with trembling fingers. I top it off with the Coke, and she lifts it like a shield, takes a deep swig before speaking. 'I suppose I should start from the beginning,' she says, her voice barely above a whisper.

I sink back down on to the sofa and clutch my own glass, fear and anticipation swirling in my gut. I lean forward, scared to hear, but desperate to know. 'Go on. I'm listening.'

Chapter Nine

Nicola runs a hand through her dyed blonde hair and puffs out a breath. She surveys the room and wonders why she even bothered tidying it up. She tried sprucing up the saggy settee by half covering it with a green throw she found in a charity shop, but that's made it even worse. The scuffed bamboo coffee table with its scratched glass top actually looked more respectable under piles of old mail, empty takeaway containers, and dirty crockery. And it would take a bazaar's worth of rugs to cover the stains on the worn carpet. 'Brilliant,' she mutters to herself. 'Welcome to the palace.'

It's never going to look anything other than what it is — a rundown social-housing flat in a grotty part of Middlesbrough that's too hot in summer, and freezing in winter — like now, on this dank, grey February afternoon.

She's annoyed at herself for trying to make the effort. Why should she go to all this trouble for her sister after Penni more or less abandoned her? Penni rarely visits anymore. In fact, the two of them have hardly been on speaking terms for fifteen years. It was after the tree incident occurred that things started to go pear-shaped between them.

She flops on to the lumpy sofa, fishes a cigarette from a crumpled pack, flicks her lighter until a yellow flame shudders to life, and takes a long, steadying drag. Smoke drifts towards the ceiling as memories of that awful day come racing into her brain. After Nicola's screams brought their foster mother, Janet, bolting from her bedroom, Penni was rushed by ambulance, lights flashing, to the hospital with serious abdominal injuries and a suspected concussion.

Nicola had sat in the waiting room in shock, numb, as doctors in scrubs whispered 'internal bleeding . . . concussion . . . life-threatening.'

Nicola was convinced that her sister would die.

But she didn't.

Thankfully, Penni made a full recovery, and Nicola couldn't wait for her to be well enough to come back home. Only, things didn't work out like that.

When she finally came to, Penni let slip to one of the nurses that Nicola had instigated the tree-climbing and had accidentally pushed her. A sliver of betrayal that rippled through social workers' notes, through hushed meetings with Mike and Janet, until Nicola was deemed 'a risk' and packed off to another home.

Nicola wasn't stupid; she gleaned snippets here and there and was horrified that they thought she was a bad influence on Penni. They even wondered if she'd tried to deliberately hurt her sister. But she really hadn't! It was just a terrible accident, wasn't it? Yet, somehow, they poisoned her sister against her.

Penni wasn't keen on visiting Nicola at her new home, and whenever they did meet, she was quiet, withdrawn. Nicola couldn't get her to open up. To be like she used to be. Like they used to be. Something between them was broken.

Since then, unlike Nicola, Penni has thrived. Mike and Janet ended up adopting her. She did well at school, went to university, and married Paul Newbury, a successful estate agent who originated from down south. While Nicola lurked in the care system, was expelled from school aged fifteen and drifted from one poorly paid job to another in between long bouts of unemployment. And now, here she is at twenty-four years of age with nothing to show for her life.

The doorbell rings, yanking her back to the present. She opens a window – a slap of icy wind rattling the sash – grinds out her cigarette against the exterior wall, drops the butt on the concrete slab, then stuffs a tab of gum into her mouth.

Nicola's heart hammers. She doesn't want to open her door, and yet she desperately does. Penni is her other half. Without her, she's felt cut adrift, like she could float away into outer space. But she knows her sister doesn't feel the same way about her. If she did, she would never have stayed away.

The doorbell chimes again, making Nicola jump. She steels herself, strides across the threadbare carpet, and pulls open the door.

Penni stands in the drizzle, cheeks pink, chestnut curls clinging to her face. Hazel eyes clear and bright. They share the same face, but Nicola sees a very different person to the one she sees in the mirror. Behind her, a man walks up the front path, tall in a dark overcoat, polished leather shoes tapping the pitted concrete. Paul. Nicola's heart sinks. What's he doing here?

'Hi, Nic,' Penni says, her voice hesitant.

Nicola's throat tightens. She juts her chin. 'Hi.' She steps back. 'Come in before you freeze.'

They shuffle past her, brushing damp against her sleeves, wafting expensive perfume and aftershave that Nicola doesn't recognise.

Penny and Paul live in Whitby. It's only a forty-five-minute drive away, but it may as well be the moon. She's never been invited into their home, but she snooped on Rightmove to see that it's a beautiful, detached period cottage overlooking the sea. Because of course it is.

Nicola follows them into her tiny lounge and closes the window. It still reeks of cigarettes, and now it's freezing too. She sees the room as they must see it – depressing.

Silence stretches.

'Do you want tea?' Nicola asks. She knows she sounds surly, but she doesn't know how to be hospitable to the pair of them. Beneath her skin, bitterness swirls.

'I'm fine,' Penni replies. She exchanges a glance with Paul, who waves away the offer.

Nicola gestures to the sofa where they both sit gingerly. She's now glad she covered up the coffee stains with the throw.

Penni draws in a shaky breath before she speaks, voice wavering: 'Nic, I can't have children. It's official.'

The sentence lands like a brick. Nicola freezes. She's heard the facts once before in a teary phone conversation from Penni – abdominal trauma that led to the development of scar tissue and adhesions, blocked tubes. But hearing it again, face to face, cuts her. Her fists clench.

Penni presses both hands to her belly. 'There's nothing we can do.'

Paul's jaw twitches. 'We wondered . . . we'd . . . like to ask something . . .' He shifts in his seat, hands still shoved into his coat pockets. 'Would you have a child for Penni? For us.'

Nicola's pulse stutters. She laughs, a metallic sound. 'You want me to have a baby? For you?'

Penni nods, eyes brimming. 'I know it's huge. I know you're struggling. We'll cover all the expenses.'

Nicola's gaze slides from Penni's teary face to Paul's hopeful tilt. The rundown flat feels smaller than ever.

Nicola imagines herself pregnant. Imagines herself handing the child to her sister and Paul. Imagines the empty feeling after they leave. The stretchmarks and postnatal slump. 'No, I'm sorry. I really am. But I can't have a baby for you. It's just . . . too much. I work cleaning offices. It's a physical job. What if I get morning sickness, or some other complications?'

'I know it's a lot to ask,' Penni acknowledges. 'But you're our only hope of having a child that would be genetically ours. We'd make sure you were looked after.'

Nicola breaks eye contact and shakes her head. The reason Penni can't have children is because she fell out of that tree, and it was Nicola's fault she was up there in the first place. Okay, it was an accident, but it was still her fault. Penni and Paul don't say as much, but the accusation is there in the room with them, mingling with the stale smoke and damp air.

'I don't know if this helps,' Paul says, 'but we're willing to pay you a substantial amount of money.'

Penni's cheeks flush at his offer. They must have talked about it beforehand, but it's clear they both find it distasteful to bring up. Nicola's heart beats a little faster. This might change things. Big money like that would never normally come her way. Her life has been a relentless struggle, a slow slide; maybe this is the rope to haul herself up with.

'How much are you talking about?' she asks, knowing how mercenary she must sound, but unable to phrase it any other way.

'Enough to set you up with a nice flat of your own,' Paul replies.

'Okay.' Nicola swallows. 'I'll think about it.'

Penni's features light up with a fragile hope. 'Really?'

Nicola doesn't respond. Just gives her sister an irritated glare that's shorthand for 'yes'.

'Thank you, Nic.'

Nicola nods, letting the words settle between them, realising that everything is about to change.

Chapter Ten

'I can't believe you're doing this, Nic!' Penni's voice cracks, the last consonant jagged, as she stands by the side of the hospital bed. Her arms are folded, fingernails digging angry half-moons into her skin, tears streaking her face.

Nicola looks up at her sister from the pillows, the sweat-damp hospital gown clinging to the soft ruins of her body. She's never felt so depleted or, paradoxically, so defiant. 'You wanted a baby, so I'm giving you a baby,' she replies, her voice trembling.

Paul pops his head tentatively around the door. His face is pallid, eyes flitting from Penni to Nicola. He looks like he wants to intervene – he always does – in his half-measured, chronic-people-pleaser kind of way. Penni says he's not like this in business. That, apparently, he's tough – ruthless, almost. A different person. But Nicola can't imagine it. She only knows this version of her brother-in-law. Penni flicks her hand towards the corridor, shooing Paul out as though he's a fly. The door clicks softly behind him. It's just them now. Like it always was. Like maybe it always should have been.

Nicola grits her teeth. Her sister clearly thinks it will go better if she speaks to her alone. But she's made up her mind. She won't be swayed on this, no matter how many tears Penni cries. She should be grateful, not guilt-tripping her, after she's just had a hellish nine months of sickness, swollen ankles, and pre-eclampsia, followed by an emergency C-section.

If she'd known what pregnancy actually involved, she would never have agreed to go through with it. But then Nicola glances over to the crib by her side. No. That's not true. She wouldn't change it for anything.

After agreeing to have a baby for her sister, Nicola had been stunned to discover she was carrying twins. This wasn't what she had signed up for. Being pregnant with one child was enough of an adjustment, but carrying two . . . She assumed that having twins must be a genetic thing, berated herself for not having anticipated it, what with her and Penni being identical twins. But the doctor disagreed. Explained that it was rare to be an identical twin, and even rarer for a twin to give birth to identical twins. That it was nothing more than a fluke. Well, whatever the reason, it had happened to her. Nicola was pregnant with twins.

She'd been apprehensive about telling her sister. What if they reneged on the deal? What if they couldn't handle two babies? The thought of them leaving her in the lurch with a couple of newborns made her sick with anxiety. But she needn't have worried. Penni and Paul were thrilled.

Not anymore.

Penni's nostrils flare, and her jaw tics up and down as if she's chewing on all the words she wants to throw at Nicola. 'You're giving me a baby!' she parrots back. 'That's what you think this is? A fucking gift? You're splitting them up, Nicola. Splitting up twins! Do you even hear yourself?'

Nicola does hear herself. She hears her sister, too, but mostly she hears the drumming in her ears, the high-pitched whine of adrenaline still spiralling through her system from the emergency C-section that ended only hours ago. Her whole body floats in a chemical stew of anaesthesia, morphine, and residual terror. It's a miracle she can even talk straight. But there's a kind of clarity that comes after you've been cut open and sewn back up for the sake of someone else — you realise you don't have to be just a conduit, a vessel, a means to someone else's end.

The whole experience has been traumatic. From having the doctor carry out the artificial insemination, where the sperm was deposited directly into Nicola's uterus, to the birth itself, there was nothing about it she enjoyed. Even worse was the sickening joy she witnessed from Penni and Paul when she told them she'd fallen pregnant. Honestly, her sister turned into a complete stranger. She fussed over Nicola like a mother, which would have been nice, but Nicola knew she was only doing it to ensure their babies were taken care of. After they got their hands on them, she had no doubt they'd go back to keeping her at arm's length. They wouldn't want to be reminded of where their children came from.

Nicola couldn't wait to get her body back, her life back, and enough money to buy her own place. The only thing that kept her going was obsessing over property sites in search of her perfect pad. That, and the fact she was able to cut down on her work hours. Although she'd have taken double shifts over the morning sickness, which made her feel like she was going to die.

Penni drags a chair over and sits right up close to her. Too close. 'Think back to when we were younger, Nic. Think back. It would have been unbearable if we hadn't had each other. And yet that's what you want to do to our babies. You want them to be alone!'

Nicola knows she's right, but pushes away the memories of the two of them together. She's too filled with bitterness and spite. She doesn't know where this fury has come from. She doesn't know why she wants to wound her sister so badly. She tries her best to sound reasonable. 'Yes, but this will be different because they'll each have a mother who loves them. We didn't have that.'

Penni's voice splinters. 'We agreed, Nic. We agreed that Paul and I would take them both. Everything's been arranged. We've bought two of everything. I've already fallen in love with them. Both of them. But . . .' She pauses. 'I'd rather you take them both than split them up.'

Nicola hates how sanctimonious her sister sounds. I'd rather you take them both than split them up, *she mimics in her head.* 'I know it's not how we planned it,' Nicola replies. What she really wants to scream is, It's not how you planned it for me.

'But . . . I can't look after twins on my own, and I can't bear to let them both go. I've made up my mind, Pen. They'll be sisters. They'll know each other. But one of them will be mine.'

'Can't you think about them, rather than about you?' Penni spits. Her voice breaks and she falls silent, pleading with her eyes.

The room is so quiet, Nicola can hear the plastic tubing of her IV line flexing as she clenches her fist. She thinks about the contract they signed, about the solicitor's thick, officious glasses and the way he scratched his beard as he explained the legalities: 'The law is clear in the UK. The gestational mother is always the legal mother at birth. Intended parents must apply for a parental order.' She nodded back then, pretending his words didn't apply to her. Pretending it was all perfectly arranged. That the scribble of ink on paper would keep her heart in check. But those words he spoke wormed their way into her subconscious.

Nicola thinks she already knew deep down that she was never going to be able to give both babies away. She just didn't know she would say it out loud, didn't know she would torch her sister's faith in her so completely in a high-dependency hospital room with a view of the car park and the constant shriek of ambulances as background music.

Now, seeing Penni's face — her body rigid, her soul lodged somewhere between horror and heartbreak — she almost wants to take it back. Almost. But then she looks at the white swaddled shapes cradled in the Perspex crib beside her bed, and the fierce, latent thing she never thought she had in her — maternal instinct, maybe, or just the urge not to be a pawn — roars up and pins Nicola to her decision.

Penni wipes a sleeve over her cheeks, smearing mascara in thick clumps. 'You'll ruin everything, you know that? They'll never forgive you. And neither will I.'

'I don't need forgiveness,' Nicola says, but the words taste sharp and metallic, and not quite true.

Penni's eyes are bloodshot, her chest heaving. 'Fine,' she spits. 'I hope you're happy, Nic.' She turns and walks out, shoulders hunched, head bowed.

Nicola listens to her footsteps recede, the noise of her departure loud in the hush. She doesn't know if they'll ever recover from this.

It's not until the room is empty that she allows herself to really look at the white-swaddled lumps in the crib. They're tiny, smaller than she expected, with faces that are both familiar and completely unknown. She reaches for one, and the effort makes her incision burn, but she doesn't care. She wants her. She needs her.

The nurses come in and out, sometimes offering congratulations, sometimes only checking her blood pressure or refilling her water jug. One of them, a round-faced woman named Sima, looks at both cribs with a kind of professional sadness. She doesn't ask questions. She just pats Nicola's hand and tells her she's brave.

After the initial whirlwind, after the paperwork and the phone calls and Penni's scene in the hospital room, it's suddenly astonishingly quiet. Paul and Penni's baby, who they name Bella, is wheeled out to the nursery, and Nicola is left with . . . hers. With her. Her daughter.

She names her Jade. She likes the sound of it – bright, sharp, and precious.

The next few days in the hospital tumble out like a deck of cards, shuffled and unpredictable. Penni doesn't visit, but Paul comes sometimes, usually when Nicola's asleep. She wakes to a faint waft of his aftershave or to the sound of him murmuring in the hallway to a nurse. He never comes in when she's awake, only stands on the threshold, looking at Jade like she might break into a dozen pieces if he steps closer.

When they finally discharge Nicola, it's raining. She wraps her daughter in two blankets and takes a taxi back to her flat. The driver, an old guy with a battered Honda and a generous silence, doesn't comment on the fact that she's alone, or on the way she keeps looking sideways, expecting Penni to materialise next to her in the back seat with a court order. He just drives, and when he pulls up outside her peeling, yellowing block of flats, he helps her with the carrier without being asked. She wants to thank him, but the words stick in her throat.

Inside, everything is exactly as she left it — the half-packed suitcase in the hallway that she didn't have time to bring, the dirty dishes in the sink. There's a note on the doorframe from her new friend, Leila, who she met at antenatal classes, offering to pick up groceries and nappies. She wants to call her, to tell her everything, but she also wants to crawl into bed and sleep for a decade.

She hears the text message ping long after she's settled on the couch with Jade splayed across her chest. It's from Paul: Can we talk? We'd like to see you. Please.

She doesn't answer. Not yet.

The next message comes at midnight, this time from Penni, though it's clearly written by Paul: Let's talk. We'll come over tomorrow morning at ten.

She's about to delete it when Jade begins to cry — a thin, reedy sound that's more bewildered than angry. Nicola gathers her up, pressing her close. She smells of the hospital and the promise of something new and untarnished.

The next morning, with Jade in her arms, Nicola opens the door to see Penni and Paul on the doorstep. Penni looks different, older — her eyes ringed with red, her lips a thin, defensive line. Nicola wonders if she looks the same to Penni.

Penni doesn't speak, just steps inside, followed by Paul, with Bella tucked into an expensive-looking car seat, and they stand there in the compact hallway. For a moment, no one speaks.

Finally, Penni says with a note of sarcasm, 'She looks like you.'

Nicola looks at Bella, then at Jade. Both so new and so breakable. Both so obviously theirs.

They sit in the lounge. The same lounge where the three of them planned this whole charade. Now it's littered with bottles and breast pump parts and a half-opened pack of nappies.

Penni speaks first. 'We need to work things out.'

Nicola nods. 'I'm not letting Jade go.'

'Thought you'd say that.' Penni presses her lips together.

Paul tries to smile, but it comes out as a grimace.

Penni speaks coldly, clinically. 'If you're determined to split them up, then Paul and I think it's best if we do it properly.'

'What do you mean?' Nicola asks, her heart beginning to thump louder.

'Paul, Bella and I will live our lives without you and Jade in them,' she replies.

Nicola's chest constricts at the thought of never seeing Bella. 'You mean, they won't get to know each other?'

'It will be too weird and upsetting for them, knowing that they're twins who've been separated, don't you think?' Penni's gaze is piercing, accusing. She wants Nicola to know that this is her fault.

Nicola doesn't know what to think. She's panicking. Feels blind-sided. But she can't seem to formulate a coherent response. Doesn't know what she wants to say. Except that it all feels wrong.

After some back-and-forth conversation that she can barely remember, Nicola signs a pre-written contract they brought with them that states she won't contact them or her other daughter. She doesn't want to sign it, doesn't even know if it's legally binding, but it's either this or they'll walk away and leave her with both babies and no lump sum, which she wouldn't be able to cope with.

She gets the feeling that Paul isn't happy with this arrangement, but is going along with it for the sake of his wife. After all, he's the biological father of both babies, and he's agreeing to never see Jade again. Maybe it's for the best. Maybe this is the closure they all need in order to get on with their lives.

Before they leave, they bring in all the baby gear that they no longer require. That they purchased when they thought they were keeping both babies. It's all top-of-the-line stuff — hundreds of pounds' worth. Nicola already knows she'll sell most of it and buy second-hand.

Paul reassures her that they will cherish Bella and that the money will be transferred to Nicola's bank account that day. At least they're not backtracking on that part. At this point, she just wants them gone from her flat. She wants to start the process of trying to forget her other daughter. If that's even possible.

That night, Nicola tucks Jade into her Moses basket and whispers into her ear, a little mantra for both of them:

'You're mine, you're loved, and you're enough.'

She doesn't feel like the last part is true. But for now, it's all she has.

Chapter Eleven

JADE

I notice, distantly, that I'm shaking. The tea in my mug sloshes perilously close to the rim, and I set it down on the coffee table with a clatter before I soak my jeans or, worse, my sofa bed. My scalp prickles and my chest is tight, and for a few seconds I think I might cry or laugh or have a panic attack, and honestly, I'm not sure which would be better. The room feels small, suffocating, as if Mum's revelations have sucked all the oxygen out, leaving behind only this weird, heavy air that buzzes with her secrets.

I take a breath, slow and deliberate, and look at Mum, who's pretending not to notice my silent meltdown. She's nursing her own mug with that careful, unshowy neatness she applies to every-thing – small sips, a napkin tucked beneath for the inevitable ring. According to her, she wasn't always so neat and tidy. But I can't imagine her any other way – as if the world might fall to pieces if she ever let herself get messy. I wonder, suddenly, if her twin is the same. And what about *my* twin? Does Bella fold her napkins and sip her tea carefully? Or is she the opposite – wild, carefree, effortless? I don't know, and that unknown gnaws at me in a way I can't explain.

'What the hell, Mum?' I whisper. 'How could you have kept all this a secret? *How?* What am I supposed to do now?'

Mum sets her cup down and says, 'There's nothing you need to do now, Jade. It's all in the past.' She's using her calm voice, the one she reserves for dealing with tricky customers at the pub or with me when I'm being 'impossible'. For a second, I want to scream: *How can you be so blasé about this? I have a twin. My life is basically a soap opera now!* But I don't. Partly because I know she'll just retreat further behind that calm mask, and also because if I start shouting, I might never stop.

Her words hang in the air, daring me to contradict her, to break the flimsy peace she's trying to manufacture for us in this musty one-bedroom flat. The sofa springs dig into the backs of my thighs, and I think about how many hours I've spent here, killing time, half watching Mum's old dramas on the TV, bored out of my mind and wishing I had someone who really got me. I always imagined that if I had a sister, even a weird one, we'd at least have each other. Now I know I do, and she's just . . . somewhere else. With a life I can only picture, richer and brighter and better than mine.

'I can't believe you never told me,' I say, my voice brittle.

Mum's gaze, which was fixed somewhere over my shoulder, snaps to me. 'It wasn't relevant. My sister made her choice. She didn't want us in her life, so I didn't see any point in telling you. What good would it have done? I mean, look at you now, you're all riled up, annoyed, upset. It's a waste of all our energy.'

'That's a bit harsh.'

Mum shrugs. 'Sometimes life is harsh. Sometimes that's just how it is.'

I almost laugh. The woman who cried when she ran over a hedgehog last spring, talking about harshness as if it's just weather. I want to ask her if she's ever missed her sister, if she's ever sat awake at night and imagined a parallel Mum somewhere, drinking expensive wine and talking in a posher accent, unknown and unreachable. But I don't, because I'm not sure I want to know the answer.

Instead, I pace to the window and stare out. It's late, and the streetlights turn everything jaundiced – the peeling paint on the bus shelter, the half-dead shrubs in the garden, the crappy cars parked with two wheels up on the pavement because the road is so narrow. Sometimes I try to imagine who I'd be if we'd never moved here, if I had a dad, if I'd gone to a fancy school like Bella must have done. Would I be more like her? Or would I just be a slightly posher version of myself – still angry, still restless, just with better skin and hair?

This must be why Mum is always so disappointed in me. Maybe she thinks she's been landed with the wrong twin and has ended up with waste-of-space Jade. Well, maybe if I'd had a different mother, I'd have turned out happier and more successful. Like Bella.

Something else hits me like a ton of bricks. 'Her dad?' I ask, my voice little more than a whisper now. My heartbeat twanging against my ribcage.

Mum nods. 'Her dad is your biological father.'

Elation and fury war in my chest. 'And he just left me? You told me my dad never knew about me. That you split up before you knew you were pregnant. You told me you didn't know how to get in touch with him!'

'I'm sorry. I thought it was for the best. I didn't know—'

'You didn't know I'd find out the truth,' I interrupt, shaking my head, bitterness filling my mouth. 'So, what you're saying is that he chose Bella, and left me behind.'

'He didn't want to leave you, Jade. Penni and Paul wanted you both.'

I pause at this, but I'm not ready to let Mum off the hook. 'So it was you who wanted to split us up!' I spit.

'I wanted to keep you. I didn't want to give you up. Couldn't bear to! You're my child!'

My head is about to explode. The only thing I know for sure is that I am not okay. Not with this. Not with any of it. What else has Mum not told me? What else about my own life is a lie or a secret, or 'not relevant'?

I want to head back to Lymington right now and demand answers from a complete stranger who is, apparently, my twin sister. But I also want to throw up. I settle for running my hands through my hair until it sticks out in a halo of static, and then slumping back on to the sofa.

'I have to speak to them,' I say, feeling sick at the thought.

'They don't want us, Jade. And I don't even know if they've told Bella about you.' Mum's words are hurtful.

'Well then, I'll tell her.'

'No!'

'You can't stop me.' I get to my feet.

Mum stands too and grabs hold of my arm. 'Please, Jade. They don't even know we live here. I came down south to try to be closer to them, but I never acted on it. I always kept my distance.' She lets go of my arm and mutters, 'Couldn't stand to see them as a happy family. They probably think we're still up in Yorkshire.'

'Then it's about time they found out we're not,' I snap, striding out into the hall where I slip on my battered trainers and my ancient parka.

'Jade! Don't do this.' Her eyes are wide, her face the same shade as the magnolia walls.

I shake her off and walk out into the evening. The air is sharp and cold, and I welcome it. It feels more honest than the air in the flat. I half hope I'll see someone I know, even one of the girls from school who pretend not to remember me, so I can spill my secret and watch their face twist in confusion. But the streets are empty, the only movement a fox scavenging near the bins and a drunk couple arguing outside the Turkish takeaway.

I have no intention of going to Lymington to see my newfound family right now. I'm too worked up to think straight, let alone have a coherent conversation. But it won't hurt for Mum to stew in her own juices for a while. See how it feels to have all control taken away. I know, deep down, that I'm being mean. That I'm lashing out. But what does she expect? She's lied to me all these years and kept me apart from the person who could have been my ally. My best friend. I've been going through life on my own, always feeling like something's missing. Maybe this is why. Maybe that hollowness in my chest is because we were separated.

I roam aimlessly until I realise I'm close to Zac's parents' house, a small terrace in a nicer part of town than mine, but not by much. I hesitate, debating whether it's worth the hassle of dealing with Zac's mum's disapproving stares, but my feet keep moving until I'm at the door. I ring the bell, and immediately regret it – maybe he's already gone to the pub. Maybe he's with some new girlfriend, the one I'm always convinced he'll leave me for. But then the porch light flicks on, and Zac answers, hair tousled, eyes pinched and glazed from one of his gaming sessions.

'Hey,' I say, suddenly exhausted.

'You came.' Zac's eyes light up. 'I was just about to leave for the pub. Shall we go now, or do you want to come in for a bit first?'

'Do you mind if we don't go out?' I ask.

'Really?' His face drops. 'Jed and Cal are expecting me.'

I give him a look, and his shoulders drop too. 'But, no, yeah, that's cool. We can stay in. I'll message them.'

'Thanks.' I stand on my tiptoes and press my lips to his.

'Close the door, Zac! You're letting all the cold air in,' his mum calls from upstairs.

'Sorry!' he calls back.

Inside, the house smells like toast and air freshener. Thankfully, his parents are already in bed, so Zac leads me up to his room, dodging a stack of laundry and their cat, Leo, who hisses at me as usual.

I sit on the edge of Zac's unmade bed, and he immediately starts fussing, clearing away crumpled clothes and beer cans, and putting on some music.

'You okay?' he asks, sitting next to me.

I shake my head – a small, tight movement. He puts his arm around me, and for a second, I let myself collapse into him, breathing in his familiar scent of sweat, shampoo, and rolling tobacco.

We sit like that for a while, both of us silent except for the low hum of the computer fan and Zac's breathing.

Eventually, he breaks the silence, wanting to know what happened when I confronted Mum, but I ask if we can leave it for now. It's too big to talk about. And I don't know what I'm going to do. Not yet. A brief image of the bailiffs pops into my head, but I don't want to talk about that either.

Instead, I distract him with my body and my lips, kissing him harder than usual, like I'm trying to ignite something in the dead air. He responds, surprised but not unhappy, and soon we're tangled up together, in knotted sheets and desperation. I want to forget, for just a short while, that there's another me out there, a better or worse version of Jade, living the life that could have been mine.

Lost in our bodies, I don't stay quiet, and he keeps shushing me, putting his hand over my mouth. His parents go to bed at some ridiculous hour as they have early starts, which means we have to keep the noise down. Zac is being such a drag about it that I pull away, the moment lost. I reach down to the floor and yank one of his old T-shirts over my head before lighting one of his roll-ups.

'You can't smoke in here, Jade.'

'So open a window,' I retort, knowing how mean I sound but unable to care.

He shakes his head, but does as I ask, then takes the roll-up from me and inhales deeply. The more Zac takes shit from me, the more he annoys me. I know I'm being an irrational bitch, but I can't help it. My mind is all over the place. I want to cry. I want to smash something. I want to do something terrible.

I take back the roll-up, lie next to Zac and stare at the ceiling, tracing the cracks in the plaster. 'Do you think people can change?' I ask.

'Dunno. Not really. Why?'

'Just wondering.'

He props himself up on one arm, peering at me with that intensely sincere look he sometimes gets. 'You're not your mum, you know. Or your dad. Or anyone else. You're . . . you.'

That's the problem, I want to say. I don't know who that is. I'm just a collection of habits and reactions and now, apparently, a twin-shaped emptiness no one bothered to mention to me.

Zac doesn't press. He just wraps his arms around me and holds on, like if he squeezes tight enough, I'll stay here and not drift off into the ether of other people's choices. I want to believe he can anchor me. I really do.

Chapter Twelve

Nicola walks the drizzly streets with four-month-old Jade bundled warmly inside her pram. It's July, but a British July, which means cold rain and grey skies. Her thoughts are sliding all over the place. She doesn't feel like herself.

The past few months have been a blur of exhaustion, resentment, and fear. Fear that she's made the wrong decision. That she's messed up her life. That she's going to mess up Jade's life. Her days are dictated by her daughter's wailing and her insatiable hunger. When she sleeps – which isn't often – Nicola slumps comatose on the sofa or dozes fitfully under her unwashed duvet.

Sometimes, when she looks at Jade, she feels a surge of pure uncut love – physical, like being punched in the heart. Other times, she feels nothing at all, just a blankness, a sense of going through the motions. She worries that this makes her a bad mother, but she read in a magazine that many women feel the same way. That apparently there are mums who love their babies and hate them in equal measure. She takes comfort in these articles. It makes her own failings feel less unique.

When Jade was six weeks old, the social worker said that she thought Nicola had borderline postnatal depression, and so her GP referred her to a therapist. She started seeing her the week after Easter. Her name was Helen, and she wore chunky jewellery and never asked about anything unless Nicola brought it up first. She liked that about her. Helen let her talk about her childhood, about the day Penni fell out of the tree, about how she and her sister had previously sworn never to let anything come between them. She didn't tell Helen she regretted breaking that promise. She just told her she didn't know how to fix it.

'You're grieving two separate things,' Helen said. 'The future you thought you'd have, and the relationship you lost with your sister.' She sipped her tea and waited for Nicola to speak. She never did. She just let the words hang there, solid and irrefutable. That was the last time Nicola attended. It was too real. Too painful.

Now she's living a new reality with her daughter. Just the two of them. It's lonely, but she doesn't have the energy to fix that. To go out and talk to people. She met up with Leila, the girl from antenatal classes, a couple of times. But, aside from their babies, they didn't have anything in common. Leila's married with a supportive husband, and a big, loving, noisy family close by. Nicola felt too overwhelmed by all that, as well as a little envious, so she pulled back, made excuses not to meet up. She knows it was a silly thing to do. Leila was sweet, generous, good company. But Nicola couldn't handle it. It made her feel socially awkward and unworthy.

So, here she is, pushing a pram along the streets of Middlesbrough alone. Drizzle turns to great splattering raindrops that ping against the rain guard like popcorn in a pan. Cars sweep past, spraying puddles, and Nicola is soaked through, her hands frozen and stiff as they grip the handle. It's at moments like this when she understands how big a mistake she's made. What the hell is she doing with a baby? She's single with no family, hardly any friends. She's only twenty-nine years old, and her life feels like it's over. Part of her really did want to keep Jade, but the other part did it to spite Penni. She can admit that to herself. Although if she were given the opportunity to go back and reverse it, she knows she never would. Jade has somehow burrowed her way into Nicola's heart.

Penni and Paul haven't been in touch, other than to tell her they're moving down south because of the business. Bullshit. *Nicola suspected they might do something like that. That they'd want to get away from her. Penni's probably scared Nicola might try to lay claim to her other daughter. If Nicola had a partner, she probably would. But it's enough to deal with one baby on her own. Two might finish her. At least she has Paul's money to tide her over for a few months, along with the lump sum to buy a nice little terraced house. That was the plan, anyway.*

But now that Penni and Paul are relocating from Whitby, Nicola has the germ of an idea. It's not definite yet, but it's something that could become a reality if she makes it happen. Once her sister is settled down south, Nicola is going to find out where. It shouldn't be too hard, as they're moving their business too. She seems to remember that Paul's originally from Hampshire, so maybe that's where they're going. Once they're established, Nicola will use her funds to buy a little flat nearby. Not too near that they run into one another, but close enough that she can keep an eye on her other daughter. To stay close to her. To shorten the mother—daughter cord that will be painfully stretched to breaking point if she's taken too far away.

The rain is hammering down now, so Nicola takes refuge in an empty bus shelter. She rubs her hands together to warm them and wipes the droplets from her face before peering into the pram to see her daughter sound asleep.

Despite the hardship and the loneliness and the fear and sleep deprivation, despite the fallout with her family, and the slow road to her mental and physical recovery, she still can't believe this little human being is hers. She can't believe any of it. For the first time in her life, she feels like she has something to lose. And she's going to do everything she can to keep it.

Chapter Thirteen

JADE

The next day, I creep out of Zac's house with the stealth of a cat burglar, my trainers making no sound on the stairs. Much as I was grateful for his arms last night, I'm not in the mood for conversation today.

Outside, the sky is as grey as a bruise, the air filled with the sound of birds who have urgent business. I cut through streets that feel unfamiliar in this light, like the world's been freshly shaken up and all the shops have moved an inch to the left. I don't want to go home, but there's nowhere else to go.

At the flat, I hold my breath in the lobby and slide the key in slowly and carefully, imagining the sound waves radiating through Mum's cheap-arse door. She'll be out for the count, I hope, shrouded in Primark sheets, breathing like a congested pug. I tiptoe to the lounge, debating whether to make toast.

I settle for a cup of instant coffee and take it over to the sofa, remembering my phone's nearly dead. I dig the charger out of my bag (it's not even mine, it's Zac's, stolen with no shame), plug it in, and watch the screen flicker slowly to life.

And then I google her – like it's an accident, like my fingers just kind of slide on to the keyboard and type 'Bella Newbury' out of muscle memory. It's not an ordinary name, so the first hit is her, capital-H Her. A piece from a couple of years ago catches my eye – she's on the front page of some local business rag, all teeth and ambition. She's the owner of Newbury New Forest Property Group – a bit of a tongue-twister, but it's a sleek little empire of lettings and sales, with more than a few million-pound mansions on the books. The kind of business my mum rails against when she's had more than three vodka tonics. Now I know why she has an aversion to estate agents.

The article calls Bella 'a disruptor in the housing market', which makes me want to gag, and there's a whole spiel about how she took over her parents' company and doubled its size within a year. There's a photo of her at some charity ball, arms linked with the local Tory MP, the kind of girl who stands in the centre of every photo. I'm halfway down her Insta, scrolling through shots of her in velvet blazers and swanky offices, when I hear the death rattle of Mum's bedroom door.

I freeze, thumb poised mid-scroll, listening to the familiar rhythm: the pause, the sigh, the shuffle of her slippers on the carpet. She appears in the doorway, last night's mascara smudged, her grey towelling dressing gown open over an ancient Sainsbury's tee. I cock an eyebrow and pretend I'm just watching TikTok videos.

Mum makes us both tea and then slumps on to the sofa next to me, clutching her mug like a talisman, and looks at me. Just looks, for a full thirty seconds, until my skin starts itching.

'So . . .' She speaks finally, her voice gone all soft. 'Did you talk to her?'

I shake my head. 'Went to Zac's.'

She exhales. 'Would have been nice if you'd let me know.'

I shrug, unable to form the word 'sorry'.

'You okay?' she asks.

I shake my head again, but only a tiny bit, so she can pretend not to see.

Mum exhales hard. 'I'm sorry, Jade. I should've told you. Should've told you years ago.' Her eyes go all watery, and she makes this strangled noise like she's trying to swallow a sob. 'I just . . . I didn't know how.'

I want to shout at her, to throw my phone at the wall like a reality TV star, but all I do is blink at her. 'Yes, you should have,' I say, but it comes out small.

She looks so wretched, I almost feel bad. Almost.

'I found her online,' I add, just to twist the knife.

She winces and nods. 'Of course you did. You always were good at digging.'

I can't stop myself. 'She's loaded.'

Mum's mouth twitches at the corner. 'Yeah, well. Some people have all the luck, eh?'

'Would've been nice to have a twin,' I say, hearing the acid in it.

She flinches, and I hate that I feel a flicker of guilt. 'It was never that simple.' Mum pauses, and then she launches into this monologue about how hard it was, how abandoned she felt by everyone, her twin with a new, better life, her parents, who she never knew, but found out later were both dead from overdoses, no one on her side except herself. I hear it as if from a distance, like I'm underwater. She says the other woman – my 'Auntie' Penni – was so desperate to have kids that she begged Mum to 'consider her situation'. I almost feel sorry for Mum, except I know she's leaving out all the bits where she made her own choices.

'What about the money they gave you?' I ask, because I remember that part, and I want to see her squirm.

She sighs, the sound full of ancient exhaustion. 'There was a bit. Not a fortune, but enough for this place. Could've got more for my money up north, but . . .' She shrugs. 'Even with the flat paid for, I was still skint. Still am.' She emits the bleakest laugh I've ever heard.

'I thought you rented this place.' I suddenly realise I've never seen her fill out any paperwork for the flat, never seen a landlord's letter.

She looks away, sheepish. 'I didn't want to have to explain how I got the money to buy it. So I let you believe I rented,' she says, the words heavy as wet socks.

'So you own it outright?' I stare at her, genuinely gobsmacked.

Mum's cheeks go pink. 'It's not The Ritz, love.'

'But you make me pay rent.' I fight the urge to laugh or cry, I can't tell which.

'I still have bills, Jade — water, leccy, gas, council tax, insurance . . . shall I go on? They don't pay themselves.'

'Fair enough.' I raise my hands in surrender. 'So, was it worth it? Losing a kid for a grotty flat?'

Her face freezes, and for a second I think she's going to scream at me, or hit me, or dissolve into snotty tears. Instead, she just whispers, 'God, Jade. You think I don't regret it every day?'

I shrug. 'I dunno. You never said. Why didn't you tell Perfect Penni to piss off? You were just kids, and it was an accident. She had no right to ask you to give up a child.'

Mum's lips twist. 'I felt guilty. Course I did. I knew the tree thing was an accident, but that didn't stop me feeling terrible about it. I ruined her chance to have a family. And there was me able to have two beautiful daughters.' She takes a breath, and some old wound in her seems to close over. 'You weren't supposed to know,' she says. 'None of it. I tried to do my best for you.'

I roll my eyes. 'By lying to me?'

She shakes her head. 'By giving you a clean slate. A proper life. Less mess than I ever had.'

I want to argue, but what's the point? She's not strong enough to accept the truth of what she did, and I'm too tired to force it on her.

◆ ◆ ◆

That night, at the pub, I pull pints like a robot and watch the regulars drift in, all of them oblivious to what's boiling inside me. My head spins with possible futures, none of which seem plausible. I try to imagine meeting Bella – the real Bella, not the goddess-tier version I've built up in my head from her online presence – but it makes my stomach flip. She'll be smarter, richer, prettier. I hate that I'm already rehearsing the way she'll look down on me. I need to get my life together.

Maybe she'll pity me, maybe she'll ignore me altogether, and which would I prefer? Neither, if I'm honest. What could I do that might turn my life around? I don't have a family that'll gift me a business; I need to find a way to make something of myself on my own. I want her to envy me, just for a second, but I can't think of a single thing she would want from my life. Aside from maybe – the thought comes unbidden – to meet her birth mother. *My* mother. Or maybe she won't. Maybe she's perfectly happy as she is.

It's quieter behind the bar now, the screens glowing with football scores, and I lose myself in the rhythm: pour, wipe, pour, wipe. Underneath it all, my mind starts running through options, a desperate little algorithm of self-improvement. I could go to college, but I don't have the money for tuition, and besides, I was shit at school. Maybe I could get a grant, or one of those hardship funds, but they'd probably want to see some actual 'promise'. I could join a gym, be a personal trainer – there are loads of them on Instagram, and they all seem to be mega-successful. I could reinvent myself as the fitness twin, but considering my smoking habit, I'd probably die of emphysema before I made it to the taster session.

The idea of bettering myself freaks me out, but also . . . it kind of excites me. For the first time since I can remember, I actually want to achieve something. Not a lottery win or a scratchcard miracle, but something earned. It's pathetic, but I cling to it – the fantasy of turning up at Bella's fancy office, with a life, a version of myself she can't ignore. It's the most awake I've felt in months, maybe years.

I start jotting notes on a bar receipt, all the ways I could remake myself – night classes, online diplomas, fake it till I make it. Maybe I could get a job in property, work my way up from junior to top negotiator, or whatever they call themselves. I know I could do it. I'm smart. I've just been lazy. I could start calling myself Jade Newbury, just to see how it feels. I'm so lost in the daydream that I don't even hear the bell for last orders.

Chapter Fourteen

BELLA

I draw on a sweep of eyeliner with a proficient flick, and cap the pen, sitting back to admire my handiwork. For a fleeting second, the mirror reflects a version of me who looks together. Like the kind of woman who's never had to google 'how to negotiate a business overdraft' at 2 a.m.

I pop my lips, admiring my favourite shade, *Damson Ambition*, and glance over the rest of myself – clear skin, hair wanded into careful waves, blouse uncreased – and permit myself a half-smile.

My bedside clock ticks at me as I stuff my feet into my boots, already mentally rerunning the coming conversation. Another day, another make-or-break meeting, only this time my audience is the bank. I've spent a week psyching myself up for this.

After my failed attempt to land an investor, today's pitch is that I need to extend the business overdraft to bridge the gap until sales pick up, which sounds rational enough if you ignore the numbers. Staring out of the bedroom window, I force myself to believe this is fixable.

My secret weapon, if I can call it that, is Fritz Marsden. Of all the bank managers in the world, mine is a guy I half know. We overlapped at school – he was a couple of years ahead – but we really bonded during a school ski trip to Chamonix. There was a night when four of us snuck out after curfew with the intention of buying weed from a lift operator, but after getting lost and arguing in the snow, we ended up with a bottle of glühwein, three chalet maids, two ski instructors, and a hangover that wiped out half a day's skiing. Fritz, bless him, made up some lame excuse about us getting stuck in a ski lift, and basically saved us from getting put on report. I haven't seen him for years, but he's been fast-tracked and now manages the branch in town.

I'd be lying if I said the connection didn't comfort me, even if it is remote and awkward and ancient history. For a week, I've been running scenarios in my head: Fritz, jovial in an old-school way, rubber-stamping the overdraft and maybe catching up over coffee. I never factor in the possibility of rejection. I can't bring myself to even consider it.

I take one last look in the hall mirror: charcoal-grey trouser suit, checked for lint; plum silk blouse; black patent boots, buffed to a gloss; hair half pinned. Despite a watery sun, October has wasted no time making it clear that summer is gone, so I add my most businesslike black wool coat and a lightweight, patterned scarf. Okay, that'll do.

Walking up the High Street, the wind is so fierce it makes my eyes water. I keep my head down, realising too late that the tears are probably ruining the eyeliner I was so proud of. By the time I get to the bank, I'm sniffling and can barely focus.

Inside, the air smells of printer paper and carpet glue. There are three people ahead of me in the queue for a cashier, but I head straight to the help desk. The woman behind the counter is maybe forty, with the brisk, managerial aura of someone who could transition into aviation security without missing a beat. Her badge says 'Marion'.

I clear my throat and paste on a smile. 'Hi, I have an appointment with Fritz Marsden for nine fifteen. Name's Bella Newbury.'

'Of course, Ms Newbury. If you'd like to take a seat?' Marion's voice is professional. She disappears into a door marked 'Staff Only', and I perch in the designated waiting area – a corridor with a row of seats facing a pale green wall with black and white prints of Lymington Quay. Part of me wants to twiddle with my phone, but it seems unprofessional. Instead, I peer down the corridor to the queue where a woman's trying to fill in a form with a pen on a chain that's too short.

Five minutes pass. Then ten. My nerves start to chew at my insides, nibbling at the confidence I built up all morning. I go over my pitch in my head, but it's starting to sound like excuses. I clutch my phone like a talisman.

At 9.32, Marion reappears, this time with a look of apology that I know all too well from years of managing angry landlords.

'So sorry, Ms Newbury, Mr Marsden has had to step into an emergency meeting this morning. He sends his regrets, but we can reschedule if you like?'

My stomach drops. I try to keep my face neutral, but I can feel it stiffen.

'Or, I can see if one of our other business managers is free to see you?'

I weigh up the options. It took me two weeks to get this meeting with Fritz, and I don't think I can afford to wait another two. 'Yes, please. Another manager should be fine.'

'All right.' Marion nods. 'Charmaine Taylor should be free in ten minutes if you're able to wait.'

I glance down at my phone, pretending to check my calendar, then look up. 'That would be great.'

'Super. I'll let her know you're here.'

Marion vanishes again. I sit and try to recalibrate. Charmaine Taylor – not a name I've heard before. I imagine someone steely, with little patience for sob stories. But maybe, I tell myself, a fresh face will mean a fresh perspective. I rehearse the pitch all over again, but now the lines feel wrong. They were prepared for an old friend, not this unknown business manager.

Eventually, a door opens, and a woman calls my name. She's taller than me, maybe forty-five, wearing glasses, dressed in a cheap black trouser suit with a coral necklace. The handshake is brisk, dry-palmed, more of a statement than a greeting.

'Bella Newbury? I'm Charmaine Taylor. Why don't you come through?'

She leads me into a small, sterile room with no windows, like a police interview room – not that I've ever been inside one of those – and two chairs arranged at a diagonally non-confrontational angle. The table between us is cheap laminate, peeling at the edges. There is nothing on the table but a tissue box and her laptop, which she opens as soon as we're both seated.

'Newbury's estate agents, right?' she says, taking a seat behind the desk.

It's Newbury New Forest Property Group, but I don't correct her. 'Yes, that's right.'

'So, Ms Newbury. What brings you in today? The business, or your personal account?' She looks up; her smile is professional but doesn't reach her eyes.

'The business.' I confirm, a little worried that she's not up to speed – I thought she was supposed to be a business manager. 'I had a meeting planned with Fritz, but . . .' I splay out my hands. 'He's busy.'

'Let's have a look.' She shifts her gaze to her laptop screen, and there's a bit of to-and-froing while she tries to find the account. This isn't filling me with confidence, but I can't very well get up and leave now.

I launch into my rehearsed explanation about 'cashflow volatility' and 'short-term liquidity challenges', careful not to sound too desperate. I talk about the buoyancy of the property market how our agency is on the verge of securing a big developer (a little white lie, but not beyond the realms of possibility), how an increase in overdraft is just a 'tide-over' until the commissions hit from the deal I'm lining up.

Throughout my pitch, Charmaine types, occasionally lifting her eyes to interject: 'Mmm' . . . 'I see' . . . 'Go on'. Her accent is tricky to place – somewhere between London and Hampshire.

'And what's the current arrangement with your overdraft?' she asks, tapping keys. Her nails are short, unpolished, and unforgiving.

'It's meant to be thirty, but I'm currently two and a half over that.' I force a smile, as if it's just a harmless oversight, nothing to worry about.

'For how long have you been over that?' She doesn't blink.

'Three. Maybe four weeks.' In reality, it's closer to six.

Charmaine can clearly see all this information on her screen, so it feels like she's twisting the knife by asking me to repeat the facts to her. She gives a thin smile, the kind that says *I've heard all this before*. Her fingers rattle on the keyboard, and then she swivels the screen to face me: a spreadsheet, full of red numbers and negative signs that make me feel nauseous.

'I've looked at your account performance over the last year. It appears there have been repeated periods of exceeding the facility, sometimes by as much as twenty per cent. Would you agree that's accurate?'

I swallow. 'There were a couple of times, yes, but it's always evened out. We had some delayed payments from clients who—'

'The problem is,' she interrupts, 'banks don't like unauthorised borrowing. And your business hasn't grown its net income year to year, which would make a temporary increase less appealing.'

Her tone is professional, but the line is clear. I try my original tack, mentioning that the potential new client is a game-changer and that I'm due to meet with them soon.

'Do you have a contract or a letter of intent from this developer?' asks Charmaine, eyes flat behind her rimless glasses.

'Not yet, but they've agreed in principle to give us sole agency on their new units.' The embellishment comes out before I can stop it, and I can only pray my confidence might become reality.

Charmaine interlocks her fingers on the desk, glances at the computer, and says, 'I'm afraid that without a signed contract, it's very difficult to extend additional credit on your account. What I can do, though, is discuss the option of transferring your whole overdraft into a loan. It would lock in a fixed repayment schedule and take away some of that month-to-month uncertainty.'

Translated: the overdraft is being shut down, but we'll happily sell you a loan at a higher interest rate.

I try one last option, keeping everything crossed. 'Could I add a further ten to the loan?' I ask, hopefully.

'I'm sorry, but that won't be possible.'

I start to argue, but I see the futility of it, and my words peter out. She's already moved on to explaining the paperwork. My mind jitters, panic rising from my gut. The silence in the little room is dense with my disappointment. I sign the form because there's no other option. She prints a copy, paper still warm from the machine in the corner, and hands it to me.

'You'll receive confirmation by email in a couple of days,' she says, standing, the meeting already over in her mind. This handshake is as brisk as her first, and she shepherds me into the corridor with a practised arm gesture.

As I step out of the bank, the cold is immediate and numbing. I stand for a minute, blinking into the wind, cowed by shame and the taste of impending disaster. I think of all the things I should have said, of how differently it would have gone if Fritz Marsden had been there instead of Charmaine Taylor, who clearly wouldn't care less about our Chamonix adventure or the fact that I got a B in GCSE Economics.

I wish with all my heart that I'd agreed to wait and see Fritz.

But now it's too late.

Chapter Fifteen

JADE

I shove a slice of pale white bread into the toaster and push the lever down. The whole counter is scattered with the remnants of a half-arsed attempt at lunch – cheese slices, a bit of squashy tomato, and a supermarket tub of margarine. I fumble with the lid, and the foil cover snaps open with a metallic burp, slicing across the side of my ring finger. 'Shit,' I hiss, cradling my hand.

The cut stings in a sharp, sudden way, tiny beads of red swelling and then dripping anaemically down towards my wrist. I shove my finger between my lips until the pain lessens, like Mum told me to do when I was a kid. For a second, I remember her soothing voice, her hands, the way she'd hold me tight whenever I hurt myself. Now, she just finds new ways to criticise me.

Her silhouette fills the doorway, arms folded over her dressing gown, one eyebrow raised. 'Are you bleeding all over the food again?'

I grab a sheet of kitchen roll, wrap it around my finger, and glare. 'It's not on the food. It's fine.'

She tuts, shakes her head, and marches forward.

Before Mum can get a word in, my phone buzzes, and for a second, the tension shatters – a notification, a lifeline, a promise of somewhere better.

I wrench my phone out of my hoodie pocket, dropping but then catching it with my good hand. The world goes quiet as I see the sender – Harringtons, the agency I begged for an internship. My pulse spikes. Maybe this is it, the golden email, the start of my real life. I thumb open the message, scrolling straight to the body. It doesn't even pretend to be personal. 'Thank you for your application, but we regret to inform you that, after careful consideration, your skills and experience do not currently match our requirements . . .' I whisper the words aloud, numb, then let my head droop.

I pinch the bridge of my nose. The toaster explodes my bread into the air just at that moment, as if even it feels my humiliation and needs to punctuate it. 'Another bloody rejection,' I mutter, voice flat as a pancake. I collapse into one of the vinyl kitchen chairs.

Mum steps forward. 'Well, it's hardly surprising, is it? Are you going to clear up this mess?'

I ball up the bloody tissue, lob it at the bin, and miss by a mile. I reach for my phone again, fingers trembling, and scroll numbly through my inbox. Just more automated rejections, more notifications from job boards, reminders I'm never going to escape Every ping is a fresh cut. 'Thanks for the sympathy.' I don't bother to hide the sarcasm.

She ignores it, bringing the toastie I abandoned and parking it in front of me. Then she dramatically loosens her dressing gown and slides into the chair opposite.

For a second, we just watch each other.

'I am sympathetic,' she eventually responds, sounding anything but.

'Could've fooled me.' I pick at the crust of my toastie.

She opens her mouth, changes her mind, then tries again. 'But—'

'Oh, here we go.' I cut her off, feeling the pressure rise up my spine, setting my teeth on edge.

She presses her lips together, then powers through. 'But,' she continues, 'you barely scraped your GCSEs, and your CV's just . . . what, odd jobs followed by four years of pulling pints? Why would any interior design firm want to hire you?'

I want to scream. Instead, I fish for something to say, anything that sounds less pathetic than the truth. 'Because . . . I'm creative. I have life experience, I know how to talk to people. I'm . . .' I search for another, more compelling word, 'hard-working.' I force myself to meet her eyes.

Mum's nose wrinkles. She exhales. 'Jade, my darling, I love you dearly, but *please*, since when are you creative? And I hate to break it to you, but you are not the most hard-working person I've ever met.'

I flare my nostrils. 'Fine, so I don't have a degree or other fancy qualifications. Maybe I'd be more motivated if I had something worth working towards. But no one will even give me a chance. How do you get experience if no one will give you experience? I'm not even asking for any payment! I'd be giving them free labour. I just need a short internship to get me started.'

Mum clicks her tongue. 'It's hardly free labour. Training people is a pain in the backside. I should know – I had to train *you*.'

'Very funny.' I think back to those early days when Mum kept losing her shit over all the little mistakes I made. Maybe she has a point.

'It's all very competitive these days,' Mum adds unhelpfully.

'Tell me about it,' I grumble.

'If you're really serious, you need basic qualifications – do a course, build a . . . a whatchamacallit . . . a portfolio. Have you actually ever designed anything?'

I want to argue, but she's right. I have nothing but desperation and a folder of half-baked ideas, all screenshots and Pinterest boards and daydreams.

'Surely they must have programs online where you can create something,' she continues. 'They have these apps where you can design a room. Why don't you do that?'

Why don't you do that? I mimic her words in my head. *Ugh*, I feel like screaming. I know what Mum says is true, but it all just feels so hard, so long-winded, so impossible. I stare at my phone and will the rejection emails to set themselves on fire. The longer I sit here, the more the room closes in. The smell of the burnt toast. The ancient whirr of the fridge. The pressure of Mum's relentless, suffocating interest.

'I'm going to have a shower,' she announces, getting to her feet.

My chest tightens and my vision goes blurry and spotty for a moment. It feels like a marathon I haven't trained for. I've already spent endless nights creating an exaggerated CV, trawling through design company websites, drafting letters, researching universities and college courses – none of which I can afford or am qualified for. I'll be at retirement age before I get anywhere.

And all the while, the clock is ticking while I watch Bella's life unfold on Instagram: sunlit café breakfasts, glittering events, champagne laughter. I wouldn't be surprised if she was awarded the Nobel Peace Prize next week. My twin swans around beautiful Lymington like a princess with everything handed to her on a plate, while I'm stuck here in shitty suburbia, sleeping on a couch, scraping by.

The bitterness is a physical taste, sour and thick. I want to text her, or even just comment something snarky on her latest post, but of course I don't. I know I'm only feeling this way because of my frustration. Instead, I scroll back through the rejection email, reading and rereading the line about my 'skills and experience' not 'matching requirements', like maybe if I stare at it long enough, the words will change.

As Mum gets up to make a cup of tea, a possibility floats towards me like a lifeline in a choppy ocean. It's a cute idea and vaguely reminds me of a storyline in a movie I once saw. What if I applied for a job – any job – at Newbury's? I could look to see if they're hiring. And then, when I show up at the offices for my interview, I'll come face to face with Bella, and we can be like – *what the hell?*

The fantasy grows in my mind – me, walking into Newbury's offices for an interview to find Bella sitting across a glass conference table. The moment hangs there, cinematic, like something from a Netflix special. Will she do a double take? The possibilities spiral out – will it be this cosmic reconnection, the universe righting a wrong? Will she be speechless? Maybe she'll cry. Whatever, it's a better story than the one I'm living now. It would make for a great 'first meeting' anecdote. I can picture us telling people later: *It was such a crazy coincidence! What are the chances of my own twin coming in to be interviewed for a job? Neither of us could believe it. We were stunned.* Local media will want to interview us. Maybe even national. I shake away my overactive imagination and get back to practicalities.

I'll probably have to lie heavily on my CV in order to score an interview, but that's okay because I won't really be going for the job. I'll just be using it as a fun way to get to meet my sister.

Mum shuffles back to the table, clutching her tea. 'What are you up to?' She eyes me suspiciously.

'Nothing,' I reply. But I can't stop the smile tugging at my lips as I open Newbury's website. It's all navy and gold, full of stock photos of people shaking hands and laughing over laptops. I navigate to their Careers page. There's a load of waffle about '*Being Exceptional* and *Building a Bright Future*', but I scroll on until I reach the Positions Available section, where there are two jobs listed. One: Senior Negotiator, requirements laughably out of my league. Two: Internship, open to 'passionate individuals with a keen interest in property and customer service'. I feel a small pulse of hope. I could be passionate. I could show a keen interest in property. Despite my lack of success applying for other internships, I'm optimistic about this one. It feels as though it's fate that I was rejected by the others, because I was meant to apply for this one. And when Bella and I do finally meet, perhaps she'll even offer me a proper paid job with the company. It would be perfect.

I lean back in my seat and take another bite of my cheese toastie, feeling the first swell of proper excitement I've had in months. In years.

I glance up at Mum, who's now sipping her tea and scrolling on her phone. I get up from the table, carry my plate to the sink, and retreat to the sofa where I pull up my CV – the one I've been 'customising' for every different application, made up of equal parts truth, exaggeration, and outright fiction. I start tweaking. 'Barmaid' becomes 'Licensed Beverage Consultant'. I invent a few more extracurriculars: volunteered at local food bank, coordinated pub-quiz nights, mentored new recruits. It's not exactly a crime, I reason, if I'm only trying to get a foot in the door so that I can reunite with my long-lost sister.

The next part takes longer. 'Why do you want to work for Newbury's?' the site asks. I stare at the blinking cursor, willing it to answer for me. I type: 'I have always admired Newbury's innovative approach to customer relationships and value your commitment to supporting young people within the community.' I delete it and try again: 'My lifelong interest in property, combined with experience handling high-pressure customer service situations, makes me uniquely suited to the team.' I delete that, too. Try again: 'I believe I would be a perfect fit for the friendly, ambitious culture at Newbury's, and am eager to learn from the best in the field.' It's all bullshit, but it's the kind of bullshit professionals like. At least I hope it is.

I attach my Frankenstein's monster of a CV, triple-check my email address, and hover over the submit button. Maybe I should give it the overnight test. It's probably best to let it marinate for a while. My finger trembles. I think of Bella's Instagram page, of her glossy, unbothered smile. I think of Mum, probably already drafting a group chat update for her friends about my latest 'failure'. I think of the possibility, however slim, that I could actually get an interview. That I could actually meet my twin up close, like looking in a mirror for the first time.

I hit submit before I can overthink it, then slam my laptop shut. There's a jolt of panic, but also a strange excitement, like the first drop on a roller coaster. I hug my knees to my chest and let the anticipation fizz through me while I wait for my sister to respond.

I think this could turn my life around. I think this might be amazing.

Chapter Sixteen

JADE

I'm slouched on the sofa, eating a Snickers, scrolling on my phone, bored, frustrated and antsy. I tried watching TV, but I can't seem to concentrate on anything. Mum's on a double shift today so the flat is quiet and empty. She left a note on the counter about defrosting chicken Kievs for tea, but even the promise of carbs later can't unstick me from this mood.

I can't go and see Zac because he's still in Devon, at the world's most tragic family get-together – his words, not mine, though I agree with him. He's apparently stuck in a cottage with no Wi-Fi and three generations of relatives all trying to tell the same stories, and he keeps texting me updates about his existential agony, but I haven't replied to any of them. I know if I do, he'll call me, and I don't want to hear his voice right now.

He asked if I wanted to go along on the trip, but I couldn't think of anything worse, so I told him I had to work. Actually, the real reason I didn't go is because I know his parents don't like me, and I don't think I could have stood days of forced politeness. Zac always tells me I'm imagining their dislike of me, but I know I'm not wrong. Maybe I should have gone just to spite them. It would be better than this desperate feeling of hanging around and waiting for my life to begin.

I toss my phone on to the sofa, harder than necessary, so it slips and lands screen-down in a pool of toast crumbs. I almost want it to break – then at least I'd have a new problem, something tangible instead of this endless gnawing at the base of my stomach. Normally I love a bit of daytime TV or TikTok scrolling, but lately I just can't seem to drum up any enthusiasm.

I lean back, wedge my hands under my thighs, and stare at the ceiling, tracing the cracks where Mum's last attempt at DIY filling has already started to flake. I try to tell myself that it's just the change in seasons. That I always get like this at the end of summer, when the air turns damp and the mornings smell of leaf mould and the shops start putting Halloween stuff on the shelves. Mum always says autumn is her favourite, that it feels like a reset, but for me it's the opposite – a slow, claustrophobic tightening, a warning that sooner or later everything will grow cold and freeze. But it's not really the weather, or Zac's absence, that's got me so twitchy. No, it's the fact that I'm still in limbo. The fact that, despite all my big ideas and best intentions, nothing has changed.

It's been two full weeks since I submitted my application to Newbury's, and in that time I've checked my email about a thousand times, sometimes waking up at 3 a.m. to do it, just in case some late-night HR person is working overtime and has decided to send me a letter of acceptance. But every time, all I see is the same junk mail – offers for hair removal, debt consolidation, the occasional desperate voucher from the pizza place down the road.

I reach for my phone again, unable to stop myself opening Gmail for the fourteenth time today and staring at the empty inbox, as if I might will a reply into existence through sheer force of disappointment. I click the search bar and type 'Newburys' again, just to make sure I haven't missed anything, but all that comes up is the original automated receipt, cold and impersonal. 'Thank you for your interest in our internship programme. We will contact you if your application is successful.' I know this email by heart. I could recite it word for word.

I open up my CV and read through it for the millionth time. It's good – more than good. Definitely worth an interview. Why haven't they responded? I read it through again – there's nothing new to add, but it's become a nervous habit, like checking your hair in every passing reflection. I scroll through, looking for missed typos or pieces of information I could punch up, but it's already been through the wringer a dozen times.

My finger freezes on the line that says 'Excellent interpersonal skills'. The irony is so sharp it's almost funny. I can hardly manage to call a company without my hands shaking, but here I am pretending to be the kind of person who wows people at parties and can schmooze with the best of them. I should probably just accept that I'm not cut out for this, that I'll be stuck at the pub forever, pulling pints and listening to Mags complain about the dishwasher. I almost laugh, but the sound catches in my throat.

It can't hurt to call them, can it? Check they received my application. I inhale and try to stay calm. I don't normally get nervous, so why do I feel so clammy and short of breath? It must be because this is such a big deal to me. This is about meeting my twin sister. About us finding each other after years of being separated. It's no wonder I'm freaking out.

Every time I imagine it, the details change, but the sensation is always the same – a nervous, electric hope that fizzes in my chest and makes the whole world feel slightly out of step. It's ridiculous, of course. I know that. I'm not twelve anymore. Separated-at-birth twins in real life don't get happy endings. But I can't let go of this idea that if I just get close enough, if I can just find my way inside her orbit, then everything will make sense. That the jaggedness inside my head will finally smooth out. That maybe, just maybe, she's been waiting for me, too.

But I don't want to just call her or show up out of the blue. I don't want her to think I've tracked her down. I want our meeting to be more natural. That's why this internship idea feels so right.

I realise I've opened Newbury's website and I'm already on the Contact page. I click on the phone number and wait as it connects and then starts ringing. My heart thumps, but I try to stay calm and channel a professional persona.

The call clicks through to a menu option and I select 'sales'.

'Newbury's, this is Ben Hutton.' The voice on the end of the line sounds young and posh.

'Oh, er, hi.' I curse my bumbling words and try to sound more confident. 'Sorry, my name's Jade Morgan, can I speak to Bella Newbury please?'

'Can I ask what it's in relation to?' he says, obviously primed not to put any old pleb through to the boss.

'Um . . . Yes, it's about a job application.' I pause and then add, 'For the internship.'

'Oh, right, Talia Benson's dealing with that. I'll put you through.'

'Hold on.' I try to catch him before he transfers the call.

'Yes?'

'I was speaking to Bella,' I lie, 'so if you could put me through to her, that would be great.'

'Hang on. I'll see if she's available.'

He puts me on hold and classical music starts playing – something pretty and uplifting. I vaguely recognise it from somewhere. It cuts off abruptly.

'Hello, this is Bella Newbury, how can I help?' Her voice is clipped, and not very warm, but my heart flips, nevertheless. This is my sister on the end of the line, and she's talking to me.

My mouth goes dry, and I wish I had something to drink. I clear my throat and try my best to sound bubbly yet professional. 'Hi, my name's Jade, Jade Morgan, and I applied for your internship position a few weeks ago. I haven't heard back yet, but

I wondered if I could come in for an interview. I think I'd be great for the position.' I figure estate agents like people who are 'salesy' so hopefully this might do the trick. I hope she'll appreciate my proactiveness.

'Oh,' she replies, dismissively. 'I'm sorry, but the calibre of applicants was very high this year. If you haven't heard back from us, then I'm afraid you haven't been successful on this occasion.'

My heart plummets down to the worn carpet beneath my toes. My disappointment isn't just because the position has gone, it's because of her tone. She sounds like she's talking to an unwanted cold caller she can't wait to get rid of. Like I'm a nobody.

I need to give this another go. 'That's a shame,' I come back with. 'Do you have any other positions going? Even something short-term, like a week's work experience?'

'Are you at school or college?' she asks.

'No, I'm in my mid-twenties.' I'm twenty-eight, but whatever.

'Sorry, our work-experience slots are only for people in full-time education.'

I'm desperately wracking my brain for something else to say. To win her over. But I can hear in her tone she's already dismissed me.

'Maybe you could make an exception?' I try. 'I'm a quick learner.'

'I'm afraid not,' she says, rudely ending the call, her mind no doubt already on to something else.

I drop my phone in my lap and slump back into the sofa with a grunt. Suddenly, I feel a spike of anger. Not at myself, but at them – the people who get to decide. The ones who never have to worry about impressing anyone because their names do the work for them. Bella Newbury. Even the name sounds like old money. Who does she think she is? She might be my twin, but she sounded like a right snooty cow. What was I even thinking, wanting to go and work for her? I bet her employees hate her.

I try not to think about my pathetically naive plan to surprise her. To see her face when she meets me for the first time. I try to forget all the imagined conversations I had in my head with her. About how excited we'd be to have found each other. I'm such an idiot. Of course she's not going to be anything like me. She's been brought up with wealth and luxury. I'm just some pleb who happens to share the same genes.

She'll take one look at me, at my life, and she'll think I'm a total loser. She wouldn't be wrong either. I fist my hands, knuckles whitening. So that's it. All those hours spent thinking about our reunion were a complete waste of time. I get to my feet and pace over to the kitchenette and then across the lounge towards the window. I stare through it, not really looking at the crappy view of the street, my mind too steeped in disappointment, replaying Bella's snooty voice in my head. I mean, logically, she didn't know who I was, she thought she was talking to a stranger, but I still feel hurt by the rejection. If this was a movie, we would meet up and have an incredible reunion. Instead, this is real life and it sucks.

I turn away from the window and sink back down on to the sofa, bored of this room, bored of this city, bored of my life and bored of my thoughts.

Although . . . thinking about it, maybe it wouldn't have been great to meet on such unequal terms. She's this hotshot business owner and I'm a nobody. It might have been humiliating. She might have been embarrassed to have such a loser for a sister. I might have felt awkward and lesser. Even though I know she's had a better financial start in life than me, it still might have been a bit humiliating.

Not for the first time, I wish I'd made a bit more of my life. Maybe gone to college or started my own online business or something. Anything, really.

I make a decision. I won't contact my sister again. Not yet anyway. Instead, I'm going to try to undermine her a little. I won't go too far, just little things to create cracks in her perfect existence, to tip things out of balance. I don't want to ruin Bella. I just want to level the playing field. Then, maybe, once she's not so high and mighty, once she's toppled off that pedestal and is back at ground level, I might finally introduce myself, and we can start out on a more equal footing.

'Hello, sister,' I'll say. 'Sorry you've been having a rough time. I know just what that's like.' I'll be her confidante, her lifeline. And she'll owe me. She'll be grateful to have me in her life. Excited to have such a caring sister.

Maybe a bad review. Maybe a rumour. Maybe just a phone call at the wrong moment. Sabotage by increments. Like death by a thousand paper cuts, if you want to be dramatic. Normal, pain-in-the-arse hassles, so she'll know what it's like to be me. To be dealt all the shit cards in life. I need Bella to have a taste of that frustration. To have her confidence rattled.

Suddenly hungry, I reach for my half-eaten Snickers, every mouthful a little victory. With renewed enthusiasm, I reopen Newbury's website. Looks like Bella's running an 'empowerment' seminar next Thursday. It's booked out, but there's a waiting list. I sign up three times under fake names: Tiffany Sharp, Mia Hutchens, Erin Palowski, all the girls who were bitches at school. Next, I draft an email from a burner address. 'Dear Ms Newbury. I am wondering if your "feminist" principles extend to your actual hiring and firing practices? Because some of the stories going around social media about your treatment of junior staff are shocking . . .' I don't hit send – yet. But I let it sit in drafts, like a grenade with the pin pulled but not released.

For the first time in years, I feel powerful. I scrunch up my empty chocolate wrapper, pull my legs up on the sofa, phone in hand, and start planning what I'll do next.

Chapter Seventeen

BELLA

Midday in November is a strange hour; the sun is already slanting west, the air crisp but not quite freezing, and the town has that out-of-season, slightly brittle feeling. The High Street glitters with what's left of this morning's frost; all the shop windows have swapped off-season discounts for Christmas bunting, and everywhere you go there's the faint, spicy aroma of mulled wine. This close to the marina, the air also has a tang of salt and diesel, and the cries of the seagulls sound like spoilt children.

I'm nervous. Nervous in the way people are when every aspect of their last six months has led up to a single, hour-long midday appointment. I'm about to meet a potential new client – Joe Sainty. It's funny that I lied to my bank's business manager about having a deal lined up with a developer, but now my lie could actually become true. Maybe I've somehow managed to manifest him into reality.

Our lunch is at one of Lymington's swankiest restaurants, Portofino, so I've dressed to impress. He's booked the table for 12.30 p.m. and I messaged an hour ago to double-check we're still on. *Looking forward to it*, he replied.

My parents are going to be so proud of me if I pull this off. It will be the biggest deal of my career. It might even eclipse their own highlights.

Joe is looking to offload an entire block of new-build apartments. Twelve, to be exact. None listed below £800,000. If he signs with us, and if I move even a quarter of them before the end of the financial year, I could pull the business out of its current death spiral.

I can't blow it. Not after the disaster with the investors over the summer – which still wakes me at 3 a.m. some nights thinking about the financial security I watched evaporate in a fog of unreturned calls – and that one awful final meeting with the bank where they refused to increase my overdraft, instead saddling me with a loan I have to pay back in crippling monthly instalments. Since then, I've been cobbling together my finances with bubble gum and denial, secretly hoping for a Hail Mary like this one meeting. If the universe is going to start rewarding hard work and perseverance, now would be the time.

I check my reflection in the glass before opening the door to Portofino. My cheeks are flushed. I brush off imaginary fluff from my navy wool coat and take a long, grounding breath, exhaling like some maiden aunt in a BBC drama. I smile at my own melodrama. I need to take a leaf out of my mother's book. She always enters a room with her chin up and eyes ahead, like the world owes her an audience.

Tony, the owner, spots me immediately. 'Bella, Bella!' he calls from behind the bar, his voice ringing out so loud that two men at the nearest table turn to glance at me with interest. It's the jokey greeting he gives me in his gorgeous accent every time he sees me. Mum sold him and his wife their beautiful quayside home a couple of decades ago, so he's known me since I was a child.

He comes around with arms outstretched, and we do the air-kiss routine, cheeks barely grazing, but the scent of his aftershave lingers. His hair is more salt than pepper now, but his warm smile is the same.

'Coat?' he asks, already slipping it from my shoulders before I can say yes. 'I put you right in the window, best spot in the house. I didn't know this reservation was for you. It's a Mr Sainty – a client, yes? Or perhaps a lover!' He grins.

I lightly shove his arm. 'Don't let my boyfriend hear you talk like that. He's already jealous enough that I'm spending my lunch hour with another man.'

'Ah, yes.' Tony winks. 'The lucky Reece Kernan-Jones. You're still not married? What's he waiting for? You date my son, TJ, he'll have a ring on your finger by March.'

I laugh, not because it's funny but because I need the release. Tony's been making the same joke for years, ever since his son and I shared two botched dates in year 12, one of which ended with TJ slipping out early and leaving me to pay for the Nando's.

I shake my head. 'Thanks, but I'm not the marrying kind.'

Tony pulls a face of mock horror, clucking his tongue. 'You all say this, then one day – husbands, babies, dogs. You see. I remind you of this when you bring me the wedding invitation.'

'Don't hold your breath,' I quip, already feeling lighter just from the exchange.

He guides me to the table – a small, round affair with a view of the High Street, currently thronged with pensioners and that one street musician with the accordion who turns up, rain or shine. 'You're the first to arrive.' He hands me the oversized leather-bound menu, mischief still in his eye. 'So what you like to drink? We have a beautiful new house rosé, very light, very easy.'

I hesitate, but shake my head. 'Sparkling water, please. It's a business lunch; I need to impress my client, not embarrass myself.'

Tony raises his hands in surrender. 'I remember, you always so serious. One day, you let yourself have some fun, eh?'

I grin. 'Maybe after I close the deal. For now, I need a clear head.' He nods, already drifting towards the bar, and I run my finger over the cool, white linen of the tablecloth.

Tony's easy banter has relaxed me, and I sink back in my seat, going over the pitch in my head. I'm flattered that Joe got in touch with our agency. It's good to know all our PR and advertising is having some effect – it certainly costs enough.

A waitress glides over with a bottle of San Pellegrino, slices of orange and lemon in a chilled glass, and I imagine for a moment what it would be like to be the sort of person who lingers in places like this for pleasure, ordering a single espresso or a glass of wine, reading the paper, nothing else pressing to do with the day. I see women like that sometimes – usually in tailored coats with caramel-blonde hair, air-kissing their friends, never flustered or stressed.

I'm not one of those women. I'm the kind who sneaks half a Twix in the stairwell on the way to her next showing, or who does her mascara in the bathroom of the out-of-town Sainsbury's because she's running a little late. Not that I should be complaining. I know I'm in a privileged position to have been handed the family business. It's just so . . . all-consuming.

My phone vibrates in my pocket. I check it, but it's just a notification from our office group chat, which has devolved into memes and mild passive aggression over who keeps leaving dirty mugs in the sink. I should crack down on it – it's supposed to be a business-related chat – but I've got too much else to worry about at the moment. No text from Joe. I check the time. 12.27. Too soon to worry. Maybe he's one of those decisive types who likes to arrive on the dot, make the meeting all business, no unnecessary small talk.

I glance at the menu but can't process the words. Instead, I rehearse my pitch in my head again, running through the points I want to make. I've even prepped a little speech in case he tries to haggle our commission down – I'm going to reference the last three developments I sold ahead of schedule, the glowing testimonials, the Instagram campaign that tripled footfall at our last show home. Okay, so they were at a much lower price point than Sainty's apartments, but I won't dwell on that. I try out a few lines under my breath, too quiet for anyone to hear.

The kitchen door thumps open, and I catch a whiff of garlic and rosemary. My stomach growls. I realise I haven't eaten anything since a banana at eight o'clock. Maybe I should have ordered an appetiser. I check my phone again. It's 12.38. Still no sign of Joe.

Another customer walks in – a woman in a North Face gilet and leggings, pushing a pram so expensive it probably requires its own insurance plan. She orders a flat white and settles at the table next to mine, frowning into her phone while her baby gurgles at the ceiling. Another woman joins her. I recognise her vaguely from yoga, but I don't make eye contact. I don't want to be asked what I'm doing here alone, waiting, pretending to look at the menu.

12.50 passes. I check my phone again. I realise my palms are damp and wipe them on the napkin under the table.

I try calling Joe, letting it ring three times before hanging up, worried about seeming desperate. I text him, breezy: *Hi Joe! I'm here at Portofino, looking forward to meeting you. Let me know if you're running late or want to reschedule!* I tack on a smiley face, instantly regretting it, then tell myself it's fine.

I check my work email, then my personal, then the DMs on Instagram, God knows why. Nothing.

At 12.59, Tony comes over brandishing a cocktail, stuffed with lime and mint. 'Virgin mojito, no alcohol, on the house.'

'Thank you,' I reply weakly.

'No sign of your man?' He's soft about it, and I'm grateful.

'He's probably caught in traffic.' My voice quivers a fraction. 'Developers, you know. Always busy.'

Tony nods, sympathetic. 'If he does not call, you let me know. I bar him from the restaurant, for life.' He makes a slicing motion through the air.

'That's sweet, but I'm sure he'll be here,' I say, though I'm not sure at all. My chest tightens. I start to imagine all the ways I could have blown it already: maybe I got the wrong date or time. Maybe he changed his mind. Maybe he checked my LinkedIn and decided I wasn't experienced enough. Maybe he's sitting at another restaurant, texting someone else, telling them I'm the one who's late.

13.07. Still nothing.

Eventually, I stop pretending to read the menu and simply stare out the window at the people bustling by, wondering which of them are on their way to something important, and which are, like me, waiting to see if the world will offer up a little mercy.

By 1.15, I know it's over. I send another message – just in case – then put my phone face down on the table. I wonder if I should order anyway, if it would be less humiliating to eat alone, or to simply leave and hope Tony doesn't mention it the next time I'm in. For a few minutes, I just sit, letting the sunlight through the glass warm my face, feeling the edges of disappointment close in, sharp and cold.

Tony returns with a bread basket and a sad smile. 'Bread always makes things better,' he says. 'Especially our bread, warm from the oven. You wait as long as you want, Bella. You are always welcome.'

I nod my thanks, break off a piece of focaccia and chew, trying to taste anything, trying to decide what to do next.

But Joe Sainty is a no-show, and he's not answering his phone. I'm gutted.

Chapter Eighteen
JADE

I borrowed Mum's silver Renault Clio without asking, but it's so much easier than the bus. Public transport is a joke in a suburb like ours – four buses a day, and one of those is a myth. I'd have had to leave at dawn, and the idea of sitting in a bus full of chattering pensioners and screaming toddlers is enough to put me off the whole mission. Not that I'm on a mission, exactly. But there's a reason I've driven the forty-one minutes to Lymington with the windows down, even though it's a freezing November day. I'm trying to clear my head since the idea for this little experiment popped into it, setting my pulse hammering.

Anyway, Mum's at work, so she'll never know about the car, and I'll be back long before she's home. I'll have to top up the petrol, and hopefully she won't check the mileage. Although you never know with Mum; she can be quite fussy about those sorts of things.

I park on the outskirts of Lymington, where the roads are emptier, and consult Google Maps to get my bearings. Finally, I check the time, lock the Clio, and walk into town, shoulders hunched. I have a navy baseball cap jammed low, tinted sunglasses, and my parka zipped to the chin. I'm nondescript and unrecognisable, I hope. Though I'm aware that from a distance, my posture and gait are probably hers. That's the problem with trying to stay inconspicuous when you're a twin.

Despite the precautions I've taken to appear invisible, now that I'm here, I don't feel concealed enough. I worry about my face being too on display. I cross the High Street like a spy, duck into a charity shop, and buy a wool scarf that smells a little too musty for comfort, just for the extra layer, pulling it up over my chin and part of my mouth. Then I double back and stake out the Portofino restaurant from the safety of a café across the road. I order an overly frothy cappuccino I don't want, so I can sit by the window and watch the show.

Bella is already there, seated at a prime table with an uninterrupted view of the entrance and the street beyond. I marvel at her face. My face. I don't think I'll ever get tired of looking at her. It's so weird. I can't explain the feeling it gives me. An unexpected rush of emotion wells up in my chest, and I take a breath to try to dispel it. A little voice in my head tells me to abandon this charade and just go and speak to her. *Get to know her like you were going to do originally. She's your sister, for goodness' sake.*

But then I remember how dismissive she was towards me on the phone. How up herself she was. I look at her now, at how put-together she is — as I knew she would be — hair in a neat chignon, make-up flawless, the black suit jacket with the subtle velvet lapel — and I know that I'm right to continue with my course of action. Every time I feel a flash of guilt, I have to remember why I'm doing this. She has to have a taste of what it's like to have a bit of bad luck. Of how it feels to not have everything go your way. I need to stay strong and not weaken for a moment. If I do, I'll wreck everything.

She's scanning her phone, jaw set, pretending to look busy, but I can see she's really on edge, chewing the skin around the edge of her acrylics. The moment is so achingly familiar that I almost laugh; she's displaying the same fragile insecurities as me. Watching her is like watching myself – if I were rich.

She's waiting for Joe Sainty, the phantom developer I invented a few weeks ago. I created him in an afternoon with a Gmail account, a carefully doctored LinkedIn profile, and a mobile number routed through a burner SIM. I sent emails, played hard to get, teased enough to keep her biting. She's come here thinking this is the final pitch, the one that will land her a juicy contract worth thousands. Instead, she's going to leave with nothing, and I know because I'm the one who arranged for her to be stood up. I booked the table in the window, told her what time to arrive. It's amazing the power you can wield if you choose to.

I squash any misgivings, sip my coffee, and watch the minutes tick past. Bella's shoulders tighten every time the door opens, and she glances up, hope flickering and then dying as each new arrival turns out to be not the man she needs to impress, but a bunch of pensioners in bright fleeces, gym mums, or a family with sticky-fingered kids. She stays for almost an hour, eyes fixed on her phone, refusing to admit defeat even as the waiters begin to hover and the lunch crowd thins. I admire her tenacity, her professionalism, and I wonder what excuses she's made for him – a meeting that's over-run, or he got the time wrong and thought it was one-thirty rather than twelve-thirty. Maybe a traffic accident where he got snarled up in a tailback.

Eventually, she realises he isn't coming. I watch her try to pay for her bottle of water with a credit card, but the waiter waves it away. She must know him – either that or he's taken pity on her. She heads towards the exit with her back ramrod straight, pretend-ing it's all gone exactly as planned.

I almost feel bad. Almost. Until she steps outside, and I see her ice-cold expression. I already know she can be a bit of a bitch. She's used to things always going her way. And my earlier twinge of guilt is replaced by a low, hot satisfaction. This is what it's like to have the upper hand, for a change.

But as she disappears up the High Street, I realise this is barely going to register for her. At best, it's a blip, a mystery to solve, another minor annoyance in a life that will always tilt in her favour. I'm sure the loss of one potential client happens a lot in her line of work. No. If I want to affect Bella – properly affect her – I'll need to do more than catfish her with fake emails and a no-show meeting. I'll need to keep piling on the pressure.

In the café, my hands start to shake with equal parts adrenaline and horror because I've already crossed a line I didn't even know I'd drawn. The reason I know I've crossed it is because I wouldn't dare tell Mum or Zac what I've done, or what I'm planning. They'd both be appalled. I could walk away now, go home, return Mum's car, and chalk this up to one more failed experiment. But I know I won't do that. The urge to continue is too strong. I want to knock Bella off her axis. I want to ruin her days, the way she ruined mine.

I start tapping ideas into Notes on my phone, and by the time my third cappuccino is cold, I have a list. *Change her diary appointments. Leave more bad reviews for her business online. Leak something to the local press about a shadowy deal.* All minor things, but if you add them together, they'll do the job. I wonder if she has a boyfriend . . . My heart is pounding with possibilities.

When the High Street is all clear, I slip out of the café and circle back to the Clio, careful to keep to side streets and alleyways. I drive home with the radio blaring, one eye on the mirror, half expecting to see someone tailing me – the police, Bella, Zac. Of course, that's just me being paranoid. No one knows what I've done, or what I'm going to do. And, anyway, like I keep telling myself, they're only little things. Nothing really bad or illegal. The important thing is the escalation. That, and the sense that there are new rules now – *my* rules.

As I pull into Mum's parking space at the back of the block, I try not to remember my elation when I first discovered I had a twin (after my initial shock, of course). I was stunned to realise I have a sister. It felt like someone had given me a gift. A built-in best friend for life. A soulmate who might travel by my side and support me. I can't think like that anymore, not after her careless dismissal of me on the phone. True, she didn't know who I was, but it still felt like a punch in the gut. I think about Mum's ruined relationship with her own sister. For her, it sounds like it's always been a duel. Like fencing, but with secrets, and guilt, and an endless struggle over who gets to be the best one. The real one.

So I'm not taking any chances. I refuse to be the loser twin, the one to be pitied. I'm going to be the one in control. I exit Mum's car and slam the door, striding to the flat with a renewed sense of purpose and a sly smile that refuses to stay off my face.

Chapter Nineteen

BELLA

It's barely 8 a.m. and I'm already on my second cup of coffee. Reece hovers in the kitchen behind me, stirring eggs in an enamel pan and humming along to the radio. There's something in his easy swivel, the way his back muscles move beneath his shirt, that makes being around him in the mornings both unbearable and necessary, like magnets pushing and pulling.

He turns to me, cocks an eyebrow, and smiles in that way that reminds me of the first time I saw him. He steps closer and trails a finger down my spine.

Goosebumps travel up my arms.

'Felt you staring,' he says, with that crooked grin. 'I've got time if you want to go back to bed.'

I desperately do want to, but I'm already zipped into my navy sheath dress, hair smoothed, make-up done. I set my mug in the sink. 'Tempting, but I've got to run.'

He wraps an arm around my waist and tugs me nearer. 'Nice warm duvet. Nice warm hands.'

'Don't you have to get to work too?'

He shrugs, lips grazing my ear. 'Yes, but there's no rush.'

'Lucky you,' I reply, snagging a slice of his toast and taking a bite of its warm, buttery deliciousness.

I turn at the sound of the mail landing on the mat. The usual waste-of-paper circulars, along with an ominous brown envelope that looks suspiciously like it's from HMRC. For a wild nanosecond, I allow myself to imagine that maybe they're giving me a rebate.

Ha, as if.

I drop Reece's toast back on to the plate and head into the hall, bending to retrieve the envelope. I rip the letter open rather than giving in to the urge to toss it in the bin.

AUDIT.

HMRC are doing an *audit.* I feel the blood recede from my hands. The word hangs in my head, echoing with bureaucratic venom. I scan the letter again. It's not a summons or a court date, but still . . . an audit. There's no reason given, only instructions, and it feels personal, like a grudge. My saliva dries out. I fold the letter quickly before Reece can read it. I don't want him to see me panic about money. It's a weird pride thing, maybe. Or self-preservation. I'll have to call Jenny, my accountant, see if she can shed any light.

'Everything all right?' Reece's voice floats over my shoulder.

I fold the letter back into its envelope and shove it in my handbag. 'What? Oh, yeah, fine. Just tax stuff.'

He nods, but I feel his gaze lingering. I wonder if I should say more. That I'm worried, that I always feel like I'm one mistake away from disaster. I want to tell him about the late-night spreadsheets, the little lies I tell my accountant so she doesn't judge. But I don't. It isn't the kind of relationship where we talk real talk, even after all this time. I guess you could say it's a little superficial. I'm not sure how or why we've ended up this way – maybe we're both too worried about scaring the other off. Or maybe Reece's life really is that perfect, and I'm too afraid of showing him that mine is not.

'You sure?' he asks, and there's a softness to it that makes me uneasy.

I wonder if I should tell him. If I should unload my problems, or at least this one. But what if he isn't sympathetic, or he brushes it off? Reece always tells me he was attracted to my boss-bitch energy. That he loves how independent I am. If I show him my vulnerable side, might it make us stronger? Or would it ruin what we have?

I think about my parents, how they communicate in code, never quite saying the thing directly. I was raised on subtext. My mother's way of apologising is to cut up fruit and leave it on my desk. I don't think I've ever witnessed either of them cry – maybe Dad once when our dog, River, died. But Mum . . . never. Even when Dad had his heart attack, she was stressed and panicked, but I never saw actual tears. Maybe she shed them in private. Maybe not. I adopted all their defensive strategies, and now I barely know how to have a feeling in front of another person unless I disguise it as a joke.

I force a smile, zip my bag shut. 'All good,' I reply, kissing Reece goodbye. My breath feels stale, my teeth too big, and while I'm not a crier, I get the weird urge to sob.

By the time I'm at the car, the sky has collapsed into a classic winter drizzle, cold and grey and relentless. I fire up the engine and sit for a full minute with my hands on the wheel. I have to show a house in half an hour. I have to pretend none of this is happening.

Traffic is an insult – endless lorries and a yellow double-decker with the nerve to break down on the roundabout near my flat. I tap at my steering wheel like I know Morse code, but it doesn't make the van in front of me move any faster. All the while, that HMRC letter pecks away at my brain, the word 'audit' hammering at my skull.

My phone buzzes with two new messages, both marked 'urgent'. One from Jenny, and the other from Talia at the office. I don't read either of them.

The showing I'm meant to attend is at a new 'luxury eco-village' development along the A337. The kind of place that has marketing copy about 'elevated living' and 'village amenities' but is actually just a bunch of identical boxes with a sculptural bike rack and a pond masquerading as a lake.

When I finally swing on to the road, I'm only five minutes late, but my clients – an engaged couple who want to buy before their wedding next spring – are already there, huddled under a green umbrella that's too small for both of them. Usually, I like to get to a property early so I can turn off the alarm and check the place over first. No chance of that now.

The property itself is a two-storey eco-home with a biometric lock and dark solar panels that gleam from the roof even in this muted light, but . . . *what the hell?* The path to the front door is no longer a path. It's a mudslide. Someone has dumped a literal mountain of wet, brown earth and rubble right in front of the house, so the walkway is blocked from kerb to door. There's no way around it except to wade through the grass, which is a soup of rain and clay.

Is this some construction delivery gone wrong?

I leave the dry interior of my car and step out into the drizzle, having left my brolly at home. I plaster a smile on and power-walk towards Molly and Ted, boots immediately saturated, skirt catching splatter. I briefly fantasise about the ground opening up and swallowing me whole.

'Molly and Ted?' I say, breathless and smiling like this is all perfectly normal.

They nod, and I thrust out my hand. 'Hi, I'm Bella Newbury. Charming weather, eh?'

Molly smiles half-heartedly.

'Is this the property?' Ted asks. 'Only we can't see the house number behind all this . . .' He gestures at the mud.

I ignore the lump in my throat. 'Yes, this is it!' I reply brightly. 'There's a bit of construction happening, but it's all part of the neighbourhood's new landscaping plan.'

The couple exchange glances, their faces tight with British politeness and the raw, biting cold.

'Should be done by next week!' I add, trying my best to smooth things over.

Molly gives a brittle laugh. 'Will we be able to get in?'

'If you wouldn't mind waiting here a sec, I'll see if I can skirt around and get to the front door.'

My shoes sink into the soggy fringe of grass, and I feel the squelch of waterlogged earth through my boots as I edge past the mound that's almost at head height. With a sinking heart, I see that it's been dumped right up to the entrance with no space to get to the door. The door itself is spattered with flecks of brown, like the house has contracted a skin disease. I'd have to get a shovel to clear a path, and I'm not doing that.

I turn to the couple and hold up a finger, asking them to wait a minute. Maybe I can get in around the back. I push at the six-foot-high wooden side gate, but it's not budging. Must be bolted from the other side. I give the vendor a quick call, but it goes to voicemail, so I leave an urgent message.

I take a moment to collect myself – wet, muddy, out of breath, and one soggy misstep from a total breakdown. Then, resigned, I limp back towards the prospective buyers, who are silently watching me from the safety of their umbrella. Molly flashes me a look of commiseration, while Ted's jaw tics in the way I imagine people's do when they're plotting a one-star Google review.

'I'm so sorry,' I say, cheeks burning. 'There's no way in. I've left a message with the vendor to find out what's happened. As soon as I hear back, I'll give you a call to reschedule.'

Molly gives me a sympathetic smile, but Ted huffs his annoyance. Irritatingly, this listing is also on with another agency. I hope the pair don't decide to go with them instead.

'I truly am sorry,' I repeat.

I watch them pick their way back to their car, umbrella bobbing with each step.

I let a sigh leak out, roll my eyes at the rain, and trudge back to my own car, where I sit behind the wheel with my sodden coat on the passenger seat. I reach for my phone, see five missed calls and two urgent texts, all from people who would almost certainly like to yell at me or, worse, demand things I can't possibly deliver.

I don't answer any of them.

I stare at the windscreen, tracing the way the droplets race down the glass, forming rivers that collide at the bottom and disappear. I like to imagine that if I could hitch a ride on one of these droplets, I'd end up somewhere far away from all of this, preferably somewhere warm and dry. Instead, I start the ignition and pull out of the development.

On the way to the office, I stop at a petrol station to pick up something for breakfast since all I've eaten today is a bite of Reece's toast. The place is empty except for a cashier so deep in a TikTok scroll that she doesn't notice me at all, which suits me fine. I grab a Red Bull and a packet of prawn cocktail crisps, then add a Snickers for good measure, because why not? The cashier rings me up without breaking eye contact with her phone, and I tap my business card on the reader.

Back in my car, I rip the crisp packet open and eat with desperate, greasy fingers, letting the crumbs fall where they may, imagining the entire audit team at HMRC laughing at my expense claims while sipping taxpayer-funded tea and biscuits. I down the Red Bull next, enjoying the buzz. My plan was to save the Snickers for later, but I'm already tearing the wrapper off.

I'm not ready to go back to the office. Not yet. Maybe not ever. But I have to, because everything relies on me being a functioning cog in my own life. I dust the crumbs from my skirt, take a breath, and finally – *finally* – pick up my phone to answer my messages.

I click on my accountant's first: *Bella, please call me as soon as you get this.*

My stomach clenches, and I drop the phone back into my bag, all my good intentions evaporating.

Chapter Twenty

JADE

I'm at work, behind the bar at The Oak, doing my usual routine – pouring pints, collecting glasses, stacking the dishwasher. The entire room is humid with the smell of lager and aftershave. I blend in perfectly. I'm part of the furniture here. There's a kind of energy in the place on Saturdays – nervous and a bit desperate, like the punters are all trying to drink away the memory of their week. Mags already put up the tired Christmas decorations at the start of the month, like she does every November. She says it puts people in a more festive, spendy mood, and she's right – the decades-old tinsel and a few gold-sprayed pine cones definitely increase the bar takings.

There's a group of three lads at the bar, wearing footie tops and Lynx. They're showing off for the benefit of some girls over by the fruit machines, trying to outdo each other with stories about who can drink the most and who once nearly got scouted by Southampton FC. One of them leans over the bar so far that I can see the blackheads in his pores. 'You'll go out with Tommo, won't you?' he says to me, nudging the supposed Tommo – a lanky bloke with a gormless expression whose only reaction is to try to grow taller still, as if he can impress me with his height.

I hold out the card machine. 'I'd love to, but I'm married.' I give them a regretful smile while flashing my left hand, where a cheap gold band shines dull under the bar lights.

The ring is fake, obviously. I bought it from Claire's Accessories in a two-for-one set with a cubic zirconia engagement ring. I started wearing it after I realised it cut down on chat-up attempts by about 80 per cent. The other 20 per cent persist, but the story of my MMA-fighting husband is handy for those triers.

The lads groan, all faux heartbreak, but at least they pay and move away, back to hassle the fruit-machine girls, jostling and snorting as they go.

I used to get angry, or at least stung, by the way the customers treated me – a weird mix of invisible and hyper-visible, like a prop with boobs. Now it just slides off, most of the time. I have bigger things on my mind.

My next customer is Dodgy Steve, the local supplier of bootleg perfume and 'designer' handbags.

'All right, Jade?' he says, sidling up with his usual air of conspiracy. 'Got a new shipment in, if you fancy summat. Gucci. Real snakeskin.'

'Sorry, Steve, I'm skint at the moment.' But he already knows I'll have a look at his wares in the beer garden after clocking off. It's a ritual.

If you'd asked me a few months ago whether I enjoy my job, I'd have laughed in your face. Back then, work was something to endure, an endless carousel of sticky floors, pretending to be nice, and night buses that never arrive. Now, though, everything's changed. Not because the work is any better – God, no – but because there's something on the side. My secret project. Having a mission, even a petty one, takes the edge off a lot of life's daily shit.

It gives me something to look forward to. A reason to think, and plot, and scheme in the quiet moments between orders.

For example, last week, before my shift, I went to watch the house on Greenway that Bella's agency is showing. I parked two streets over and observed her from my car, clocking her Fiat 500 as she swept up the drive to show *me* – a no-show – the property.

That's not the real story, though. The real story is the builder's rubble I arranged to have delivered a few days later. I'd seen the ad on Freecycle: 'Rubble hardcore for collection or delivery – FREE.' All I had to do was ring the number and supply contact details. I gave them the address of Bella's listing, so it would make a lovely surprise for her next round of viewings. It's the little things.

I didn't get to see her reaction, which was a shame, but I picture it anyway – Bella's perfect face twisting with confusion, then smoothing over as she tries to explain the problem to her clients.

It's not just no-shows, annoying deliveries and effed-up empowerment seminars. I've also rung the Revenue anonymously to grass her up for tax dodging. I've signed her up to weird mailing lists that fill her inbox with spam. I even sent her a fake parking fine. I soothe my conscience with the thought that none of this will actually hurt her. I tell myself these are mosquito bites, nothing more. She'll brush them off, tell a funny story to her fancy friends, and move on with her pristine day. But my pricking conscience is warring with my desire to really impact her life. To do something far more serious . . .

The sound of a glass smashing brings me out of my reverie. At the other end of the bar, Mags is staring at me like she's been calling my name for hours.

'Jade!' she shouts over the din. 'Customers are waiting to be served.'

I blink and look over. 'What? Oh, sorry, Mags.'

Mags is a local legend, sixty if she's a day, and knows more about The Oak's regulars than their own spouses do. She gives me a look that would turn water to ice. 'What's wrong with you at the moment?'

'Uh, nothing.' I force a smile.

She arches a brow, not buying it for a second. 'You've been away with the fairies for weeks.'

'I'm fine,' I insist, but the lie sits weirdly in my mouth.

'Well, then act like it,' Mags retorts, and gestures with her chin towards the loved-up couple at the end of the bar. The guy is making a show of putting his arm around the girl's waist, and she's giggling so hard her nose wrinkles up. I almost feel jealous, until I realise he's already looking interestedly past her at some other girl.

I sigh, head down the bar, and take their order. All I can think is, I bet Bella doesn't have to deal with people questioning her every move. I bet she gets to do and say what she wants, and everyone just worships her, like it's the word of God. Even when she acts like an absolute bitch, no one would call her on it because Bella's the boss.

Another replay of last month's phone conversation slips into my mind, and my face grows hot at the memory of her casual rejection. I bet she never even gave me a second thought after ending the call. I was just a momentary nuisance to her. Imagine if I had her life. That kind of confidence, that arrogance. Like a jacket you can just throw on and zip up, instead of something stitched together from scraps, hoping it holds.

There's this voice in my head more and more, lately, that tells me it's time to stop playing small. That if I don't do something real, something proper, I'll end up exactly like all the other staff who work here – worn down, hunched over, dreaming about how things could have been different. I'm starting to believe the voice. That's the scariest part. And I don't like to dwell on it, but my debt isn't something that's going away. I need to find a solution to it before those bailiffs show up again.

On my break, I slip my phone from my pocket and scroll through Bella's socials for the tenth time today. New photo: her in a set of gym leggings, smiling with her hair up and a bottle of green juice in hand. The caption is some bollocks about 'self-care Saturdays' and #bossbabe.

I stare at the picture until it blurs, and then my fingers slowly slide across to open a new Google tab and I start typing 'how to change identity' into the search bar. The results fill the screen – some are motivational speakers or psychology blogs, but others are geared towards people escaping their lives or the criminally minded. I skim a few, my heart pounding even though I don't know why. It's not like the cops are watching me, is it? I bookmark a couple of links, then close the browser and shove the phone deep into my apron.

For the rest of my shift, I'm on autopilot. Wipe, pour, smile, repeat. But the plan won't leave me alone. I probably wouldn't have the nerve to do it – but just say I did. How would it look?

By the time we're locking up, I'm already hypothetically figuring out phase one. Next payday, I'll buy the dye and book a cut at the salon by the bus station. No. That won't work. I'll have to do this properly and splash out on the hair – spend money I haven't got to make it convincing. The hairstyle is everything. Get that wrong and I may as well forget the whole thing. Maybe I can save money on the clothes. I could try the charity shops in a posher area of town. I'll have to get my teeth whitened, or at least clean the coffee stains off with bicarbonate of soda. I'll also need to lose a stone or two and tone up a bit. If anyone were to notice my new look, they'd just think I was trying to better myself.

Focusing on the steps calms me, gives my brain something to chew on that isn't just envy or bitterness. It's almost comforting to have a plan. I picture myself living Bella's life – waking up in clean sheets, reading the paper over Waitrose granola, driving to work with a latte that costs more than my hourly wage. I picture the way it would feel to walk into a room and have people's faces light up at the sight of me.

There are obstacles, obviously. The biggest one being Bella herself. She's not just going to roll over and let me step into her shoes. I'll need to think things through a bit more.

Dodgy Steve is waiting for me outside, like I knew he would be, with a battered duffel bag of handbags, sunglasses, and purses, and a couple of pre-made roll-ups. He hands one over, and we light up together, standing in the yellow spill of the streetlamp.

'You look like you're up to something,' he says, squinting at me. 'I can always tell.'

'Maybe I am,' I reply, and for the first time all day, it feels natural to smile.

Chapter Twenty-One

BELLA

Reece and I step out of his BMW – a sporty, slate-grey M5 that still smells new even though it's clocked enough motorway mileage to have acquired a few battle scars. It locks with a soft clunk. The engine ticks as it cools. The driveway undulates around us, the gravel glittering with frost.

My parents' house looms at the top of the carriage drive, a white Georgian with three and a half storeys and a sprawl of outbuildings that have been stitched on to the sides over the past two centuries. It's both beautiful and brooding, the way grand old houses often are – the kind that stir up nostalgia and awe in equal measure.

The house sits in grounds of almost two acres of lawns and ancient woodland, and has views over the Lymington River. I grew up here, built forts and played hide and seek in the woods, learned to drive on the rutted gravel, and hosted illicit sleepovers in the garden cottage. I see it all with the double vision of nostalgia and the nerves that have started to grip me. I take a deep, cold breath and try to remember that this is just my family's home. Nothing to worry about.

Reece saunters up the wide, shallow steps as if leading a diplomatic mission, one hand buried in the pocket of his winter coat, the other holding a bouquet of pale pink roses. If this house is impressive, his parents' main home is the full stately-home fantasy – helicopter pads and Jacuzzis, a billiard table in every wing.

Mum's already standing in the doorway of the porticoed entrance that sits between the two bay windows. 'Hello, darlings,' she cries, her voice carrying across the frosty drive in a burst of warmth. She's already in full-on Christmas hostess mode, festive scarf thrown over a chunky knit. Her hair is still a rich shade of chestnut, though the shine is more salon dye and conditioner than genetics these days. Her arms are open, ushering us forward as if we're the prodigal children returning from some epic adventure, rather than a ten-minute drive along the B3054.

Reece offers her the roses, and Mum beams, inhaling the scent and then bundling us both into a hug. 'These are gorgeous. Come in, come in!'

Reece sniffs the air, and I see him register the aromas of cooking apples and fresh-cut pine with a barely perceptible nod; as much as he plays it cool, he loves this sort of curated domestic bliss. The entrance hall is orchestrated for maximum seasonal effect. The traditional ten-foot tree stands to the left of the central staircase, decorated with tasteful cream and gold ornaments, and topped with the cracked angel I made in year 4 art class. A collection of winter blooms sits on the console table, and a low hum of classical music plays from hidden speakers.

'Tree looks great, Penni,' Reece comments, shrugging off his coat and handing it to Mum, who takes it along with mine and hangs them in the cloakroom.

'Thank you,' she replies. 'I had to badger Paul into getting it up in time for today's lunch. We're so late organising everything this year.'

'Christmas is still a few weeks away, Mum. Plenty of time.'

She kisses my cheek, and I catch the scent of her Jo Malone perfume. 'You say that, but it all goes by so quickly. We seem to have even less time now we're retired.

'Where's Dad?'

'Cooking, obviously.' Mum rolls her eyes, but you can hear the pride underneath. 'He's been fussing over the roast like it's a NASA launch. Come through to the drawing room. We'll have a glass of something in the meantime. Reece, did you drive? Are you drinking? You should both stay the night in the cottage, head back in the morning.'

Reece turns to me, and I shrug my agreement. 'Great.' He rubs his hands together. 'What have you got behind the bar, Mrs N?'

Mum giggles and leads him into the lounge, where they head over to the drinks cabinet.

'Just going to say hi to Dad,' I call through the door. I drift past the staircase, breathing in the layers of wax polish, woodsmoke, and citrus cleaner, the smells of a house that I can't imagine ever belonging to anyone but my parents. I run my fingers along the banister, then head for the kitchen.

Dad is exactly where he always is on a Sunday – in front of the range, sleeves rolled, face ruddy from the heat, glasses steamed. The kitchen is big enough to stage a musical, all exposed beams linked to a wooden-framed conservatory that overlooks the river. He looks up, sees me, and smiles.

'Munchkin!' Dad shuts the range door, sets down the oven gloves, and engulfs me in a hug that is all shoulders and wool jumper and the faint scent of cologne. Dad was ruthless in business, but always gentle at home.

His arms make me feel safe and loved, and for an instant, I relax, remembering how he used to lift me on to the worktop to 'help' peel carrots or stir soup. The memory makes me wish

I could rewind the past twenty years and go back to being that cherished little girl without a care in the world. I picture summer mornings having breakfast at the oak table in the conservatory, the French doors wide open to the lawns and river beyond. Fishing and boating with Dad, making daisy chains in the garden with Mum. Although I realise I'm romanticising quite a bit – we were always ridiculously busy, often apart, and the magic was patchy at best. But sitting here now, smelling my father's cooking, I almost believe in it again.

'Taste this,' Dad insists, turning back to the hob and tapping the edge of a small orange Le Creuset pan. He stabs something on to a fork, blows on it, and offers it to me.

I chew thoughtfully. 'Chestnut?'

He grins, delighted. 'With mushrooms and a hint of sage. I'll add sprouts for Christmas lunch. You two are coming, right?'

'Of course. But we're doing Boxing Day at Reece's parents'.' I try to sound upbeat, but already feel the scheduling headache blossoming behind my eyes. 'Do you want a drink?'

Dad raises a glass of sherry. 'Way ahead of you.'

'Need a hand?' I ask the question, but I already know the answer.

'No, all under control.'

I stand by the French doors for a moment, enjoying the feel of weak sunlight on my face. I catch Dad glancing over at me, like he's trying to gauge my emotional temperature. I try to project an air of serenity, but the pressure of the week – of the year – is coiled in my chest like an unpopped balloon.

'Get yourself a drink, Munchkin,' Dad says.

I turn and smile. 'Good idea.'

I wander back to the lounge, where Mum and Reece are deep in debate about the merits of sherry versus vermouth, each defending their choice with the intensity of a seasoned barrister.

They both look up when I enter, and Mum beckons me over with the old conspiratorial smile. 'Bee, you'll back me up, won't you? Sherry or vermouth?'

I point to a bottle of Harvey's Bristol Cream and she crows in triumph.

'Traitor.' Reece smiles.

Mum pours a measure of sherry into a thimble-sized glass and hands it to me.

There's a kind of agreeable hush in the room – not silence, but a lull between punchlines, punctuated by the snap of the wood-burning stove and the soft Christmas playlist. The room is a nest of comfort. The deep-blue velvet chairs are as ancient as the house. The Persian rug is faded along the main walking paths. The Tiffany lamps throw out a warm, forgiving light, like permanent golden hour. On the sideboard, a bowl of clementines sits next to a tray of mince pies under a glass dome, and the chessboard by the hearth is already set up for a new game.

I take it all in, and the contrast makes me almost dizzy – the world outside is cold, hard, and indifferent, whereas in here, it's a thermal blanket of cosiness and tradition.

I let myself drift for a bit, half listening to their friendly banter, sipping my sherry and gazing out of the bay window on to the frosty drive. If I squint, I can almost convince myself that nothing in the world is wrong. That the only anxiety in my life is whether Mum will go easy on me at Scrabble later, or if Dad's remembered the pigs-in-blankets – Reece's favourite. But the tension in my skull keeps humming.

At the table – set for four but able to seat twelve – Dad has gone all out. He's plated everything with restaurant precision, garnishing the potatoes with sprigs of rosemary and the parsnips with a glazed honey drizzle. We settle in around the table, napkins folded just so, ruby red wine glinting in cut-glass goblets. The conversation is easy, everyone on their best entertaining behaviour, but the longer it goes on, the more aware I am of my inability to join in fully. I keep fussing with my hair, shifting in my chair, refilling my glass before it's empty.

I know Mum can tell something's off. She keeps glancing at me with the same look she used when I came home with a grazed knee or an unexplained D on a maths test – concern fused with a desire not to make a fuss.

As the food and alcohol cruise through my system, instead of feeling more relaxed my anxiety heightens, but I need to keep it in check because I don't want my parents to worry about me, especially not Dad.

'Everything all right at work, darling?' Mum asks gently, as Dad and Reece argue about the world's most overrated football manager.

'Yes, of course. Just a bit of a frantic week, that's all.'

She gives me a searching look. 'You're sure?'

'Absolutely.'

Mum purses her lips in that way she does when she knows my surface-level answer is a lie, but she lets it go and tries to lighten the mood. I know she's also wary of opening a can of worms that could load any stress on to Dad. 'You're not working yourself ragged, I hope. Reece, you've got to make sure she actually sleeps. If she comes home looking like a raccoon at Christmas, I'll have words.'

Reece laughs. 'Noted, Penni. But you know Bella and her commitment to Newbury's.'

Dad's already refilling my glass. 'Hardest-working woman I know, our Bee.'

They mean it affectionately, but each time they say something like that, I feel the weight of pressure increase. I hope my smile looks genuine. I try to make more of an effort, contributing half-remembered stories – the water balloon incident in year 6, my brief and spectacular failure at dressage, the time Dad burnt an entire Christmas pudding to a blackened meteor and tried to salvage it with brandy. I'm performing an expected normality – the amusing daughter, the loving girlfriend, the stable adult with an apartment, a business, and a bank account that definitely isn't running on fumes.

Because I can't tell my parents about the looming threat of the Inland Revenue or the avalanche of other business troubles that are crashing down on me. Not now, not when Dad's health is finally stable and they're enjoying their retirement. They've worked so hard all their lives – too hard. They deserve a break from the stress. I have no choice but to handle this storm on my own. Hopefully, I'll be able to fix it and they'll never find out. Although I know that's probably wishful thinking. I'm frantically trying to keep a lid on it all, to stop the chaos from boiling over. Yet the fear grips me, a paralysing dread that it will all detonate in my face, leaving nothing but ruins.

'You're sure you're fine?' Mum says later, while we're in the kitchen clearing up, stacking plates like it's a competitive event.

I nod, too quickly. 'Promise. It's just the Sunday evening blues. I'll be a different person in the morning.'

She leans in and kisses my temple. 'I hope not, Bee. I like you exactly as you are.'

I nearly tell her everything in that moment, but the words snag on my teeth. I want to confess, but I can't bear the look I imagine passing over her face – the flash of worry, then shame, then effortful reassurance. I am supposed to be the perfect daughter who doesn't need rescuing.

When the dishes are done, we find the boys in the lounge. I burrow in beside Reece, feeling suddenly childlike, listening to the grown-ups talk as if I'm not one of them. We do the ritual of leftovers and drinks and, eventually, round two of pudding and coffee. My anxiety thaws a little with the heat of the fire and the gentle hit of the sherry. I get quietly giggly and cling to Reece, who cradles me with a tenderness we don't usually have time for.

It should be enough, this warm room and this safe moment, to insulate me from what's coming. But the spiral is tightening again, even on a Sunday, the phone in my handbag vibrating with a new email, and already I'm running disaster scenarios in my head and rehearsing apologies I hope I won't need.

When Dad falls asleep in his chair and Mum starts dropping not-so-subtle hints about 'young lovebirds' needing their privacy, Reece and I take our leave with the promise we'll be back to the main house for an early breakfast before we need to dash off to work.

The night air nips my face as we cross the drive to the little garden cottage. Inside, the heating is cranked, and the room smells faintly of clean linen and Mum's perfume. We head up the rickety stairs to the bigger of the two bedrooms, where Reece strips to his boxers and dives under the covers, patting the space next to him.

'You all right?' he asks.

I nod, climbing in beside him. He wraps himself around me.

'You're stressed,' he says.

'No, I'm not.'

He snorts. 'I can feel the tension in your whole body. Bells, what's going on? Have I done something to upset you?'

Again, I want to hand him the whole story. I want to say, *I am failing, I am terrified, I can't do this, and I don't know why anyone ever thought I could.* But, again, I don't. I can't. Instead, I brush it off. 'Course not. It's just work stuff.'

He doesn't push it. Just burrows closer and kisses my forehead.

For a second, the pressure lets up just enough to allow me to breathe. The smell of Mum's fabric softener and the faint whoosh of the ancient radiator soothe me. I lie very still, listening to Reece's breathing as it slows, and the far-off hoot of an owl. I could stay here forever, safe in this womb of luxury, but already my mind has gone to the alerts on my phone, the emails, the voice memos lined up like dominoes. At some point, I know I might have to tell them the truth about everything. But not yet. Tomorrow, I will get dressed, eat toast with proper jam, and be the Bella they all want to see.

Chapter Twenty-Two

JADE

Lurking in a busy Lymington gift shop, I pretend to be captivated by a display of overpriced candles, as a playlist of instrumental Christmas carols bleeds tinsel-bright into the air. The windows are fogged with the breath of shoppers and the bite of winter rain.

'Can I help you with anything?' the manager asks, sidling up, with the tone of someone who's come across enough shoplifters to be wary.

'Just browsing, thanks.' I'm turned away, and wearing my usual disguise of parka, hat, and monstrous scarf wound loosely over the lower portion of my face. I keep my hands neatly behind my back, the model of an innocent browser.

She's not deterred. 'Those candles are made locally,' she says, moving closer. 'Gorgeous, aren't they? Feel free to take off the lids and have a sniff.'

'I will, thanks,' I reply, telling her to *piss off* in my head.

My prayers are answered when a real customer, a mum with a toddler clutching a bedraggled-looking cloth duck, pipes up at the counter about gift-wrapping a mirror. The shopkeeper's attention pivots, and I can breathe again.

For the past few weeks – whenever I've been able to use Mum's car without her noticing – I've been embarking on these little field trips through Lymington, spending time in cafés, newsagents, salons, anywhere a local would go. Visiting all the likely Bella haunts, trying to get to know the place, just so I don't feel like a stranger. Of course, I've had to wear my usual disguise and keep my head down, but that's easier in winter when I can stay bundled up.

Working at the pub, Mum, Zac – they all feel like irrelevancies now, taking me away from my new purpose. I can already feel myself leaving them behind, preparing for my ritzy new life.

When I'm not in Lymington or at work, I've spent every other moment watching YouTube videos on how to become an estate agent. There are hundreds – tips on sales patter, scripts for cold calls, how to plant self-doubt in buyers while oozing charm. It's all about confidence and micro-expressions. I watch with headphones in, a notebook open, scribbling down phrases and mannerisms like I'm revising for exams. I'm not letting the practicalities faze me – by the time I'm Bella, I'll be able to charm an OAP into a shoddy retirement flat before she's put the kettle on.

Obviously, I won't need to take an actual course because, once I'm Bella, I'll be magically qualified. This research is just for my own peace of mind. So that once I step into her shoes, I'll be convincing.

I've already dyed my hair back to its natural brunette shade – Bella's shade. It's a bit flat, and the cut isn't quite right, but I've got time. With a little more effort and maybe some hair products and vitamin supplements, I can bring it up to glossy, shoulder-grazing health. I now can't believe I ever wanted to go blonde. This shade suits me so much better. For now, I keep it tied back in a low ponytail like she sometimes does when she's on the job. Occasionally, I catch my reflection in car windows and have to do a double take because I don't look like me anymore.

Of course, Mum's had plenty to say about my new look and, for once, she's been quite complimentary. Although I've noticed her giving me a few funny glances when she thinks I'm not looking. But if she has any suspicions, she hasn't said anything. Hopefully, she simply assumes I've been inspired by Bella's style since finding out about her. Ever since coming clean about her past and my sister, Mum has avoided all conversation about it. At first this annoyed me, but now it suits my purposes for her not to be asking any questions.

As well as Bella's look, I'm also trying to learn everything I can about her mannerisms, in case they're different from my own. Luckily for me, Newbury's has created a few videos, and she's in most of them doing walk-throughs of the properties. I'm going to have to polish my accent. Bella sounds like she went to private school, so I'd better get practising. It's actually quite fun. I feel like an actress. It would be easier if I could really get into character and carry it on at home and work. But everyone would take the piss, accuse me of trying to be posh.

So I have to be content with recording myself on my phone and playing it back. Sometimes I overshoot and sound like a BBC weather presenter, which would make Mum die laughing if she caught me. I only let myself practise when she's out.

A few times, I work up the nerve to do a dry run in public. I'll order a coffee or ask for directions to the city centre with Bella's accent, and watch the baristas and dog walkers for funny looks. Nobody's commented. I think I'm getting good. And the more I do it, the more I enjoy it. I think people seem to respect me more when I'm her.

My favourite training ground is the estate agency itself. Over several days, I've watched from across the street as Bella comes and goes in her parade of smart coats and expensive boots.

This afternoon, from my vantage point in the gift shop, I see Bella popping into the café next door with her boyfriend – I've seen him a couple of times before – a posh twat. He could be a fly in the ointment, but I'm not worrying about him for the moment. The two of them sit in the window of the café. He leans in intensely as if they're having a serious conversation, but she looks distracted, scrolling through her phone. And then I realise she's not carrying her handbag. I guess the boyfriend is paying.

This could be my in.

There's only one other staff member in the agency today, an older guy sitting at a desk near the back – possibly the manager, possibly not. He's busy talking to a couple. They're hunched over, engrossed in what he's saying.

Ten seconds, maybe less. I leave the gift shop, cross the road – pocketing my beanie and fluffing my hair – and slip through the agency door. My heart is drumming so loudly I worry the guy at the back might hear it, but he's wrapped up in his spiel about 'fixed interest rates' and 'life insurance'. I pray he doesn't look up and notice I'm wearing a completely different outfit.

Bella's desk is immaculate – her screen locked, in tray neat, an angled photo of her and her mum and dad at a regatta. No sign of the handbag.

Okay, I can do this.

I head confidently into the back office, exhaling when I make it without being questioned. The room is small but tidy. There are two sofas, a kitchenette, a corner desk with . . . *yesss!* Her black YSL handbag sits on top, just inviting me over to have a rummage. Quick as anything, I unzip it.

The keys are there, next to a contactless credit card, a driving licence, and a packet of Nurofen. No time to hesitate. I clock the address on her licence – Flat 12, Seafoam Court – pocket the keys and the credit card, then re-zip the bag.

I duck out of the room, stride through the front office and out the main door, nearly colliding with a buggy on the pavement. I toss the mother a dirty look as she apologises and I walk briskly up the street, forcing myself not to run. I can't draw any attention now.

There's a key-cutting place further down the road. Behind the counter is a man with a beard so big it looks like it could swallow a padlock. He's hunched over the machine when I arrive, doesn't look up at first.

'Hi, Bella,' he says eventually, glancing up with a nod of recognition.

Shit, he knows her. 'Hi,' I reply, trying out the accent, bright and airy. 'Any chance of doing a rush job for me? I need a spare set of keys.'

He grins. 'Always in a hurry, eh?' He holds out his palm. 'Whatcha got for me?'

I hand over the keys, steady as I can. He inspects them, eyebrows peaking at the Fiat key.

'This one's got a chip, so you'll need to go to the dealership, love. Sorry. But I can do the others.'

'That's fine.' I shift my weight. 'Could you do them in, like, ten minutes? Emergency at home. I can pay a bit extra.' I put on my most pleading smile.

He considers, then shrugs. 'I can do them in twenty. But I won't take any money, not after what you did for our Leah.' He gives me a solemn nod.

Clearly, Bella's a Good Samaritan. I mentally file this for future reference. 'You're an angel. Just got to nip to the bank. Be back in a bit.'

He nods and turns back to his key-cutting machine. I just have to hope he doesn't say anything to Bella about it. She seems to know everybody in Lymington. She's like Princess frigging Diana, everyone just loves her.

I wander down the street, my head bowed, trying to kill the allotted twenty minutes. I'd rather have waited in the shop – the fewer people that see me, the better – but I can't risk an ongoing conversation with the key man in case he realises I'm not who I say I am. This impersonation malarkey is harder than it looks.

After eighteen minutes, I return to the shop. He greets me with a grin and hands over the set in a little brown envelope.

'You're a lifesaver,' I say, and mean it.

'Only repaying the favour,' he replies.

I shrug a smile and leave, heading back to Newbury's, but, to my dismay, I spy Bella leaving the café with her boyfriend, the two of them returning to the office. That was a quick coffee – I thought for sure they'd be longer. If she notices her keys are missing, she might get someone in to change the locks. *Think, Jade, think.*

I dart into a charity shop opposite and hover near the window, peering through a rack of ugly Christmas jumpers. Bella and her boyfriend chat with her employee, laughing about something. With a sinking heart, I watch her disappear into the back. After a min-ute, she emerges and leaves with her boyfriend – this time with her handbag over her shoulder. *Damn.*

Once they're out of sight, I dart across the road, heart racing, and slip back into the agency. This time, the guy at the back looks up and frowns. *Shit, can he tell?*

'Forgotten something?' he asks with a smile, followed by another frown as he, no doubt, tries to work out why I'm now wearing a thick parka.

'Yeah, just got to . . .' I give a short laugh and shake my head at my scatterbrained antics. I walk briskly past him, into the back office. Once there, I congratulate myself on fooling another person that I'm Bella. Then, I place her original set of keys on the floor, beneath the desk where her handbag was. Hopefully, she'll accept that she dropped them.

I walk out with a cheery 'Bye again!' As soon as I reach the street and walk a few steps, I let myself breathe. My hands are trembling, my whole system charged with adrenaline. Yet I feel lighter, freer. I've done it. The keys are mine.

But I know that today is nothing compared to what comes next.

The most nerve-wracking part of all is what I'll have to do to truly become my twin. Getting the keys, learning the accent, walking in her footsteps, that's just prep work. The real transformation requires a blank canvas, and as long as Bella's still here, I'll only ever be the knockoff. I'll have to get her out of the way. The thing I need to ask myself is whether I have the courage to do what needs to be done. Whether I have the capacity for . . . I daren't even say the word. Not even to myself.

It hits me in the stomach first – a cold, electric jolt. Then it ripples outward, curdling into a strange, weightless clarity. It's not horror, not really. It's relief. Because I know, without a wisp of doubt, that I can do this.

Chapter Twenty-Three

JADE

Bella's fresh-cut key copies are cold in my palm, gleaming with promise. The knowledge that I could let myself into Bella's flat at any time is both intoxicating and terrifying. But I don't go in. Not yet.

I stand beneath a bare-limbed tree outside Bella's building, heart pinging off my ribcage, and weigh my options. On the one hand, I'm itching to see the inside of her apartment, but on the other, I think about the credit card of hers I snagged, now tucked into my purse along with my own card, driving licence, and Tesco Clubcard. A few hours and she'll notice it's missing, a couple more and it'll be cancelled. And it's unlikely I'll have any more chances. Anyway, she could return home at any moment.

Decision made, I turn and head back to Mum's Clio. I'm at the wheel before I know it, skimming every yellow light, radio turned up to eleven. The traffic is blissfully light for a Monday rush hour; maybe the universe has decided to give me a pass today. The city blurs past – lights, concrete, billboards.

Westquay looms like a cruise ship – tiered parking, walkways, lights that never switch off. Thankfully, it's open for late-night shopping. I park, and take a moment to breathe, the scent of diesel and petrol making me wrinkle my nose.

The lift is slow but gives me a moment to wipe my palms on my jeans, check my reflection, and reset my game face. Not even a hint of nerves – just the cool, ordinary mask of someone who spends every other week in John Lewis and Zara.

My last shopping trip was ages ago, with Zac, back in the summer, when I felt that familiar stab of guilt every time I bought something, even though I told myself it didn't matter, that it would just get added to my credit card bill. This time, I'll have free rein to buy what I like, courtesy of Bella Newbury.

The doors open, and the mall's noise engulfs me – music, chatter, the click-clack of heels, the drone of announcements. I'm swept along in the crowd, letting their energy push me forward. This close to Christmas, the whole place is a shrine to excess – Christmas trees on every level, animated snowflakes projected on to walls, sparkling decorations, and lights.

I buy one item at a time, taking turns in each store. The salespeople don't look twice at me, and the card works on every tap. I'm careful not to overdo it, keeping every individual purchase under £100. One chunky cardigan, a couple of pairs of Levi's, a Superdry coat, and a stack of band tees that will start a feeding frenzy among the Depop set.

The thrill ratchets up with each beep of the card reader. No one questions it, no one stops me. In the beauty hall, the card goes through for a bottle of Chanel Gabrielle perfume and a skincare set I know retails for double online.

A beauty consultant with shell-pink nails offers to do my make-up, and for a moment I'm tempted, but the call of Bella's credit card is too strong, so I regretfully decline. I buy Charlotte Tilbury, La Mer, Yankee Candles. All the stuff I know I can get great resale value for in the run-up to Christmas. The timing couldn't be better.

At the Apple store, I select a screen protector, a charger, and Bluetooth headphones. The sales assistant doesn't even blink. My phone buzzes in my pocket, and for a second, I'm sure its Bella herself asking me what the hell I think I'm doing, but it's just a spam email from a college that rejected me, reminding me that my future awaits. I snort, nearly dropping my shopping bag.

Even with all this, I'm not careless. When I get to the till at John Lewis, I try to read the sales assistant's face – will they notice the tense set of my jaw, or the sheen of sweat on my top lip as I start to worry that I might be pushing my luck? But all she does is smile, hand me the paper bag, and ask if I want to sign up for a reward card. I tell her I don't have time today, thanks, and walk away.

The spree is like a fever. In Lush, the smells are deliciously sweet, like cake and sherbet, and the sales staff descend on me with buckets of glittery bath bombs. I take six, because why not, and add a shower gel that's dayglo purple. At the till, the guy gives me a little speech about their recycling programme. I smile and nod, thinking about how every drop of plastic in this city will outlive us all, piling up in landfill with our darkest secrets.

It's here that the card finally gets declined. I fake irritation, and mumble something about calling my bank and coming back once they've cancelled the block. Security don't even glance my way. I have seven bags swinging from my elbows, and a surge of power that makes me want to run back to the car and just drive until it runs out of petrol.

Instead, I pause at the food court. I skipped breakfast and lunch, and so my stomach is a pit of acid and adrenaline. I treat myself to a bubble tea, using my own card to pay. A reward, really, for a job well done. I sit at the table surrounded by my loot and watch the shoppers swirl by for a few moments. Next, I go through the receipts, making a mental tally of the total haul. If I can flip it all online quickly enough, I'll have a decent chunk of money – not enough to see me through the next phase, but it's a start. I don't even consider using any of it to pay off my debts. They'll be behind me soon enough.

Keen to share my high with someone, but knowing I can't, I text Zac a photo of the boba with an 'x' and nothing else, then I remember my lie to Mum and add a line: *If Mum asks, I drove you to Southampton General this afternoon in her car because you dislocated your thumb ;)*

Zac texts back straightaway: *Are you high?*

I laugh and slurp the last of the tea. *No, but that sounds nice.*

Haven't seen you for ages. You free later?

I pause, feeling momentarily nostalgic for his kisses, but then I remember that my life has changed, and I don't have time: *Sorry, really tired.*

The line of dots indicates that he's typing, but then it disappears.

Shaking away a brief spark of remorse, I get to my feet and start walking back to the car. The high is already wearing off, the weight of the bags leaving red crescents on my fingers. As I cross the food court, I get the eerie feeling of being watched – a prickling at the base of my neck. I scan the mezzanine but see nothing out of the ordinary. Still, I keep my head down, beeline for the exits, and let the crowd carry me away.

There's a moment, just as I'm unlocking the Clio, when I think I see someone across the car park watching me from the shadows. I worry it might be a security guard that's on to me, but it's a man in a blue windbreaker, slouched against the rails. Did he follow me? He flicks a cigarette over the edge, shoves his hands in his pockets, and walks away. I exhale. Must be getting paranoid. I dump the bags in the boot, get in, lock the doors, and drive.

I exit the car park with the radio off, letting my thoughts knot and unknot in the dark. It's late, and I'm suddenly starving. I should have ordered some food along with the tea. I head out of

Westquay and make a pit stop nearby to satisfy my craving for a Burger King. Then I get back in the car and head for home

The city is a maze, but tonight it feels like I know every short-cut, every alley. As I barrel down the dual carriageway I'm riding the high of the day, the feeling that I've done something, made a dent in my world, however small, however crooked.

Mum should still be out at bingo with Pam tonight, so it'll be safe to bring my haul into the flat. I catch a glimpse of myself in the glass panel by the entrance door – flushed, triumphant, a little dangerous. I almost don't recognise her.

I wonder, then, if Bella's found out. If right now, in her sleek flat back in Lymington, she's checking her bank balance, or getting a text from the fraud people. Calling them to cancel her card. I drop the bags on the sofa, which gives a little sigh under their weight, and I stand back to admire the loot, and start planning my next step.

In the glow of the muted TV, I open my phone and create a fresh seller profile, username and all. I'm clever enough to use the free VPN that Zac installed for me, set up for this exact moment. There's a weird satisfaction in knowing I can go from thief to entrepreneur in a single day.

I take pictures of every item against a white duvet cover. Every click of the camera is its own little hit. I arrange the clothes so they look expensive, like they belong to someone with a proper life. I write captions with just the right ratio of exclamation marks, make the listings feel both urgent and effortless. They virtually write themselves – 'Rare!' 'Sold out everywhere!!' 'Get it in time for Christmas!' In less than twenty minutes, the first bids start rolling in, and by eleven-thirty, I've answered four messages from buyers, all desperate to pay over the odds if I can ship tomorrow. It's almost disappointing how easy it is, how little anyone cares as long as you'll post tracked and next-day.

Above the TV, Mum's wall clock ticks, and for a split second, I do feel a twist of guilt. Not for Bella, but for Mum. If she ever found out, it would break her in half. Aside from that, I feel efficient, like I've unlocked a new level of myself. Maybe this is what Bella feels all the time: hungry, invincible, always one step ahead. I watch as the bids creep higher and the dopamine rushes in, electric and pure.

In the end, the only other thing I feel guilty about is how easy it is. I hide all the bags behind the sofa, change into one of the stolen tees, spritz on some of the new perfume that I've decided to keep for myself, and crawl under the white duvet in a blanket of satisfaction, the telly still murmuring. I prop my phone on my chest to keep refreshing the app. The bids climb higher. I run the numbers in my head – a few hundred quid, easy.

Then I remember the keys in my coat pocket, and the reason I took them – access to Bella's flat. That's tomorrow's plan sorted.

Eventually, I drift off, clutching my phone to my chest, and dream that I'm in a house made entirely of other people's things. Staircases of stacked jumpers, walls of perfume bottles, a garden of headphones, and glittery bath bombs. In the dream, I can never find the front door; I just wander from room to room, pushing at the possessions as they pile up around me until there's no air left to breathe.

Chapter Twenty-Four

BELLA

I push the door shut behind me and collapse on to the sofa, my shoulders still aching from the day's tension. Yesterday's calm at my parents' feels like a cruel joke now that Newbury's is already under the tax inspector's microscope. They arrived right after my lunch with Reece, commandeering the back office and rifling through every spreadsheet and receipt. I've been sick with panic all afternoon, not helped by the fact that I thought I'd lost my keys. One of the auditors found them under my desk, which didn't give a very good impression of my capability. I keep replaying the woman's cold expression as she handed them to me. I need a distraction.

I call Reece to see if he wants to go out this evening. I could do with a few drinks to calm down. He picks up after two rings, and I'm greeted by the roar of beer-soaked laughter.

'Which pub are you at?' I ask. 'I can be there in ten.'

'Sorry, Bells,' he says, voice muffled by the pub crowd. 'Last-minute outing with the boys this evening.'

'Is there any way you could duck out? I've had a shit day, Newbury's is having a tax audit and I've had this miserable pair of inspectors at the office all afternoon. Think they might be here for days. I could do with cheering up.'

'Oh, shit, that's annoying. But you'll be okay, Bells. You're always on top of your paperwork. Just let them do their thing. They'll be out of your hair before you know it. Why don't you call Tori, see if she's free to go out? I would meet up, but we just found out it's Rob's birthday so we're having a big night.'

I take three measured breaths, counting each one, and try to convince myself that this is an entirely reasonable turn of events – that my boyfriend is not obliged to drop everything for a minor existential crisis, that Rob's birthday isn't some grand betrayal, that I shouldn't expect anyone to anticipate my need for rescue. It doesn't work. The feeling of rejection burns, and worse, it's not new, it's familiar, like a bruise being pressed.

I want to hear Reece's voice drop into that private register he saves for me, telling me not to worry, that he'll pop round with a takeaway and a bottle of wine and distract me with a movie and sex until the dread ebbs away. I want him to be the person who makes it easier. I want to matter more than his friends, just this once.

'No worries.' I try not to let the bitterness seep into my voice. 'Have a good night.'

'Cheers, Bells. You too. We'll do something tomorrow, yeah?'

'Sounds good.' I end the call, my fingers trembling with disappointment as I'm left in a silent flat rippling with emptiness.

Reece was so sweet last night at my parents' house. The perfect, attentive boyfriend. But it always changes when we return to our real lives. We snap apart again.

I pace the living room, phone in hand, thumbs worrying the edges of the case until the silence becomes unbearable. I open WhatsApp, flicking through my chats as if a solution might be embedded in a meme or a ten-word text from six months ago. I hover over Tori's name for a full minute. If I call her, she'll listen, but it'll all be recounted later – 'Bella was an absolute wreck last night, darling' – and whatever comfort I get will be ruined in the aftermath of whispers.

On the next shelf of options – call Mum? Immediately vetoed. For a start, I absolutely cannot tell her about the audit – she and Dad would fly into a panic. Ditto for telling her about my other worries. And if I'm vague and simply say I can't sleep, she'll just recommend drinking camomile tea and reading a good book. No. I'll have to fix my own mood. That's the way it's always been.

So, do I just crawl into bed? Face four walls and stew in dread? No. A plan seeds itself. Get out of the flat, get drunk, get back late enough that there's no time left for spiralling. I can be hungover and penitent in the morning. For now, numb is the goal.

I stand in front of the bedroom mirror and stare at my face. The day has etched new lines at the edges of my mouth and eyes, but a smear of lipstick and a bit of concealer should cheat the world into thinking I'm fresh as a daisy. I swap my jumper for a black camisole with thin straps, layer on a jacket, and let my hair down. It looks good enough, or at least not actively terrible.

I zip up my boots and head out into the chill. I can't go into any of the bars round here – I know too many people, and besides, the tax inspectors are staying locally, and the last thing I need is for them to see me getting smashed in the pub.

I spend the whole walk to the station rehearsing an alternative version of the phone call with Reece, one where I say something cutting or clever enough to make him feel guilty. In every scenario, he laughs it off and tells me to relax, which only makes me more annoyed. I replay the conversation so many times, I nearly walk past the entrance to the station.

I head briskly towards the train platform, feeling the first tremor of anticipation. When you're in a small town like this, escaping – even for a night – feels like you've pulled off a heist.

As I swipe my company card for a ticket, guilt tugs at me – should my business funds be paying for this night out? I shove it aside, board the train, and find a seat.

The countryside slides by, dark fields and distant lights, but I can't look away from my own blurred reflection. I try to empty my mind – no spreadsheets, no stern auditors, no disappointments – but my thoughts keep bouncing around like pinballs. I chastise myself – always so controlled, so proper. Maybe that's why I'm unravelling now. I can't wait to sit in the corner of a bar and drink until my brain goes numb.

The train pulls into Southampton Central. I bypass taxis in favour of a brisk ten-minute walk. It's dark and cold, but at least it's not raining. My body thrums with anxious energy. The city at night is a collage of streetlights and student laughter and, for a brief, heady moment, I feel younger than I am – twenty-one, maybe, with no obligations except to make it home in one piece. I drift down the street, letting my feet choose a direction. I pass two chain pubs, a chippy, and a kebab place, each brimming with cheerful people whose night has not yet turned. I duck into a bar that's halfway between a pub and a club – dark, with sticky floors and a soundtrack of forgettable pop.

A gaggle of teenagers shoulder past me on their way to a corner table. 'Careful,' I mutter. The girl who bumped me – definitely underage – turns and tells me to 'piss off' before catching up with her friends. Guilt and irritation war inside me. I shouldn't have snapped, but she shouldn't have barged into me.

I shake my head and continue towards the bar, trying to place the song. It's one I've heard recently on the radio, but I don't know the name. I can't believe I've reached a stage in my life where I no longer know band names and song titles. How did that happen?

'Can I help you?' A cute barman with dark curls and blue eyes comes straight over to me, ignoring the other punters at the bar and earning himself some dirty looks. I'm flattered. It feels nice to be noticed. 'Two double vodka tonics please.'

He looks over my shoulder. 'Who's the other one for?' he asks in a soft Irish accent.

I think about saying 'You', but I'm not quite brave enough. 'Me,' I reply instead.

He grins and reaches below the bar for two glasses, keeping eye contact. His attention stabs at the loneliness I've been swallowing all day.

I open my purse to get my credit card, but I can't seem to locate it.

'Everything okay?' he asks.

'Yeah, just trying to . . . hang on.' I rummage some more, but it's just not here. What the hell? Where's my credit card? My company one's here, but not my personal one. Did I leave it at home? On my desk? Did I lose it? I steel myself and hand over the business card.

The evening passes quickly and hazily. I spend it knocking back vodkas, occasionally doing shots with the barman, whose name is Seamus. He's over from Cork, chasing dreams with the rest of his band. I think he's at least five years younger than me, but he's sweet and I like him. He feels like the kind of person I could talk to. Be honest with. He seems kind. Or maybe it's just that I'm hammered.

While he pours drinks for other people, I become a spectator to their messes. A hen party in matching sequinned dresses; two men having a debate that devolves into a shouting match; a couple breaking up in real time, their faces flushed with rage and exhaustion. I check my phone. Reece hasn't texted. I consider messaging him something dramatic, but the thought exhausts me. Instead, I scroll through social media until my vision blurs. Seamus brings over another drink without being asked. 'On the house. You look like you need it more than I do tonight.'

As the night deepens and the music gets louder, I return from the loos to see that the young girl who barged into me earlier has taken my place at the bar, and Seamus is giving her the same twinkling smile he was giving me a few moments ago. A green-eyed spike of jealousy twists through me. But I have no right to feel it.

Time to go home.

I push through the door out into the cold night, and, for a surreal moment, I see someone on the opposite side of the street who looks exactly like me. And I mean *exactly*. She's coming out of Burger King, stuffing fries into her mouth. *What the hell?* I must be super-drunk to be seeing visions of myself. I take a few steps towards the figure and get a fright as a car honks its horn and swerves. I realise I've stepped out on to the road. Somewhere in the haze, I hear my gasp. By the time I recover my senses, the vision of me vanishes, and I stand alone on the pavement, shaken, almost sober again. I could have been killed.

Would that be so bad?

I step away from the kerb and walk a few steps. My reflection flickers in a shop window – red-rimmed eyes, smudged mascara – and as I catch the washed-out image of myself, I realise I don't want to go home. Back to my office, to those auditors. Back to Lymington, where all my troubles are waiting for me. I'm not equipped to face any of it, but I don't have the courage to admit my fears and ask for help. Or to run away and start afresh.

I'm stuck.

Chapter Twenty-Five

JADE

Early next morning, I lurk in a narrow alley next to an overflowing recycling bin, across from Bella's apartment, shivering despite my multiple layers. Her building is a four-storey white edifice in one of the nicest areas of town. Although I haven't yet seen any bad areas of Lymington.

Her boyfriend's BMW isn't parked out front, so I guess he either didn't stay over or he left already.

The street is quiet apart from the occasional dog walker, a couple of uniformed cleaners, and a few workers leaving their homes, smartly dressed, with thick coats and hats. All of them too preoccupied to notice an unremarkable figure hunched in the shadow of a bin, plotting. A dark-red Mercedes SUV rolls by with blacked-out rear windows and a stressed-looking mum in the driver's seat. I feel oddly invisible, capable of anything. My hands tremble, not just from the cold, but from a mixture of nerves and anticipation.

I continue to watch the block, breath held, blowing on my gloved hands and stamping my feet to try to get some warmth back in them. Finally, after thirty minutes of freezing my arse off, Bella's pale blue Fiat slowly emerges from the rear of the property. I get a good look at her face through the windscreen. She's wearing her hair scraped back a little too harshly, and has a thick, blue wool scarf at her throat. She looks rough, as though she hasn't slept. For a moment, I wonder if she's been up crying, or arguing, or if today she simply feels the same friction with the world that the rest of us do. She looks left and right, and peels away down the road.

The moment her car turns the corner, my body jolts from its hiding place. It's now or never. I stride over the road and up the stairs to the entrance doors. The copied key works on the first try, which gives me a sick little thrill. Inside, the hallway is empty and smells faintly of lilies and cleaning fluid.

I climb the stairs, rather than take the lift, each step steady, though my chest clangs, my system flooded with adrenaline. Bella's flat number is 12, which I'm guessing must be on the third or fourth floor, but I stop on the second to have a look, just in case. Nope. This floor goes up to flat 8. On the third floor, I spot number 12 and do a quick scan in case she might have a door cam, but there's nothing I can see to suggest any kind of additional security, so I approach the door, heart racing.

The copied keys slide effortlessly into the locks. I turn the second, and hear a beautiful little click. I push open the door, still wearing my thin faux-leather gloves, as I don't want to risk leaving any fingerprints. I'd assumed that we'd share the same prints, but apparently not. I've done my research. Everyone's are unique, twins included.

Although I saw Bella leave a few moments ago, I pause in the doorway, my head cocked, listening for any sounds of life. But all is silent. No beeping alarm either, which is a relief.

Once inside, front door closed, I do a slow pan of the flat. Small hallway with a gilt mirror above a console table. Pale oak floors, high ceilings, and white sash windows. Black-framed glass doors leading to a huge lounge-kitchen-diner. A wood-panelled door, open a crack to reveal a bedroom in pale green and muted creams. I push open another door to see a guest-bedroom-slash-office, and another door reveals a tasteful limestone shower room with brushed-gold fixtures.

I can barely comprehend that if everything goes to plan, this could be my new pad. It doesn't feel real. But I can't stand here gawping all day.

I move with purpose. First, the mahogany desk in the spare room. I open all the drawers, rummaging through stationery, spare cables, notebooks, old greetings cards, and various other crap. And then, inside the bottom right drawer, beneath a stack of papers, I find a battered grey Moleskine notebook. Flipping through the pages, I'm elated to find a scrawled list at the back with her passwords, usernames, even the PIN for her phone. So predictable, so careless. I just have to hope they're up to date. I guess she did make some effort to conceal them – having written in pencil, she's erased a few letters, worried someone might find them. I'm sure I have enough info here to work some of them out.

Another upside to discovering this handwritten treasure trove is that my writing is nothing like hers, so I'll be able to examine how she forms her letters and practise. I take photos of all five pages' worth of codes.

There's a filing cabinet in the corner, the keys hanging from its lock. I open it and take photos of bank statements, bills, receipts. Not sure if I'll need anything here, but it doesn't hurt to have the information. There's nothing that I can see of any note on the bookshelves.

I leave the office and head to the living room next. Such a beautiful airy space with tasteful, comfy furniture, expensive-looking rugs, and modern artwork. How did she end up with this life while I ended up with mine? Was it simply a quirk of fate? Did Penni reach into the crib to pick up the nearest of us, and it just happened to be Bella? Or did Bella give a piercing gaze that endeared her to Penni? Perhaps it was Mum's decision, and she bonded with me first. Well, whatever it was, I'd say that Bella got the better deal. Twenty-eight years of living in luxury, while I've had to scrape a living and rack up debt just to get by. I shake my head and drag my attention back to my surroundings.

I have a root around in the kitchen area, opening the cupboards, scanning the wine rack. I take one of the five bottles of prosecco – I doubt she'll miss it. The fridge is almost empty – just a couple of tubs of M&S salads, a carton of oat milk, and a lone mango.

Gorgeous as it is, it doesn't look like there's anything else of interest for me in this room, so I head to the bedroom next. This is the main reason I'm here. To snaffle a few of Bella's designer outfits so that I can really take on her persona.

I glance around the restful sanctuary, looking for a wardrobe, but I can't see one. I frown. That can't be right. There's a door to what I presume is an en-suite, but when I push it open, I'm confronted with an enormous walk-in wardrobe leading to an opulent jewel-green bathroom with a clawfoot tub at the far end.

Wow.

I've never seen so many outfits, shoes, and handbags. It's like a high-end store in here, all arranged by colour and heel height. I grab a pair of tan leather boots that look as though they'd cost a year of my wages. Should I take them? Yes, I should. I also pick out a couple of dresses, a jacket, two handbags – one of them a real Mulberry that I can sell online – and a wool coat that smells faintly of an expensive perfume. There's something intimate about rifling through her closet, as if I'm absorbing her life through osmosis.

I spot a grey garment carrier hanging next to the coats, open it, and slot my choices inside. It takes all my willpower not to stuff it as full as I can. But I mustn't tip Bella off to my visit. She can't know she's been robbed. Reluctantly, I replace the tan boots. It's winter, she'll know they're missing. I just need to be patient – they'll be mine soon enough.

The last thing I take is a bottle of Kayali perfume, unopened, with a ribbon around the box. I've never heard of it, but it looks expensive, probably a gift she never got around to using. I stuff it in my coat pocket. Bet I can get a good price on eBay.

I finish loading up the carrier and decide it's time to leave. I take one last lingering, yearning glance around the apartment, reluctant to say goodbye to what will hopefully soon become my home. But I can't risk staying any longer.

Back in the hall, I'm about to open the front door when the landing outside creaks. I press my ear to the door and listen. The sound stops. I hope that's not Bella returning. I don't have a plan for what to do if I come face to face with her. For a split second, I consider bolting back across the flat and finding somewhere to hide. There must be a space in that gigantic closet. My heart is pounding as I try not to panic. I'm sure it's just one of the neighbours. Or maybe it's nothing. I linger for a moment, wishing there was a peephole. But all seems quiet now, so I risk it and dart out—

—straight into a woman coming out of the opposite flat. My brain short-circuits. How am I going to explain myself?

She's petite, dark-haired, early thirties, dressed in a navy-blue Lycra set with neon orange piping, a smart gym bag slung over one shoulder. Her face is all angles and energy, with bright, dark eyes that glimmer with surprise, but also recognition.

She speaks first, her voice brisk and softly accented, Spanish maybe. 'Oh, hi Bella!' She beams. 'Perfect timing! I wanted to ask if you got the email from the management company?'

I respond, as evenly as I can, 'No . . . I mean . . . maybe, I've been slammed this morning. Haven't checked. What's it about?' The words come out a little high, but the neighbour doesn't notice.

She waves her phone in the air. 'It's the roof repairs. They're asking for another contribution from each flat. I thought we agreed a cap last time?'

My mind blanks for a moment. I haven't prepared for any of this, I don't know anything about 'contributions' or 'caps'. But then, feeling a crackle of something like dark joy, I lean into it: yet another person who's mistaken me for Bella.

I flick my wrist, glance at my phone, and sigh. 'God, seriously? I haven't even looked; I've been on client calls all morning. Can we chat about it later?' I say, calibrating my voice. 'Running late for a meeting!'

I start to edge past, but she shifts to block me, smiling as she replies. 'Sure, sure. But what time? You're hard to get hold of, you know?'

'Six o'clock?'

'Great! I'll come to you.' She steps aside, and I make my escape, hoping my smile doesn't look too forced.

I skip the lift entirely, terrified she might follow and spot the deception in such a confined space. I take the stairs, flying down three flights like a crash-test dummy, my feet barely touching each step, my lungs burning, legs almost buckling.

Outside, the sunlight is so stark it throws everything into high relief. I blink, momentarily disoriented by the sudden assault of brightness. The morning is so crisp it almost feels fake – the perfect blue sky, the cheerful birdsong, the distant rumble of a bus. But I welcome the icy air against my clammy skin.

I take a hard left down a side street and keep walking, my shadow stretching and shrinking on the pavement as I go. I force myself not to look back until I'm three streets away.

Only now do I allow myself to exhale and laugh, a wild, shaky bark that startles a passing dog walker. I've done it. I haven't just bluffed my way out of danger, I've been accepted. Mistaken for

Bella by someone who actually knows her well. And, okay, it was fleeting, but it was also up close, for a full minute, in a real conversation with moving parts. My resemblance to her, the mannerisms I've studied and borrowed, the voice modulated just enough. All those secret rehearsals and mirror drills – they're working. The ridiculous amount of detail I've poured into this persona is finally paying off.

But I realise it isn't enough to just look like her. I think about the passwords, the outfits, her memories, the small tics and tells that make up Bella's life. I'll have to master them all, wear them like a second skin. I can pass as Bella superficially, but will her world truly accept me? What about her parents? They'll be able to tell, surely. I might be able to fool her friends and neighbours, but her mum and dad are an entirely different matter. If they suspect I'm not her, they'll instantly realise who I am.

The thought freezes my gut. Bella's parents know her voice and body language intimately. I doubt I could fool them for five minutes, and yet I'll need to. The questions crowd in, sudden and suffocating. I try to push them away, but they cling to me like her stolen clothes. Maybe I'm not cut out for this level of con. Maybe it's time to call it off before it spirals even further. Or maybe I just need to rethink the plan. I guess, instead of taking over her current life, I could simply sell her business, empty her accounts, and run.

But I'm getting ahead of myself. Before I think about any of that, I still need to scrape another chunk of cash together so that I can get Bella out of the way. After that, things should begin to get easier.

My heart is pounding. I want to blame it on my rushed exit down three flights of stairs and subsequent zigzag through the backstreets, but I know it's proper nerves starting to kick in. I've already broken so many laws today. But that's nothing compared to what I'm going to have to do. I'm in so deep: I can't even think about turning back now.

Chapter Twenty-Six

BELLA

There's a knock at the door just as I'm wringing my hair, still dripping from the world's fastest shower.

I'm expecting to see Reece, but it's my neighbour, Marisol.

'Hello, Bella. I know it's a bit early, but I brought over a bottle of Rioja. Thought you might like a glass while we chat about the roof repairs.'

My stomach turns at the thought of drinking wine after last night's binge-drinking session. 'Hi, Marisol. Um, *roof repairs?*'

'Yes, remember? We arranged to meet at six today to chat about it.'

I scramble for the memory, but my head's still not right. It's as if everything from the last twenty-four hours has been overwritten by a single, throbbing hangover. 'I'm so sorry. I completely forgot. I have to be out this evening . . . a dinner thing.'

'Oh, okay.' Marisol's smile flickers, then frays at the edges. For a moment, she just stands there, staring at the top of her wine bottle. I feel a stab of guilt deep in my chest. She only moved here a few months ago, and this block is full of card-carrying introverts who never say more than 'morning' and 'bin day's Thursday' in the communal hallway. I don't think she knows many people. I get the sense she's not good at the making-friends bit.

'Can we make it tomorrow instead?' I ask. 'I promise I won't forget this time.'

'Sure.' Her face recalibrates, the smile reboots. 'Tomorrow. Same time?'

'A bit later, say, six-thirty? I'll get some nibbles in.'

'Perfect!' She waves and disappears back into her flat.

I close the door and exhale with such force that my vision whites out for a second. I feel rough, and I really do not want to spend tomorrow evening talking about roof-repair quotes I can already feel the awkwardness of forced small talk lubricated by cheap Rioja and supermarket hummus. I know I should do more to make my neighbour feel welcome, but everything feels so hard lately, like I'm watching my life from behind a thick screen.

I'm halfway through towel-drying my hair again when there's another knock at the door.

I open the door, and this time it *is* Reece, out of breath but grinning, wearing the dark suit I once told him made him look like a hitman. And the shirt I gave him last Christmas, the one with the subtle navy polka dots that he claimed was 'too playful' for work. He's obviously worn it this evening to try and butter me up, to get me to forgive him.

'Hey. Sorry about last night, Bells.' He's holding a small bouquet of supermarket tulips, wilting at the tips. 'Really. It was a dick move. Should've been there for you. Promise I'll make it up to you tonight.'

'Come in.' I don't respond to his apology because I'm still pissed off about his lack of support. Instead, I point at my hair and say, 'Need to finish getting ready.'

He sprawls on my king-size bed, watching me.

I hold up two tops for him to inspect: 'Black or green?' I stare at the mirror to avoid looking at him directly.

'Black,' he replies immediately. 'Sexier.'

Sexy is the last thing I feel. As well as hungover from last night's solo drinking session in Southampton, I've had another anxiety-ridden day at work.

He's booked a table tonight, so I know he's really trying to make things up to me, but the truth is I would have much preferred a pyjama night on my own, maybe an Uber Eats and some Netflix – anything but an elaborate dinner that will require three layers of make-up, uncomfortable underwear, and pretending not to be exhausted. I'm not in the mood for performative coupledom tonight. But if I bail, Reece will only think I'm sulking.

I slide the black silk top over my head and wriggle into my favourite jeans.

'Jeans?' He doesn't even try to hide the judgement. 'I booked The Carousel. You know, that new swanky place down by the Quay.'

'You didn't say there was a dress code,' I reply.

'Well, no, but . . . it's kind of . . . formal?'

I sigh, and go back into the walk-in.

'I mean, you look good in the jeans, but—'

'It's fine,' I call back grumpily.

I pick out a cream silk pleated skirt and my tan boots. But now the top's all wrong. Where's my Mulberry handbag? I'm sure it was on this shelf. Goosebumps prickle the back of my neck. There's a strange smell in here, like a fruity body spray – something that definitely doesn't belong in my flat. Has someone been in here? Surely not.

'Reece, can you come here a sec?'

He does as I ask, a quizzical expression on his face.

'Does it smell weird to you in here?' I ask, and immediately feel ridiculous.

Reece takes a deep, theatrical sniff. 'Weird how?'

'Like, chemical? Sweet?'

He shrugs, unbothered. 'Maybe the cleaner used a different polish?'

'No. Kayleigh only comes on Thursdays, and it always smells like those eco-friendly wipes. This is more . . . synthetic. Like cheap perfume.'

'I can't smell anything.' Reece takes a step towards me. 'Except you.' He nuzzles my neck, but I step away.

'I need to dry my hair.'

'You're still mad at me, aren't you?' Reece folds his arms.

'No. I'm just tired. Work sucks at the moment and my brain is scrambled.'

'Well, let's go out and forget our worries for a night.'

I hate the way he says 'our worries', like he's dismissing mine. He doesn't get it, and somehow that makes me want to cry and throat-punch him simultaneously. I think, maybe for the first time, about what it would be like to be alone every night – no negotiations, no explaining myself, no going out when I want to stay in.

I realise that this is why our relationship hasn't progressed in years. He never wants to talk about the serious stuff. Never wants to hear anything negative. It always has to be sunlight and laughter. Which, on the one hand, is also what I love about him, but it can be frustrating when there are real issues going on in my life.

'Can you see my Mulberry bag anywhere? The small one, cross-body?' I try to sound casual. 'I was sure I left it here, but it's gone.'

Reece scans the room in a slow, distracted way. 'You probably left it at work.'

'I never take it to work. Too nice for the office. I usually keep it here so I don't forget it on the way out. I think I must be losing my marbles.'

There's a silence, and I feel for a moment like I've opened a door to a possible future, a version of myself who loses things, who forgets appointments and cries in changing rooms and quietly becomes someone nobody can quite rely on. The thought makes my chest throb.

'I think you're just tired,' Reece says.

'Maybe. I just . . . I have this feeling in here tonight like someone's been around my stuff.'

He laughs, which I find infuriating. 'Maybe it's the ghosts of your old school friends, come to haunt your fashion choices.'

'Ha, ha.' I roll my eyes. But I do remember locking the door, checking twice before I left this morning. There's no way anyone could have got in. It must be Kayleigh. Has to be. Maybe she arranged to come today instead, and I forgot. Same as I forgot I was supposed to be meeting Marisol this evening. I'm going to have to ensure I put everything in my online diary instead of thinking I'll remember.

I try to put it out of my mind and return to the perma-crisis of getting dressed. I pull out another top, a forest-green one with a low scoop, and try it with the skirt. Better.

'Do you think I should get an alarm system?' I ask, half joking. Although I don't know why I'm asking, because I can't afford anything like that at the moment.

Reece's eyebrows go up. 'If it makes you feel safer, sure, why not?' He's reading something on his phone, not even looking at me.

'Or what about a doorbell camera?' I muse, sure I could pick one up cheaply. Something suddenly occurs to me. 'Hey, can you grab my wallet from the dresser?'

He tosses it to me, almost knocking over my bottle of La Mer Revitalizing Hydrating Serum. I repress a grunt of annoyance, flip the wallet open, and my blood goes cold. My credit card isn't there.

'Fuck.'

'What now?' He sounds more tired than curious.

'My credit card!'

'What about it?' Reece frowns.

'I just remembered, I went to pay for . . . something yester-day and it wasn't in my purse.' I'm not telling Reece that I went out drinking alone last night. I was hoping I was wrong, but it's not here.

'When did you last have it?'

'You sound like my mum,' I say, but I try to think. 'Not yester-day. I think it was at the weekend? I picked up a coffee from Beanz on Sunday morning, before we went to my parents' place.'

'Maybe you left it in the café.'

'Good point. They'll be closed now. I'll pop in tomorrow.'

'You should probably check your bank statement, just in case.'

That's actually a good idea, but I resent him for having it. I snatch up my phone, open up the app, and take a look at my credit card statement. 'You have got to be kidding me.'

'What?' Reece comes and looks over my shoulder.

'Superdry, John Lewis, Zara, the Apple Store . . .' I murmur in disbelief, noting that each transaction is time-stamped within min-utes of the last. In total, over a thousand quid gone in one evening.

'Had a bit of a spree, did you?' Reece asks before the penny drops. 'Oh, that wasn't you?'

'No, it bloody wasn't!' I sit heavily at my dressing table. My mind spins. Someone must have swiped my card while I was in the bar last night. Could it have been that Irish barman? Or maybe it was that young girl who knocked into me. Maybe they were in on it together. Maybe he was flirting with me to distract me, while she went through my bag. I feel like such a gullible idiot. Should I call the police?

'Shit,' Reece says, with appropriate alarm. 'You need to call the bank. Right now.'

I notice a red alert at the top of the app asking me to verify that a purchase from Lush is being made by me.

I type back 'NO' in capital letters and scroll down to the bottom of the screen to find the number for the fraud department. 'Sorry, Reece, I'm not going to be able to come out tonight. I have to sort this out.'

'The reservation isn't for another half hour.' Reece reminds me that this crisis is merely a detour from dinner.

I shake my head. 'I know. But I'll probably be on hold that long. Raincheck?'

I hear him sigh, the sound of disappointment and relief intermingled. 'I'll just . . . go, then. I'll rebook dinner for another night.'

'You're not staying?' I ask.

'While you're on hold to the bank?' He smiles. 'I'll pass. Text me when you get it sorted, yeah?'

I nod, only partly listening, already punching in the numbers. He leaves the room, his coat swishing, a soft click as the bedroom door closes behind him. I barely notice. I sit, half dressed, knee bouncing up and down like a nervous metronome, waiting for the call to connect. I can hear the thump of my heart in my ears.

A robotic voice answers, giving me a list of options.

I press four for stolen cards, and hear the front door slam, relief and disappointment tugging at my chest.

Minutes crawl. My thoughts spiral in reverse: *Where's my Mulberry bag? Did Kayleigh come today? How sure am I of anything at this point?*

I wander back to the bedroom, phone still pressed to my cheek.

The fraud operator finally answers, a middle-aged Scottish woman who calls me 'Mrs Newbury' in a fatigued voice. I try to explain I'm 'Ms', but she's already reading out the flagged transactions in a bored, methodical way. I reply to her questions. *Yes, the Superdry purchase. Yes, the John Lewis purchase. Yes, I have my other cards, just not the platinum credit card. Yes, I will cut it up if I find it.* My responses sound brittle, like I'm reading from a bad script.

She puts me on hold and then comes back, her tone slightly warmer. 'All right, Mrs Newbury, we've blocked your card permanently. The new one will arrive by Monday. You should call the police to report the theft, just so it's on file.' She's probably said this a thousand times.

My phone pings with a message. It's Reece. *Sorry for bailing. Hope you get it sorted xx.* No offer to come back. No inquiry about how I'm feeling, whether I want company or support, or even just to vent my stress into his shoulder.

I grit my teeth, disappointed in him all over again. His detachedness never used to bother me. When did that change?

I sit on the bed and let my phone fall from my hand. Is this what relationships are supposed to be like? I'm starting to realise that Reece and I have been quite surface-level. I guess that's because we've never really had any major obstacles to overcome. No bad times. Ever since we met, our lives have been plain sailing, relaxed, fun. Now that my life is hitting a rough patch, he's backing off. It's depressing and scary to think that I can't rely on him to be there for me when things get serious. Does this mean the end for us? Or am I overreacting?

I don't think I am. He knows I'm having a shit time at work. That I'm having an audit. That my credit card was stolen, and I'm worried someone has broken into my home. And what's his reaction? To leave. I sink back against the pillows with a sigh. If I'm not going to have my boyfriend to lean on, I guess I'll have to sort out my problems on my own.

Chapter Twenty-Seven

JADE

After work, I slip out the back door of The Oak, avoiding the kitchen crew's litany of shared complaints, and duck into the alley behind the pub. It's freezing – my breath comes out in dragon puffs, wreathed in the sickly glow of the security lamp – and my backpack is so overstuffed it's threatening to split at the seams. The adrenaline buzz that powered me through my shift is ebbing, replaced by the prickling tingle of nerves, like static running up my arms.

I pace in tight circles, boot soles crunching on frost, and try to keep my hands busy. Every few seconds I check my phone, skipping from eBay and Marketplace to Gumtree, Depop, and Vinted, checking my listings and balances. It's all mounting up nicely. After my initial credit-card spree at Westquay last week, I managed to sell almost nine hundred quid's worth of stuff. It was such a buzz. But I'm going to need a hell of a lot more than that. Maybe even ten times that amount. I still have Bella's taupe Mulberry bag that retails for just under a grand, but every time I went to photograph it, I got the creeping fear that she'd reported it stolen and that some hidden algorithm would trace it back to me. Luckily, I came up with another idea for how to get rid of it.

I also decided my only option to get the money I need quickly was to return to Bella's flat, while she was at work, for one last rummage. So that's what I did, fully prepared with a backpack this time.

Instead of hitting the obvious stuff – the showpiece heels and the brand-name items I know she's worn on Insta – I went straight for the back of the closet, the dead zone where even Bella's compulsive tidiness couldn't quite reach.

There, bunched between garment bags and vacuum-sealed puffer coats, I found a treasure trove – half a dozen silk tops with the tags still attached, a couple of boxed purses, even a pair of sunglasses so expensive they came with their own authenticity certificate. I got that shivery, over-caffeinated feeling as I unzipped a battered overnight bag and found it stuffed with old receipts, spiral-bound planners, and more than a few loose tenners and twenties. I took those, too. My guess was that Bella didn't even know they were there.

On my way out, I paused at her dressing table, which looked like it belonged in a movie star's dressing room – glass perfume bottles, facial rollers, a lipstick in every possible shade. I'd ignored it on my first visit, but this time I paid more attention. Nestled in the middle was a large, pink, velvet jewellery box.

I opened it, half expecting a tinkly ballerina. Instead, there were layers of chains, bracelets, rings, and earrings that I'm fairly certain cost more than Mum's flat. I picked out a few of the shinier bits and dropped them into my pocket. I also got lucky when I pulled open a couple of drawers and found gift bags of unopened make-up. I stuffed a few in my rucksack, then carefully shuffled the remaining contents so it wouldn't look like anything had been disturbed.

Stealing, it turns out, is only the first chapter. Fencing the spoils is a completely different operation, and that's where things get complicated.

Getting the jewellery appraised was a non-starter. The man behind the glass at Cash Converters took one look at me, then at the gold, and handed it back without even squinting through his magnifying glass thingy. I left the place shaking, convinced I'd already been reported to the police. That experience made me too nervous to try the local pawn shops in case they did the same.

I guess online reselling is simple enough if you're a normal punter flogging your ex-boyfriend's hoodie, but when you have a stash of ill-gotten handbags, designer clothes, and enough high-end make-up to paint a mural, you need to be a touch more creative.

So I started small, listing the least eye-catching items first – the silk tops, the boxed purses, the unopened make-up. It was a slow trickle of sales to begin with, but every completed transaction made me feel a little more invincible, like I was levelling up in a video game. Still, even with everything combined, I've barely scraped together £1,300.

So now here I am, huddled in the alley, watching my breath fog in the lamplight, until I spot Dodgy Steve loping towards me in his usual uniform of anorak and Saints scarf, rolling a spliff with the kind of efficiency that can only be achieved through a lifetime of total dedication to his art. I have to admit, I like Steve. He's funny, but not in a way that's performative; he's not trying to be charming, he just is, more often by accident.

The moment he spots me, the corners of his mouth twitch up, and he stashes the unlit spliff behind his ear. His eyes flicker with interest as I swing the heavy backpack off my shoulder. 'What you got for me, then, Jadey?'

I unzip the bag that's crammed to the brim, and let him take a look.

For the briefest instant, I catch a micro-smirk – eyebrows arched, eyes hungry – but he quickly schools his features back to lazy indifference, as if he's doing me a favour just by looking.

He picks up a pair of Balenciaga trainers, turning them over to inspect the soles, like he's weighing fruit at a market. 'Hmm, might be able to shift these,' he says, but his face has already betrayed him. He knows their value. Knows someone will bite his arm off for them at the right price. 'Where d'you get these? Off a corpse?'

'No corpses. Just an heiress with poor impulse control.' I keep it breezy. 'You can offload them then?'

'I can give it a go,' Steve replies, tucking one shoe under his arm and rummaging deeper. He finds the jewellery next, and his eyebrows shoot up. 'And what's this little treasure trove, eh? Planning to open your own Argos?'

I shrug, but my heart's in my throat. 'I figured you might have an outlet for this kind of stuff.'

'Where'd you get it?' He immediately mimes zipping his lips. 'No, best not tell me. I don't want to know, right?' He glances around, less for the police and more for rivals, then drops the gold back into my bag. 'You're a dangerous one, Jade.' He pulls out boxed purses and brand-new designer perfumes, nodding at each new discovery. Every time he finds something he likes, he gives a little grunt – sometimes a whistle, sometimes a grunt–whistle hybrid.

'That's all of it?' he asks when he reaches the bottom of the bag. 'Yep,' I confirm.

He nods. 'I'll take it all off your hands, but some of that stuff might be too recognisable, if you know what I mean?'

We spend the next ten minutes haggling. Steve starts off with a number so insulting I nearly walk away on the spot, but I can tell he's just posturing. When he sees I'm in no mood for games, he relents, and we settle on a figure that at least gets me nearer my target.

Money changes hands and, even here, away from prying eyes, it's a furtive, ritualistic gesture, like passing a note in class. I don't check the cash until I'm back home, but I know instinctively it'll all be there. Steve has his own code of honour, warped though it is.

I pass him the backpack. 'Bring me the bag back next time you're in, yeah?'

He nods. 'Planning on any more like this?' he asks airily. But I'm not fooled by his nonchalant attitude.

'Maybe, not sure.' I shrug. I don't think I can risk going back to the flat. Not unless I really have to.

'If you do, I'll take a look,' he adds. 'Not promising anything though. Have to see how I get on with this lot first.'

I nod, although I'm hoping to put this new life of debt and petty crime behind me. I need to focus on the future. On my new life of ease and comfort.

We stand awkwardly for a moment, like two kids who've just swapped Pokémon cards in the playground.

After a beat, Steve reaches up to his ear and removes the spliff. He lights up, takes a deep drag, and spits a flake of tobacco from his tongue. He grins at me with a kind of lopsided affection, and I see the gold crown on his canine flashing in the yellow streetlight. He doesn't smile like he's happy; more like he's making a bet with me about whether either of us are going to get out of this alley alive.

He offers it to me, and I hesitate just long enough to be cool, then take it. I've only ever smoked weed when someone handed it to me, and always with the same feeling, like it's a ritual you're not sure you believe in but you don't want to offend the other person.

I inhale and it scrapes at my throat in a way that makes me think of hospital disinfectant. I blow the smoke out slowly, watching it curl like a ribbon into the darkness. For a heartbeat, it looks like I'm breathing fire. Our quiet camaraderie takes the edge off the cold and the fact that I have basically become a member of Southampton's criminal underclass.

Steve looks me up and down, not creepily, more curious. 'This new side-hustle suits you, Jadey. You look good with your hair and whatnot.' He gestures to my overall appearance.

'Thanks. Gone back to my natural colour and started working out a bit.' I toke on the spliff again, and this time it hits pure in the back of my throat. I pass it back.

He takes it with a nod and, for a few breaths, we just stand here, passing it back and forth. The night is chilly enough to make my nose run, and I have to keep sniffing, like a kid in an unheated classroom. The city sounds different at this hour, the normal traffic and shouting replaced by the distant wail of sirens and the scuttle of foxes.

I let the weed smooth out the jagged edges of my thoughts. My doubts. Because, despite my determination to see this through, I can't help thinking back to when I first heard I had a twin. Back to that pure emotion when I realised this could be the connection I've been missing all my life. The thing that was going to make things better. Even now, as I teeter on the precipice, it's not too late to turn back from my plan. But once I open my mouth to Steve, that will be it. There'll be no changing my mind after that.

For a few moments, I allow myself to think about backtracking. About leaving here, calling Bella up, and introducing myself. Only thing is, I can still hear her snotty voice on the phone telling me I'm not up to scratch. Even the lies on my resumé weren't good enough for her, so what would she think about the truth? A barmaid sleeping on her mum's sofa with a mountain of debt and no life goals.

No. I shut down my doubts and harden my heart.

The plan stays.

I can feel the question growing between me and Steve, and I know that either I'm going to ask it or he's going to ask what's up, so I may as well get it over with.

'Listen, Steve. If someone was hassling me, is there anyone you know of who could . . . make it stop?'

His eyes snap up, good humour vanished. 'Who is it?' he asks, eyes narrowing. 'I'll do it for you. I'll dangle the fucker over the top of a multistorey. Tell him if he hassles you again, I'll let go.'

I get the distinct feeling that Steve isn't joking. 'Thanks, but, no. I don't want any ties back to this place. To you.'

He takes a deep inhale on the joint, weighing his answer. 'All right, depends who's doing the hassling,' he says. 'Most people can be discouraged with a fistful of dog shit through the letterbox. But if you're thinking about something more long-lasting, that's a different story.' He studies me for a moment longer. 'Who is it? Boyfriend? You in trouble?'

'It's complicated.'

He grins, but it's joyless. 'Want me to send round a couple of yobs with cricket bats?'

I'm starting to regret asking, but I can't back out now. 'No, that's not what I mean. I just . . . I need to know my options for something more serious.'

He freezes, like a video on pause, and I see the whole spectrum of calculation cross his face – suspicion, then understanding, then a kind of professional curiosity. 'Okay, right. Well, there's one bloke I know who, if you've got the cash, can handle anything. And I mean anything. You want someone scared? Ruined? In jail? Dead? You just have to say the word.' Steve speaks with unsettling calm, as if he's recommending a handyman. 'But it will cost you. A lot.'

I force myself to look him in the eye. 'How much is a lot?'

He names a figure, and it's not far off what I've saved so far – including tonight's transaction – which makes me want to laugh and cry in the same breath. My heart is hammering.

'Can you give me his details?'

He shakes his head. 'I'll contact him, then he'll contact you. Cleaner that way. All right?' I nod, and for a moment, I think we're back in regular territory. But then he leans in, voice barely above a whisper. 'Jade, don't fuck about with this. If you want a person gone, and I mean properly gone, you have to be sure. This isn't like shoplifting. You can't just say sorry and put it back. Once you go down that road, you don't turn around.'

I swallow. 'I know. I get it.' But the truth is, I don't get it at all. I can't even imagine the road, let alone what lies at the end of it. All I know is that I'm so tired of waiting for things to happen to me, of waking up every day knowing that nothing will change unless I change things myself.

Steve absorbs my reply, finishes the spliff, grinds the glowing butt under his boot, then moves on, like nothing happened. 'Anyway, I'll have the cash for you on Friday, same spot. And bring any more jewellery you can get your hands on. I can shift gold easy as anything.' He grins, reverting to his usual light-hearted self.

I nod, attempting to smile back, but all the energy's gone out of me. The transaction, the information, the realness of the whole thing – it's all a bit too much. And I'm not used to smoking dope. I think it's made me a bit paranoid. I'll stick to ciggies in future. I'm going to need a clear head for all this.

He claps my shoulder, not hard, but it still rattles my bones. 'Don't stress, yeah?'

I nod, but the tightness in my chest doesn't lift as I walk away. I try not to think about what I'm about to do. Instead, I need to focus on the outcome. On living my best life. The one I was always meant to have, but by a random quirk of fate, I was denied. I tell myself that this, right now, is just the awkward, uncomfortable, transitional phase. Once it's done, I'll be free. And then I won't have to think about debt or stealing credit cards or sleeping on sofas. About doing dodgy deals in back alleys and hiring scary people to do scary things.

Chapter Twenty-Eight

JADE

It's the early hours of the morning, the kind of pre-dawn darkness that feels like a secret. I'm in Mum's Clio parked in a gravel lay-by down a country lane that barely qualifies as a road. The engine is switched off, but the keys are in the ignition, radio on the lowest possible volume, the faint, familiar scent of Mum's body spray. The only illumination comes from the clock on the dashboard. The time reads 02.17, and I'm ticking down the seconds to the strangest, most unthinkable meeting of my life – waiting for a hitman to show up.

I can see why he chose this location. It's the back arse of nowhere. There's no CCTV, no houses for half a mile, not even a reliable phone signal, unless maybe you stand on the verge and hold the phone at a sixty-degree angle while humming. I run a thumbnail across the Clio's dashboard, tracing the outline of a sticker Mum put there years ago: 'MINIONS ARE LIFE', it says. We went to see the movie *Despicable Me* for my thirteenth birthday, and the Minions were our favourite characters.

The instructions I was sent, via my burner phone, were clinical and direct: *WAIT AT 02:30 PRECISELY. DO NOT BE LATE.*

VEHICLE WILL ARRIVE, PARK IN FRONT AND FLASH HAZARDS. GET IN REAR OF VEHICLE. It's all caps, like the sender is shouting. I imagine the other end of the transaction, another burner phone held by gloved hands, a face with no expression. There were other messages before that, all variations on the same theme – no names, no faces, no questions. I find myself reading the text chain over and over, making sure I've got all the details correct.

I keep checking my face in the rear-view mirror. Not for make-up, not for stray hairs – just to see if I look different, now that I'm here to arrange a murder. My cheeks are flushed and my eyes are wide, almost cartoonish. I look like a teenager on her way to a house party her mum doesn't know about. My hands keep finding their way to the steering wheel; they grip and relax, grip and relax, like I'm doing stress-relief exercises. I try to hold them steady, but the more I think about what I'm doing, the more they tremble.

It's been a week and a half since I first asked Steve to help me out, and I still can't believe I'm going through with it. There's a part of me that wants desperately to believe this is all a joke, or a test, or a dream. Or that any second now, Mum will bang on the window, mascara streaking, and drag me home in a swirl of angry perfume and threats to call the police. Instead, the only thing in view is the hedgerow – a knotted black mass that looks like it wants to swallow me and the car whole.

Obviously, I'm glad that Mum hasn't picked up on any of my plans, but it's also pretty crap that she hasn't noticed anything different in my behaviour. Or maybe she has noticed, but has chosen not to say anything. I get that – despite living together, we have separate lives – but it would have been nice to think that Mum paid more attention to what I do. Perhaps if she'd interfered a bit more, asked what I was up to, pushed to get to the bottom of things . .

perhaps then, I might have changed my mind. Or maybe not. I think I'm just getting the jitters.

My head is a shambles. Now that I'm actually here, the gear-stick slick beneath my palm, I feel like my whole body has been hollowed out and replaced with cold, heavy air. This is the kind of place they find missing people, months later, after the foxes have done their work.

My breath fogs up the windscreen. I wipe it away with a sleeve that smells vaguely of fabric softener and stale cigarettes. I tell myself it's fine, that this is the plan. I rehearse the conversation, try out different ways to say what I need, but every version sounds laughably naive. Steve said the guy would be 'professional', and that I should treat it like a job interview. But what questions do you ask at a job interview for murder?

I keep imagining different versions of tonight – the one where the hitman turns out to be a cop, or a sadist, or an opportunist who decides to kill me instead, just for fun. Each time I imagine that, my heart tries to climb out through my throat. I count the seconds between beats, willing them to slow down.

The minutes tick by. I fidget. 4G isn't working, so I scroll through old texts. The heater starts to make a weird tapping sound, and suddenly I'm hyper-aware of every noise, every shift in the wind.

At 02.28, a pair of headlights flares in the rear-view mirror. My body tenses, as if an electric current just ran the length of my spine. The lights are distant at first, but within seconds, they swell until they're a whitewash in the glass. My hands jerk instinctively, shielding my eyes. The approaching car moves slowly, deliberately, as if it's stalking rather than driving, its beams blinding, shining into the Clio's interior as it draws closer, no doubt illuminating me from behind. I feel exposed. My heart is racing. Is this him?

The car cruises past and pulls into the space in front.

It's an old silver Toyota Corolla, the sort that pensioners drive to Tesco on weekday mornings.

I can't tell if I'm sweating or shivering. Probably both. The Corolla's interior is dark, and the silhouette in the driver's seat is so still that, for a second, I think the car is empty. Then the passenger window cracks just wide enough for a wisp of cigarette smoke to curl into the night.

A full ten seconds pass before anything happens. Then the hazards click on – one, two, three deliberate flashes.

I review the plan – get out, don't look nervous, get in the back seat. No sudden movements. I try to imagine how people act in movies – confident, ironic, bored – but nothing feels right I almost laugh at myself for thinking this would be like in the films, where you just hand over the cash and walk away.

Psyching myself up, I square my shoulders. This is business. A transaction, nothing more. I'm just here to outsource a problem. It's not like anyone will even know about Bella Newbury going missing. That thought is comforting and horrifying at the same time.

I clumsily pull the hood of my sweatshirt up and step out into the raw, damp cold. The Clio's door shuts with a noise that sounds ten times louder than it should. As I walk towards the Corolla, my feet crunch on old grit and broken glass. The smell of wet, rotten leaves fills my sinuses. I imagine the crows in the field watching, hunched like dark-robed judges.

I keep my head down, as if that might make me invisible. I glance up once at the car, and for a second, I almost turn around and run. But I don't. I walk up to the rear door and wait. Through the open window, a voice, low and flat, says, 'Get in.'

There's nothing else. No greeting, no joke, not even a 'please'. I open the door, heart hammering, and slide on to the back seat.

The car is warm, which is unsettling. I expected it to be freezing. There's a chemical sweet smell – air freshener, maybe – as well as fresh cigarette smoke. But underneath is something tangy and metallic, a smell I can't quite name. The driver doesn't turn. I can only see his eyes in the rear-view mirror, dark and focused.

He's silent for a few seconds, just smokes his cigarette, tapping the ash out of the window.

I try to look unimpressed, like this is just a regular Tuesday for me. It's not. 'Thought you'd have a nicer car,' I say, immediately regretting it.

He blows out a stream of smoke and flicks the butt out of the window, its orange glow eaten up by the dark. 'I don't like to draw any attention.' His voice is neutral with a hint of London in it. 'The less you stand out, the less you're remembered,' he adds. There's no more preamble. 'Who's the mark and when do you want it done?' he asks, like he's taking an order for pizza.

My mouth feels like sandpaper. 'Her name's Bella Newbury. I need it done as soon as possible, please.'

'Got a home address?'

'She lives in Lymington. Flat 12, Seafoam Court, Ellington Place. I can write it down for you.'

'Nothing in writing. I can remember. Does she work?'

'Um, yeah. She's an estate agent. She owns Newbury New Forest Property Group.'

He draws a breath in through his teeth. 'High-profile? That'll cost you extra.'

I flinch. '*What?* But—'

'Or you can leave now.'

'How much extra?' I ask.

'Another five hundred.'

My heart sinks. 'I don't have it.'

'Not my problem. And I'll need it all upfront.'

I stammer out a reply. 'I thought I'd pay you half now, half once the job's done.'

'This is the real world, love, not TV. All upfront, no refunds, no "change of heart".'

My brain races, trying to think of a way I can get the extra with such short notice. 'I've got the amount we originally agreed on, but that extra five hundred might take a while.'

'Give me what you've got now,' he demands, 'and I'll text instructions on where to leave the rest.'

'I'll need proof once it's done,' I say. 'A photo, her phone, and whatever ID she has on her at the time. And the body needs to disappear without a trace. It can never be found. That's the most important part.'

'You'll get proof it's done,' he agrees. 'But you never contact me again. Understand?'

'Yes.' I pause. 'How will you do it?'

'Better you don't know.'

I realise he's right. I don't want to know. I fumble in my bag, with numb fingers, for the envelope stuffed with cash. It's ironic that the proceeds are all courtesy of Bella. That she's funded her own demise with her credit card and her designer gear. I question if I can trust him to keep his word. To do the job. I suddenly wonder if he and Dodgy Steve might be in cahoots. Maybe they'll split the cash between them without carrying out the hit.

Even though it's a lot of money to me, it seems such a paltry amount for someone's life. Like she isn't worth more than a second-hand car or a holiday in Torremolinos.

I pass the envelope to him, and he takes it without turning around.

I find myself blurting, 'How do I know you'll actually do it?'

He looks at me in the rear-view, his gaze cold, but not cruel. 'You don't,' he says. 'But my line of work runs on reputation.'

I can't decide if that's supposed to be reassuring.

'Get out. And don't look back.'

I don't need to be told twice. I fumble with the door handle and step back into the cold. The car peels off, gravel popping under the tyres, and is gone before I can even cross to the Clio, the engine noise fading into the distance.

I stand in the darkness for a while, registering the way my breath ghosts in the air. Gravel crunches under my trainers as I shift my weight, but I can't bring myself to move. My mind spins slow cartwheels around the question: *Did I really just hire someone to kill my sister?* And I wonder if I've just made the biggest mistake of my life, or if this is what the road to freedom is supposed to feel like.

An owl screeches somewhere above, and I flinch, shocked out of my trance. I realise it's starting to rain. I stagger the few paces back to the Clio. My hands are shaking so badly I can't even grip the door handle at first; I have to tuck them under my armpits, count to ten, and try again.

When I finally manage to turn on the ignition, I catch my reflection in the smeared glass of the driver's-side window. My face is flushed, eyes over-bright, and I realise I'm looking at the same face as my twin. Again, I wonder if I should have got to know Bella instead. But I squash the thought as soon as I have it. It's too late now.

I turn the key, and the Clio sputters to life. I put it in gear and drive, feeling the adrenaline start to ebb, replaced by something cold and sharp in my chest. I keep thinking about whether or not I should have asked him more questions, whether I just hired a professional or paid a con artist. My mind runs through every possible outcome, none of them comforting.

The drive home is a blur. I keep expecting blue lights to flash in the rear-view, or the Corolla to reappear and run me off the road. But the lanes are empty, and the only thing keeping me company is the splatter of rain against the windscreen and the thump of the wipers. I rehearse what I'll say if I'm pulled over: 'Just coming back from a late shift' . . . 'Got lost' . . . 'I'm picking up a friend who drank too much'. Every lie feels as weightless and useless as tissue paper.

When I finally make it home, the flat is silent and dark. Mum's asleep, oblivious as usual. I peel off my coat and collapse on to the sofa, mind racing, nerves absolutely shot. I don't know if I'm the victim, the perpetrator, or the hero of my own story. It's all a jumbled mess right now.

I shut my eyes and wait for the sun to rise, dreading the photo that will show me it's done.

Chapter Twenty-Nine

JADE

It's that strange week between Christmas and the new year, when no one knows what day or time it is, and the whole atmosphere feels somewhere between a holiday and sick leave. There's a half-eaten advent calendar propped up on the kitchen counter, empty Quality Street wrappers strewn about like confetti, and the whole flat smells like a weird combination of leftover gravy and brandy custard.

I'm curled into the corner of the settee, scrolling through social media, not really seeing anything, just killing time until I can bring myself to say what needs saying.

Mum's bustling around the kitchenette. It's barely big enough for one person, and she keeps banging her hip on the corner of the fridge and swearing under her breath. She yanks a cottage pie out of the oven and thuds it on the hob, then glances at me with an expression that's hard to decipher, somewhere between irritation and confusion. Her hair's up in a messy bun, and there's an angry spot on her left cheek. I clear my throat.

'So . . . I was thinking I might do a bit of travelling.' I try to sound casual, like it's the most obvious thing in the world for me to announce. My heart's hammering so loud I'm sure she can hear it over the whirr of the extractor fan.

She stares at me. 'Travelling?' she echoes, as if I've announced my intention to become a Buddhist monk. 'You're going *travelling*?' Her mouth opens, then closes. She pulls off her oven gloves like she's peeling off a layer of skin and drops into a chair, her whole body deflating like a paddling pool with a slow leak.

'Yeah, first Australia and New Zealand, and then maybe Thailand and Vietnam, I haven't quite figured it out yet.'

She fixes me with a suspicious look. 'Was this Zac's idea?'

Typical that she's crediting Zac, as if I'm incapable of independent thought.

'No. I'm not going with Zac.'

'You're not?' She shakes her head like she's got water in her ears.

'No.'

'So, who are you going with?'

'I'm going by myself.'

'You're going to the other side of the world on your own?' Mum's voice is weirdly soft, but she clasps her fingers together until they whiten at the knuckles.

'Why not?' I say, forcing a smile. 'You always said you wished you'd seen the world. I thought you'd be excited for me. At least you get your living room back. And the sofa.'

She gives me a long, assessing look, like she's trying to see if I'm screwing with her. But her eyes are red and tired, and she just can't carry off the hard stare anymore. 'Jade, love. You've never been further than the Costa Brava. And even there you didn't like the food and couldn't handle the heat.'

'That was ages ago,' I protest. 'And you can get burgers and chips anywhere these days. Also, my taste buds have evolved. I'm basically a citizen of the world now.' I try to laugh, but it comes out almost like a hiccup. She's still watching me, not buying it for a second. I look away at the greasy window with condensation trickling down the inside.

There's a beat of silence between us, just the hum of the fridge and the sound of my own pulse in my ears. Neither of us moves. 'It'll be good for me,' I add finally. 'I'm stuck in a rut here.'

She sighs. 'I'm not disagreeing with that, but the world's a mess these days. Look at the news – there's war and disease and all these awful things happening. It's not safe, a young woman off on her own. There are weirdos everywhere.'

'There are weirdos in Southampton too,' I say. 'You can't live your whole life being scared of what might happen. And I'll meet other travellers along the way, people like me.'

'That's what I'm worried about. You won't know who they are, what they might have done. What they're capable of doing.'

And vice versa, I think to myself.

A twinge of guilt plucks at my chest. Even though Mum annoys the hell out of me, I don't like thinking of her all alone, worrying. But if I'm going to become Bella, then I need a plausible explanation for why I'm no longer around. I blink, not quite feeling real. I can't quite believe that Mum will never hear from me again – that we'll never have another conversation. But I can't let myself get emotional. Not now. It's too late for that luxury. I have to do what's best. Things have gone too far for me to change my mind.

'What does Zac think about you going off without him?' Mum asks.

I feel a little ache in my chest when I think back to last week. To his expression when I called things off with him. He looked so forlorn. Granted, it was mean breaking up with him two days before Christmas, but I genuinely didn't think he'd be that upset. To be honest, I never treated him that well. I was actually a bit of a bitch. I thought he'd be relieved to be shot of me. His mum will definitely be celebrating – Happy Christmas, Mrs Hughes.

'Zac and I broke up, Mum.'

'Oh.' She suddenly looks older than her fifty-four years. Her skin is sagging slightly, and there are smokers' lines around her mouth. Which reminds me, I'll have to ditch the ciggies once I'm Bella. That's going to be hard – even the thought of nicotine has me gasping for a drag.

'We'd been drifting apart anyway,' I add.

Mum nods. 'Are we eating this cottage pie, or what? Although, tell you the truth, after your news, I'm not feeling too hungry right now.'

'I'll dish up.' I push down a flare of guilt, ease myself off the sofa, and walk past Mum towards the kitchenette.

As I pass, she takes hold of my hand. 'I'd have loved to go travelling when I was your age,' she says quietly.

I pause, taken aback by her confession. 'So why don't you? Go and see the world.'

'Oh, you make it sound so easy.' Mum rolls her eyes. 'But it's not that simple at my age. Bills, work . . .'

'It is that easy!' I reply, keen to deflect the conversation away from my leaving. 'You could rent this place out. Use the money to travel.'

She sniffs, then wipes at her nose with the sleeve of her jumper. Avoiding my suggestion, she asks, 'When are you off, then?'

I pause and have the grace to look a bit sheepish. 'Tomorrow.' The word drops like a grenade between us. I'm sort of impressed with how smoothly I say it, but inside, my stomach is doing backflips.

'*What?* Tomorrow? No. Jade, that's crazy. Why so soon? That's no time for a proper goodbye or anything.' She gets to her feet and stares me in the eye until I look away and busy myself locating a serving spoon.

'I wanted to tell you sooner, but then I thought it would be easier for both of us this way. No dragging out a long goodbye.' I try for honesty, or at least something that sounds like it.

She stands up, comes over to me, and for a second I think she's going to slap me, but instead she says, 'You make it sound like you're disappearing forever. When will you be back?'

I shrug. 'It's an open ticket, so . . .'

She shakes her head and sits again, stares at the wall, eyes glazed. Then, as if remembering something, she looks over. 'How are you paying for all this?'

I shrug. 'I've been saving. And I'll work while I'm away. There's loads of fruit farms and hostels, and bars that hire backpackers. It's what everyone does.'

'So you've no idea when you'll be home?'

I shake my head.

'But you'll call me every week, let me know you're okay?'

'Once I get a new SIM,' I say.

'I won't be able to call on your old number?'

'No, but—'

'Jade, I don't like the sound of this. At all.'

I can feel her fear, thick and metallic in the air. I almost want to hug her, but I don't. I never really learned how.

She stretches her lips into an unconvincing smile. 'You always were a stubborn one. I can't stop you, can I?'

'Nope. Don't worry, Mum. I'll be fine. I'll be living my best life. Same way you can do now, without me cluttering up the place.'

She snorts. 'Don't try and make it sound like this is you doing me a favour, Jade. I can't say it won't be nice having the place to myself for a while, but I still want you close by. You're my daughter.'

'And you're my mum.' I hate how it comes out so raw, like I'm five and scared of the dark. There's a long, draining moment where neither of us speaks, and her eyes go glassy, and my stomach fills up with guilt, lifting my ribs until I think they'll snap. I stare at nothing, willing the silence to settle and become manageable. Instead, it tips over the edge and keeps falling, echoing the truth that I'm not just leaving – I'm vanishing. Or at least Jade is.

I want this part to be over. To relegate Mum's hurt expression to history. I want to be living Bella's life already, without my mother guilt-tripping me.

'Come on, let's eat before it gets cold.' I scrape the cottage pie on to plates, using the motion as a way to focus on something that isn't my mother's devastated expression. Reminding myself that this is what I wanted. Remembering all the weeks of hard work that have got me here. My new life is within tasting distance.

As I hand a plate to Mum, she looks up at me, her eyes glistening. 'Promise me you'll take care of yourself, Jade. Don't do anything . . . stupid.'

I nod, even though 'stupid' is all I've ever done.

'If you hate it, you can always come back,' she adds, voice tight.

'That's not the plan, Mum. I want to see what else is out there. Even if it's just . . . something different.' I don't mention that what's out there is already mapped and measured – a house, a career, a bank account. I'm inheriting someone else's 'different' like it's a hand-me-down jumper. I change tack and try to lighten the mood. 'Besides. You'll be so busy catching up on all your true-crime podcasts, you won't even notice I'm gone.'

She can't manage a smile. 'Let's eat before it gets cold.'

It occurs to me that this is probably the last meal we'll ever have together, and immediately, I start counting every chew, every swallow, like I have to log it in my memory for later. I almost wish she'd start an argument. It would be easier than this. She barely touches her food. I wolf mine down, too fast. I want to get to the next step, the one where I'm not Jade anymore. I want to be Bella, with no history and nothing to be sorry for.

Mum goes to bed before ten, claiming she's tired, but I know she won't sleep.

Once I hear her bedroom door click shut, I go into the bathroom and stare at myself in the mirror for a long time. I turn my head from side to side, trying to see what Bella saw when she looked in the mirror. There's the same nose, same small gap in my front teeth. But where I see a jumble of bits, Bella probably saw perfection. I need to become her now, all smooth lines and easy charm.

I slide the envelope from the back pocket of my jeans. My hands shake as I open it again. The Polaroid is smaller than I remember. In the picture, she looks like she's asleep, aside from the bullet hole in her forehead and the fresh, red blood pooling around her head. The way her face is slack and grey makes my stomach drop. I read somewhere that if you lose your twin, you lose half your soul. I wonder if that's true, and if so, which half do I have left?

I take a cheap orange lighter from my pocket and hold the photograph over the sink. I flick the little wheel and see the flame spark to life. Hold it to the corner of the Polaroid and watch as the shiny image curls and smoulders, finally catching light and disappearing into ash. I drop the final corner into the sink and run the cold tap until the smell of smoke recedes.

It was torture waiting to hear back. Waiting to receive photographic proof that 'it' had happened. Wondering whether or not it even would, or if the hitman (or Corolla Man, as I prefer to think of him) would simply skip off into the sunset with my cash, leaving Bella unharmed.

I borrowed the remainder of his fee off Dodgy Steve, promising to pay him back double by the end of next month in either cash or designer gear. I've never given him any reason to doubt me, so he stumped up the money, and I managed to get it to Corolla Man the same day.

And then, this lunchtime, while Mum was working, a hand-delivered padded envelope with my name on the front came through the door. I opened it straightaway, hands shaking. Inside were two of Bella's bank cards, a driving licence, her iPhone, and the Polaroid. I almost wish I hadn't asked for a photo because, even now that I've destroyed it, I'm never going to be able to get the image out of my head. But I had to have proof.

I'm sure these numb, sick, guilty feelings will all recede in time, and I'll be able to enjoy myself again. I have to keep sight of why I'm doing this. I have to remember that her life is the one I should have had. That I'm only getting back what's rightfully mine.

And now it's done. It's finally time for me to become Bella Newbury.

Chapter Thirty

JADE

I wake up before it's even light – before the traffic revs or the bins thunder or the tenants above start to move. I don't use my phone. I don't even look at it. I swing my suitcase out from beneath the sofa bed; it's a battered thing belonging to my mother, with a half-torn sticker from Lanzarote and a broken zip tooth. I'm taking it with me for authenticity's sake. I creep into the hallway with the same care with which I used to tiptoe past monsters in childhood nightmares, although now the monsters feel more real.

For a moment, my palm hovers on the handle to Mum's bedroom. I want to see her face. *No. Best not.* I'm planning to be a ghost. Instead, I walk into the kitchen and rip out a page from a spiral notebook. My handwriting is too formal, an admission of guilt, but I keep it short:

Mum,

Speak soon. Don't forget to take your blood pressure tablets. You always forget.

Love you x

I read it twice, then add another *x* at the last second, as if a single letter could fill the space I'm about to leave behind. I set it on the countertop with my flat keys. A part of me wants to take them for safety's sake, but that would spoil the purity of the act. The police, if they ever come, will see the keys, the note, and know I intended to stay in touch.

The outside world is a dark, frozen, sodden graveyard of street-lights and puddles. I drag my suitcase across the paving slabs, which seem engineered to amplify every sound. The walk to the station feels like a held breath. The air has that grim, grey taste you only get in winter in England, like all the people and the pigeons are just waiting for sunlight to come back and make life bearable again.

At the station, I avoid the security cameras, though I know it's pointless. I buy my ticket to Lymington, pretending not to notice the stare of the man at the next self-service machine. I fumble with the ticket, drop it, and pick it up. I check the time and nip to the loo, where I remove the SIM card from my mobile, stomp on it with my heel, and then flush it away. I have Bella's phone now and, thanks to her notebook of passwords and PIN codes, along with facial recognition, I'm able to access most of her apps.

On the train, I rehearse my new name under my breath, over and over. *Bella Eve Newbury. Bella Eve Newbury.* The longer I say it, the more I grow into the shape of her. I picture the way she carried herself, the careful shoulder set, the smile that locked so self-assured. The rhythm of her voice, the way she enunciated certain words in her property videos – 'exquisite', 'delightful', 'triple aspect'. I try each one out, like a piece of exotic fruit, rolling it between my teeth. By the time the train spits me out at Lymington station, I look at my reflection in the window and see someone who will never answer to Jade Morgan again.

I walk to Bella's flat with my set of copied keys, trying to ignore my trembling fingers and too-fast heartbeat. Outside her building,

I pause for a moment to breathe. To steady myself and take it all in – the white facade, the sash windows, the peaceful, tree-lined road. This street is so well-mannered, so painfully middle-class, it feels like a film set. I walk up the path, past the clipped box hedges and the little brass plaque that says 'Seafoam Court'. For a second, I think about how the people here probably complain about the recycling bins being too ugly, or their neighbours playing Radio 4 above a polite decibel level. I imagine them watching me through the slats of their expensive wooden shutters, and for half a second, I stare back, daring them to question me.

Inside, I let the lift take me up in silence. The key slides into the lock and turns with a satisfying, expensive click. The flat is pristine, so scrubbed it smells like money. There's a rubber plant in the hallway that I hadn't noticed before, and a painting of abstract blue blobs, and when I set my suitcase just inside the door, I have this mad compulsion to kneel and kiss the pale wood floors. Instead, I take off my boots and slip into the apartment. *My* apartment.

There's a bottle of prosecco in the fridge, and when I open it, the pop echoes down the corridor like a starter pistol. I drink straight from the neck. I don't bother with a glass, nobody's watching, and that's the best bit. The prosecco is cold and bites the back of my throat in a way that tells me it's the first of many acts of ownership. I take it with me into the living room, where everything is warm and welcoming and decorated to look effortless. The kind of luxury that comes from money, but more from knowing you belong.

I flop on to the huge cream sofa, making a mental note to never eat curry on it, and let the cushions embrace me. For a moment, the anxiety drains out. All I feel is the springy give of the seat, the gentle hum of the fridge, the faint thud of my own pulse in my ears.

I do a tour of the flat, drink in hand. Through the restful bedroom and into the huge dressing room, I run my fingers across the bottles and potions on the dressing table. I unscrew the lid of a £200 face cream, scoop a little out, and rub it into my hands. For the first time I can remember, my skin doesn't feel like sandpaper. I gaze at the shoes, bags, and racks of clothes. I've seen it all before, but now I'm staring at it with the pride of ownership rather than the fear of trespassing.

I try on a pale pink, cashmere lounge set. It's cosy and comfy, the fabric so soft it's almost erotic. I spin in front of the mirror, then collapse on to the plush carpet, laughing at the absurdity of it all. I am a queen. I am a goddess. I am Bella Newbury.

As the day wears on, I nest. I remake Bella's bed with fresh sheets. Visit the deli on the corner and stock the fridge with salads, Greek yoghurt, blueberries, and smoked salmon. I use her credit card to order a scented candle online for delivery under the name Bella Eve Newbury. I'm living in her skin, and it fits. By mid-afternoon, I'm delirious with prosecco, caffeine, and euphoria. I decide to test-drive her Fiat, the keys glinting on a gold hook by the door. No more sneaking around borrowing Mum's car whenever I want to go somewhere. I've got my own set of wheels now.

The drive along the country roads is everything I imagined – hedgerows, wild wind, the winter sky egging me on to go faster. I roll the windows down and blast some bass-heavy tunes, the kind of music Bella would probably have hated, just because I can. I imagine how it would feel to get pulled over in this car, in these clothes, and to present her licence with a dazzling smile. No one would ever suspect. Although, with a sudden chill, I remember the half a bottle of prosecco I've drunk and I realise that I could be in serious trouble if I were to be breathalysed. I'd better get home – *home!* An image of my new apartment flies satisfyingly into my brain – and this time I'll stay under the speed limit.

It's already dark when I return to the flat. I eat a goat's cheese salad and watch some early evening cookery show where they're

191

making canapés. Their chatter is so inane it's almost hypnotic. I'm chewing, halfway to a second mouthful, when the entry buzzer screeches through the flat. It's not just a sound – it's a fork jabbed straight into my nervous system.

I freeze, my brain flying into a panic. I can't move. I can't even swallow. My stomach flips in a slow, sickening arc. Who could it be? I'm not ready. I don't want to see anyone, not yet. I need to get more comfortable in Bella's skin first.

I tell myself I'll ignore it. Just wait it out. If it's important, they'll call back. But the buzzer doesn't stop. It sounds again, and again, and again.

I set my plate down, the clink of it against the glass coffee table absurdly loud, and pad barefoot to the window. From this angle, all I can see is the dark, quiet street. I squint, and my ghostly reflection gapes back at me, eyes wide and panicked. My heartbeat grows loud and twangy. I need whoever it is to go away.

What if it's Bella's boyfriend? At least I know it's not her parents – Bella's diary has them on holiday in the Caribbean for four weeks. So that gives me a nice long time to get comfortable before I try to pass the ultimate test of fooling them. I take a deep, steadying breath as the buzzer takes on a rhythmic sound. There's a pattern to it – two blasts, a pause, then three more in rapid succession, as though whoever's down there is playing a tune. It almost makes me smile, as it's the kind of thing I would do if I were annoyed that someone was ignoring me.

Why am I so anxious? This is what I wanted – to take over my twin's life. And I can't do it by hiding away in her flat. I need to start the process of becoming her. And I can only do that by integrating into her life properly. And that means interacting with her friends and family.

Before I can change my mind, I head into the hall and press the intercom button, remembering to modulate my voice into Bella's posh drawl. 'Hello?'

'Finally!' It's a woman's voice. Posh, around my age. 'Are you going to buzz me in? Or do you want me to freeze to death out here?'

I hesitate. Is this someone I'm meant to recognise by voice alone? You'd think in a block this posh, there'd be a videophone. I flip through my mental list of possible suspects, but nothing fits. 'Who is this?' I ask, risking it.

A snort on the other end. 'Very funny, babe. It's Tori. You better not have forgotten about tonight.'

My mouth goes dry. *Tori.* The name rings a tiny, insistent bell from one of Bella's social media posts – some wild-eyed blonde with a penchant for tequila and outrageous outfits, always tagged in photos at three in the morning, always with her tongue out or her arm flung around Bella's neck like a lifeline. 'Oh! Um. Tori. Hey. Yes. Sorry, long day. Come up.' I press the buzzer to unlock the front door, every cell in my body screaming at me to run and hide.

I hear the entrance door click. She'll be up here any minute. I have maybe ninety seconds to remember how to be the version of myself that Bella's friends would recognise. I check my face in the hall mirror. The sight is not pretty – my cheeks are splotchy, my eyeliner smudged, and my hair has the dull, greasy sheen of someone who's spent the day sprawled on the sofa, drinking. I pull my hair into a messy bun and hope the dim interior lighting will hide the worst of it. But I get the feeling that Tori, whoever she is, won't be impressed.

I open the front door and stare nervously at the humming lift, waiting for the door to open. *Come on, where's your confidence? Where's that Jade sass when I need it?* I force myself to stand tall, shoulders back, Bella-style.

Too late, I think about checking Bella's phone to see if there are any messages from Tori that might clue me in about tonight's arrangements. I'll have to sneak a look when I get a moment.

Tori emerges from the lift in a cloud of perfume and attitude, a force of nature disguised as a woman. She's got a halo of platinum waves arranged in a style I've only ever seen on reality TV stars, and she's poured herself into a shimmering green dress that looks both absurdly expensive and half a size too small. Her jacket is fake fur, white as aspirin, and she's tottering on towering gold spike heels.

'Wow,' I say, before I can stop myself.

She does a cute little mock curtsey. 'Thank you, darling. I do try. But what in the name of God are you wearing?' She steps closer, squinting at my pink lounge set with the air of someone inspecting a suspicious stain. 'Didn't I tell you, seven o'clock? You're not even showered. We'll have to move fast if you're going to make a human out of yourself. The cab's waiting.'

She sweeps past me into the living room, pausing only to glance at the TV. 'What's this cookery shit you're watching?' She grabs the remote and switches the channel to a music video, pumping up the volume to levels that instantly make the floor vibrate. 'Much better. Party vibes, babe. It's New Year's Eve! You know the rules.'

I follow her, feeling like a guest in my own home. Tori turns, blue eyes impossibly wide, all mock outrage and affection. 'Seriously, Bells, what am I going to do with you? If you were a puppy, I'd have to put you in one of those obedience classes.' She's not waiting for my answer. She's already kicked off her heels and is peering into the fridge. She locates the prosecco and pours herself a glass without asking, then refills mine to the brim. 'Drink up,' she instructs, 'you look like you need it.'

I nod and take a tentative sip, letting the alcohol burn its way down. My hands are steadier, but only just. Tori gives me a quick once-over, then tugs me towards the bedroom with the determination of someone on a life-or-death mission. I catch a glimpse of us in the hallway mirror as she drags me along. She's flawless and bright, all technicolour and sharp edges, while I trail behind looking like I've just failed a job interview.

'We have, like, seven minutes to get you glittered and ready to go,' Tori announces, shoving open the walk-in and rifling through my clothes with zero hesitation. 'You wore the black velvet last time, so that's out. The red slip, maybe? No, I know you, you'll whinge all night that you're freezing. Oh, wait—' She extracts a sequined jumpsuit from the far end of the rails and holds it up 'This is the one. You'll look dangerous in this.'

I stare at the jumpsuit. It's not my style – not Jade's, anyway – but that's the point. Bella's life, Bella's rules. 'Okay,' I squeak. This meekness isn't like me, but I don't mind admitting to myself that I'm feeling pretty out of my depth right now.

'Go on, get changed,' Tori urges, flinging the jumpsuit at me. She's already dug out a pair of stiletto boots and is lining up eyeshadows on the dressing table like weapons. 'You do your hair – you'll need a shit-tonne of dry shampoo – I'll do your face. We'll make a transformation montage.'

I blurt out a laugh, surprising myself. The sound is thin, but real. For a second, I even feel an echo of the old thrill – dressing up for a night out, the anticipation fizzing through my veins. It's almost enough to drown out the guilt, the feeling that I'm trespassing in someone else's life, wearing their skin and stealing their friends.

In the bathroom, I quickly check my phone for messages from Tori, but I can't find anything. My hands are shaking too much, and I can't focus. I give it up, deciding to just go with the flow – it's New Year's Eve, so it'll be a party or a club or something. Instead, I peel off my clothes and slip into the jumpsuit. It's tight, but not unkind, especially around the boob area; the sequins catch every glint of light and throw it back in starbursts. I swipe some dry shampoo through my hair and blast it with the hairdryer, hoping the noise will drown out the doubts squabbling in the back of my mind. I use a comb to give the crown a little volume and then gather half of my hair back, leaving some face-framing pieces down in what I hope is a Brigitte Bardot look. It's not perfect, but I'm going for a messy, bedhead vibe. I'm going for something that will impress Tori.

When I emerge, Tori wolf-whistles. 'Look at you! From zero to hero in five minutes flat. Get over here, I'll do your eyes.' She sits me down at the dressing table and works with brisk efficiency – primer, foundation, dark glitter-shadow, winged liner that stretches almost to my ears. She leans in close, her breath warm and winey. She finishes with a flourish. 'Perfect! Red lips or pink?'

'Red,' I answer decisively, finally finding my voice.

She grins, delighted. 'There's my girl.' She slaps the lipstick into my palm and lets me do the honours while she checks her phone. 'Cab's still there, but the driver's getting antsy. You ready, or do you need to psych yourself up in the loo first?'

'I'm ready,' I say, spritzing on some of Bella's perfume, and this time I almost mean it.

We pause in the hallway for coats and purses. I slip my feet into stiletto boots. They pinch, but I don't mind the pain – the sharpness of it is a reminder that I'm finally here.

We head for the door. I flick off the lights, one by one, and follow Tori into the lift, the landing echoing with our laughter and high heels. I'm buoyed by the fact that I'm actually doing this – a new life, new friends, new chances. But as the lift door closes, sealing us into the small, mirrored box, I catch one last reflection of my face – half me, half stranger – and I feel a well of panic simmering beneath the surface, looking for a crack.

Chapter Thirty-One

JADE

When Tori told me we were going to a New Year's Eve party, I pictured a regular house party in a swanky detached home with a front drive and four good-sized bedrooms. Everyone tumbling out on to the patio at midnight to set off an Asda box of special-edition fireworks. At most, I expected a nice hotel function room – fairy lights, cava, a DJ in a Santa hat, and a buffet table groaning with sausages on sticks and Kettle crisps.

What I didn't picture was this multi-million-pound Victorian manor set in its own parkland. The cabbie got lost twice on the driveway, and it was only when we passed a pair of stone griffins and a fountain that I realised I wasn't just out of my depth – I was out of my postcode, my league, maybe even my species.

Apparently, Tori and I went to school with the owner, Madeleine Fairfield. And apparently, we don't like her. According to Tori, Madeleine is a stuck-up cow. According to a recent *Tatler* article, which I speed-read during the cab ride over, she's now an influencer and philanthropist. And according to Tori's radar for free drinks, Madeleine and her husband, Monty, throw New Year's Eve parties that are basically legendary, and Monty himself is 'a top bloke, absolute sweetheart, would literally give you the Gieves & Hawkes shirt off his back'.

As my gaze sweeps over the lavish display of fairy lights, cascades of champagne, and the clique of minor celebrities vaping near the entrance, the nerves kick in even deeper.

It's the kind of mansion whose rooms are named after dead poets, where the windows are taller than most people's houses, and the guest list comes with a pre-approved social pecking order. The moment we step on to the checkerboard marble of the vast, double-height entrance hall, Tori goes full extrovert, tossing out compliments with the speed of a machine gun. 'Mel, you look fucking incredible! Cara, that dress is criminal, hand it over!' She does a round of air kisses while I hover at the edge, trying to smile at all the right moments and not betray that I literally just googled 'posh party small talk' in the cab on the way over.

'Bells! Tori!' We both turn, and I'm proud of myself for reacting to Bella's name so instinctively. Tori drags me into a reception room where a cluster of former netball captains, now repurposed as glossy magazine editors and tech-startup founders, are propped on velvet armchairs, swapping gossip at a decibel level that makes my head ring. I try to keep track of the names, but the room is a blitz of perfect teeth, power brows, and names that sound like luxury skincare brands. The music – something house-y and relentless – vibrates up through the antique carpet, and I realise immediately that if I don't get a drink soon, I'm in danger of having a full-blown panic attack.

'Hey guys,' I say, aiming for cheerful and almost getting there. 'Everyone looks amazing. Sorry, I just need to—' I mime a drinking gesture and start to slip back towards the entrance hall, hoping no one noticed how my hand is shaking.

'Hey, Bella, where's that fit boyfriend of yours?' A petite brunette with a snake-like expression asks before I can make my escape.

I can tell her type straightaway. Predatory. Wants my boyfriend for herself.

I discovered, through Bella's phone messages, that his name is Reece Kernan-Jones. From scrolling through their chat, I can already tell he's self-obsessed, and that Bella was a doormat in their relationship. My online search confirmed that he's a bit of a dick, albeit a rich, handsome one. I can't deny I'm a bit nervous about meeting him in the flesh. What if he gives me the ick? They've been together a while, so he'll probably be able to tell that something's different. But Tori was fooled, so maybe Reece will be too. Anyway, I'm committed to pretending to be in love with him for the next five hours, and then ghosting him forever.

'He's not here yet,' I respond coolly to snake-woman before turning on my heel in search of the bar.

'Wow, boss, you look hot.' I look up to see a youngish lad with floppy hair and a cheeky grin.

'Hey . . . Ben.' I recognise him from the 'Meet Our Team' photos on Newbury's website. Although this evening he's wearing a tux, like most of the other men here tonight. 'Thanks, liking the James Bond look.'

He waggles his bow tie in response.

'Where's the bar?' I ask.

'They've never had a bar.' He gives me an odd look and signals to a waitress, who comes over with a tray of champagne flutes.

I take a glass. 'I really can't remember.'

'You've been here plenty of times,' Ben says. 'Thought Maddie and Monty were good friends of yours.'

'I have, they are,' I reply. 'Just a little out of it. Knackered and a bit . . . squiffy.'

He continues, 'If you want the good stuff, there's single malt in the library.'

'Which way is that?' I say before I can stop myself.

Ben points. 'Just follow the sound of grown men pretending they know how to play chess.'

'Actually, this will be fine.' I wave around my champagne, feeling like an idiot for asking for directions in a 'friend's' house. I hope Ben will just put it down to too much alcohol.

Behind me, a plummy voice purrs, 'Haven't seen you in ages, Bella! So glad you could make it.'

I turn to see a tall, slender woman in a floor-length cream shift dress and an emerald necklace that looks like it's the real thing. I recognise her from a quick, earlier online search. It's our host, Madeleine.

'Maddie! You look absolutely drop-dead gorgeous.' I think my accent is getting better by the minute. Being around all these public-school types is rubbing off on me.

'Thanks, Bella, darling. So do you.' She gives my outfit a cursory up and down glance, her expression saying she isn't impressed. 'But you know I hate being called Maddie.' She gives me a mock glare.

Oops. I've already fluffed the first test. 'Sorry, Madeleine, too much champagne.'

'You can never have too much champagne,' she drawls. 'Oh, and Monty's looking for you. He's in the kitchen trying to beat Richard H in an arm-wrestling match. He'll never do it.'

'I'll go and find him,' I say, before adding: 'Beautiful party, as always.'

'You're sweet,' she replies.

I head left, and Madeleine calls after me. 'I said he's in the *kitchen*, Bella.' She points in the opposite direction.

I flush. 'Silly me.'

As I make my way towards the kitchen, I wonder how much longer I can keep this up. Hopefully, everyone will start to feel the effects of the alcohol soon, and I'll be less conspicuous. The way that everyone is surprised to see me, it seems like Bella might have been a bit of a recluse.

I navigate the crowded hallway, trying not to initiate eye contact with anyone. There are doors leading into various beautiful living spaces – a dining room, a study, TV lounge, formal lounge, and is that a . . . yes, a ballroom set up with the DJ at one end, the volume slowly cranking up.

Finally, I find myself in a massive kitchen-diner with limestone floors and a barrel-vaulted ceiling. Since doing all my research into the world of estate agents, I have a whole new repertoire of property terminology. Makes me feel quite clever, and I like it.

A slightly overweight guy in shirtsleeves, with curly brown hair, waves and comes over. He's panting, and there's a sheen of sweat on his face. 'Happy New Year, Bella. How's tricks?'

'All good, thank you. How about you?'

'Oh, you know, same old, same old. Bloody Richard H is unbeatable. I just lost two hundred quid.'

'No go on the arm-wrestling?' I ask, feeling quite proud of the fact that I can spit out something other than a vague greeting.

'Absolutely humiliated me. Took less than twenty seconds. And I've been practising all year.'

'You need a personal trainer, Monty.'

'I do, don't I! Clever girl! Right, watch out, Tricky Dicky, I'm coming for you next year.'

I grin back, feeling as though this is the first proper connection I've made since arriving here. I think I'm genuinely warming to Monty.

'Now,' he says, growing more serious. 'I've been meaning to ask you, Bella. Calista's interested in getting into the property game. What's the likelihood of an internship at Newbury's next summer?'

'Um, I'm sure we could sort something out.' I think back to my months of desperation when I was trying to get some work experience, and no one would give me the time of day. Now here's this rich guy with the right connections, and he gets his sister, or niece, or whoever, an internship after one brief conversation at a party. 'Call me when I'm back in the office, and I'll check my diary.'

'Super, will do. You're an angel. An *angel*.'

'I try,' I reply with a smile.

A woman in her forties taps me on the shoulder. 'Bella, darling, so lovely to see you out and about. We haven't chatted since Miranda's birthday party in the summer.'

'Hi.' I attempt to summon another smile from somewhere, tuning out as she starts rambling on about yachts and how some stupid idiot wore heels on deck and ruined the floor. I've got to get out of here, I can't deal with this. I could probably cope with two or three conversations, but with everyone wanting to talk to me, one after the other, I feel out of my depth. Like I'm going to mess up and everyone will realise I'm an impostor. But, more importantly, how can I escape this terminally boring woman? She's barely stopped to draw breath.

I reach out to place my glass on the black quartz island, but purposely let it drop on to the floor to distract from her relentless drone. The glass smashes, having the desired effect, jolting her from her monologue.

'Oh, I'm so clumsy,' I say. 'I'd better find a dustpan and brush.'

The woman tuts. 'One of the staff will do that.' She beckons over a waiter and points to the floor without so much as a 'please' or 'thank you'.

'Now, where were we?' She moves away from the broken glass, taking hold of my elbow in a vice-like grip to drag me with her.

'Hey, Bells, there you are! Been looking for you for ages.'

I turn to see a stunningly handsome guy with dark hair and a strong jawline. It's Bella's boyfriend, Reece, and my heart flips with nerves. His timing is impeccable, though. 'Excuse me,' I say to the boring woman and take Reece's arm, steering him out of the kitchen.

His eyes rake over my body. 'You look incredible.'

My cheeks heat under his gaze. 'Thanks.'

'But how on earth did you manage to get stuck with Minty?' he adds.

Minty? Monty? Jeez. 'She pounced when my defences were down.' I mime strangling myself. 'Got me in a chokehold.' Reece laughs, and I thrill at the sound. I'm not sure if I'm more excited about having fooled him or having made him laugh. 'Honestly, the most boring conversation I've had in my life.'

'Well, duh,' he replies. 'They don't call her Monologue Minty for nothing.' He bends and kisses my lips, a light brush, nothing more, but it sends shivers down my back.

Interesting. Maybe Reece isn't going to be a fly in the ointment after all. I don't think I'll be rushing to ghost him.

With my boyfriend by my side, the night suddenly takes on a different hue. He's handsome and witty, and we laugh all night. He keeps giving me these funny looks, and I know he senses that there's something different about me, but I also know he likes it. I feel strangely powerful and confident, and I still can't quite believe that this is now my life.

Chapter Thirty-Two

JADE

'Wow.' Reece props himself up on one arm and looks at me. 'That was . . . amazing.'

I can't help but smile, breathless and a little smug. Judging from his expression, it's possible that Bella might have been crap in bed. Maybe she used sex as a currency, not as a pleasure, or maybe she was just too bored to even try. I say nothing, just roll myself closer and tuck my face into his neck. I feel his pulse against my lips, his skin warm and soft, scented faintly with last night's cologne and the citrusy tang of his sweat. 'You weren't so bad yourself,' I murmur.

He huffs a pleased sound, then starts tracing slow lines and shapes across my skin. His fingers are gentle, a little uncertain, drawing maps along my spine and hips. There's something overly attentive about the way he touches me, like he's marking out a new discovery, or maybe making sure I'm real. I feel a shiver of realisation – for the first time, I'm not pretending at being Bella. I'm actually her, in her life, drinking in all these textures and smells and emotions, letting myself float in her bed with her boyfriend in her impossibly expensive flat. I'm not acting anymore.

'Not to be weird, but . . . you seem changed somehow.' Reece keeps his voice low, as if he doesn't want to startle the moment. 'Like, since last night – I dunno. You're different.'

My stomach plummets for a second. Is he on to me? Do I seem off? Was my kiss the wrong kind of kiss, the wrong flavour of Bella? But Reece just looks at me with a sort of lazy, half-drunk admiration – like a man faced with the best steak he's ever eaten by surprise.

'Not in a bad way,' he adds. 'I'm not complaining or anything.'

I make a show of yawning and stretching, buying myself a beat. 'New year, new me.' I kiss his cheek, soft as a feather. I desperately hope it sounds like something Bella would say.

'Well, I like the new you. I like it a lot.'

'Good,' I reply. 'I want to try being more relaxed. Less work, more play.'

'Really?' Reece sits up. 'You don't know how pleased I am to hear you say that, Bells. Things have been so . . . serious lately.'

'I know. So let's have some fun. Go out more, maybe book a holiday.'

'Are you sure you can do that?' he asks. 'What about all your work commitments that you've been stressing about?'

'That's why I have staff, right?'

Reece laughs and inches his hand a little further down my back. We come together again, easy as pie, even though I feel a tiny flare of guilt that I'm not the person he thinks I am. Afterwards, with limbs tangled, he falls asleep at once, his mouth grazing my shoulder and his warm breath stirring my hair.

I lie awake in the peaceful near-dark, my eyes drifting up to the picture-perfect ceiling rose and chandelier, trying not to think about how different it is from Mum's old flat, where there was always a permanent night-time glow from an angry streetlamp in the car park or from the flickering screen of the telly after-hours. I try not to think about Zac, or the way he always wanted to snuggle afterwards.

Instead, I focus on Reece's solidity. On how he makes me feel safe and protected after such a short time. I think I misjudged him. I thought he was going to be a boring posh twat. But he's sexy, with a great body and a dark sense of humour that matches my own. And it also doesn't hurt that his family is super-rich. Although I guess I don't need to worry about that, as I now have my own money.

There was a point when I embarked on this scheme where I didn't believe I was capable of actually pulling it off. There were too many obstacles. Too many things that could go wrong. I had to set everything else aside and focus on the endgame to the detriment of my family, my relationship with Zac, my morals, possibly even my freedom. Because if anyone discovered what I was up to, that would have been it for my life. Game over. But I'm here. I'm doing it. I'm leading a charmed life as Bella Newbury. My mind is racing so much with the enormity of it all that I don't think I'll be able to get a wink of sleep tonight.

Still, I must have drifted, because the next thing I know, a slant of watery sun is creeping through the curtains and Reece is standing by the bed, stroking my hair.

'Wakey, wakey, sleepyhead.'

I slide my eyes fully open and stare up at the handsome face of Reece Kernan-Jones – *my boyfriend*. 'Hey,' I croak, as the events of last night come rushing back in a wave of unreality.

'Made you a coffee.' He nods at the bedside table where a chunky mug waits on a coaster.

'Thanks,' I reply, feeling a little shy this morning without the help of alcohol.

He runs a hand through his hair, making it stand up in a million directions. 'I've got to head over to the parents for New Year's lunch. Are you sure you can't come?'

Bella must have had a reason why she wasn't able to go, and I'm glad because, much as I'm really starting to like Reece, I don't feel quite ready to meet his parents and any other family members who might be there. I'm nervous that any little thing might give me away – the wrong laugh, the wrong wine order, the wrong reference to a childhood holiday. I know from Bella's WhatsApp history that Reece's parents are intimidating, old-money kind of people, and that she always found them exhausting. If she found them difficult, then it certainly wouldn't be a walk in the park for me, especially as I used up all my charlatan bravado last night. I need to recharge before attending any other social engagements.

'I'd have loved to, but I can't today,' I say.

'What about your promise last night to work less?'

'I meant it. Just let me get through the next few days, and I'll clear some more time.' Hopefully, my vague waffle will satisfy him.

'Okay, I'm holding you to that.' He presses his lips to mine, slow and sweet. I taste coffee and toothpaste. He lingers, like he doesn't want to leave, and I have to push him away, laughing.

He groans. 'God, Bells, what's got into you?'

'Nothing . . . yet,' I reply with a smirk.

He pulls back and looks at me with surprise.

I immediately realise that I shouldn't be so forward. This wasn't how Bella acted with him. I grin, trying to brazen it out. '*What?* I told you this year I was going to be more fun. This is me, trying.'

'Well, I like it. But I really have to go. You know what Dad's like when I'm late.'

'Go.' I make a shooing motion.

'I'll try to get away early. Then we can carry on where we left off. You'll call me later?' he asks, already halfway out the door. 'Or, you know, we could meet at the pub after?'

'Pub sounds perfect. Text me when you're done.'

He slips out, with one last bemused look, and then I'm finally alone.

Once the door slams behind him, I feel the whole flat shift and settle, like a lake surface smoothing after a boat has left the shore. I stretch out decadently in Bella's king-size. It's such a luxury to sleep on an expensive mattress, rather than Mum's saggy sofa bed. When I was little, Mum would say, 'Don't get used to things, love. Everything changes in the end.' I somehow don't think this is what she meant.

The thought of Mum back home in her flat alone on New Year's Day brings me down, so I push away the image and instead let myself marinate in the memory of last night – the dark tangle of Reece's hair in my fingers, the sharp clean smell of his aftershave, the way he looked at me with that weird, soft awe. I've never been the object of awe. Desire, sure – hunger, sometimes – but not awe.

I try not to think about Zac. But of course, I do. I think about the way he used to pull me up against him like I was a bear he'd won at a funfair. He's not built like Reece – he's thinner, paler, always a bit hunched, as if he suspects that any moment the world might swat him away. I go through the list of last night's disloyalties and count them off on my fingers. I don't feel as guilty as I should. Or maybe I do, but it's too late for guilt.

I sit up and take a sip of my coffee. Even my morning beverage tastes expensive – a little too strong, but I could get used to it. Bella has one of those bean-to-cup machines that probably costs more than the average person's monthly rent. I press the side of the mug to my cheek, savouring the warmth, and stare out at the view from Bella's window, which is mostly rooftops and a pale slice of January sky.

The flat is absurdly, impossibly quiet. No toddler shrieking from next door, no arguing couple upstairs, no creak of central-heating pipes, no tinny radio in the background. Even the fridge hum is soft and expensive-sounding, like an executive toy rather than an appliance. I take my coffee and walk around the flat just to feel the warm wood floors beneath my feet. I run my hand along the furniture, like touching it will make it more real.

The rest of the morning passes in a delicious haze of laziness and satisfaction. I shower in the beautiful, oversized jewel-green cubicle, letting the rainfall showerhead soak me from top to bottom. I tip my face straight into the deluge and let it flood my nose and eyes, feeling like I could drown right here and be happy about it.

I use too much of Bella's shampoo. It comes in a frosted glass bottle with a label that reads, in tiny serif font, 'Restorative Marine Cleansing Elixir'. I lather it through my hair and try to imagine what it would be like to have always lived like this. My hair smells like expensive holidays, like spa days and French mothers who call you *ma chérie*. No three-for-two deals from Superdrug here. Even the water feels softer and less limescale-y.

Back in the bedroom, I towel off, take time styling my hair into soft waves, and dress in cream joggers and a soft navy sweater. I don't think I've ever felt this relaxed and content in my life.

In the kitchen, I pour oat milk over a bowl of organic granola. I eat it slowly, reading the back of the box for lack of anything else to do. Every mouthful tastes like 'wellness' and 'intentional living'. I let my mind drift. I do not, under any circumstances, allow myself to think about Zac or Mum again. Instead, I imagine my life stretching out before me like one of those time-lapse videos online. I watch myself ageing in this flat, growing more and more like Bella every day, until at last no one could possibly distinguish us.

That's when the intercom buzzes. Just the once – sharp and insistent. My mind immediately serves up the memory of Mum's old flat, how people would lean on the buzzer at all hours. Random kids, bored, pressing every flat's bell at once; delivery guys wanting you to take in someone else's parcel; sometimes just strangers, lost, needing to get in from the rain. We learned to filter out the noise, even when it was intended for us. But here, in this world, no one buzzes unless they mean it.

That makes the buzz feel worse.

Maybe it's someone trying to break into the building.

The buzz comes again, longer this time. I look at Bella's phone – no new messages, no missed calls, nothing on the building's WhatsApp group. I let the granola go soggy in its lake of milk and listen to the silence that follows, waiting for the third buzz that will prove it's not a mistake.

It comes. It could be one of Bella's friends. But what if it's not? My peaceful frame of mind is evaporating fast. I know I should answer it. Put myself out of my misery, but something is telling me not to.

A few moments later, the buzzer sounds again, but this time it's not tentative. It's a long, insistent blast. After a couple of minutes, there's a heavy pounding on the apartment door. Someone has let them in to the block.

This is where every cell in my body starts to panic.

I freeze, and for a full ten seconds, I am absolutely certain that I am going to die, or go to prison, or both. The world telescopes, sharp and focused – the nail polish chipped on my thumb, a couple of dropped coffee beans on the kitchen floor, the slow, cold seep of dread into my bones.

A man's voice booms from the landing – deep and aggressive, not the sing-song tone of an Amazon or Sainsbury's delivery person. Not the friendly banter of a friend.

'Open up, this is the police!'

I drop the bowl that's in my hands. It smashes – pottery shards, milk, and granola scattering across the oak floorboards beneath my feet.

My mind goes instantly and completely blank, the way a computer screen whites out after a crash. There's a long silence as I try to process it. Then everything collapses inward, and my thoughts splinter into a thousand tiny, panicked questions.

Did they find Bella's body, or catch me on CCTV, or find some digital breadcrumb I failed to sweep up? Did someone from the party last night grow suspicious of me? Did someone at the train station recognise me? Has Mum discovered what I've done? Could Zac have guessed my plan? What about Dodgy Steve, or the Corolla Man himself? I want to blame someone, but the truth is, I have no one to blame except myself. My hands are sticky with sweat. I grab a carving knife from the block, then immediately realise how insane that looks and put it back, wiping the handle on a tea towel.

A part of me wants to laugh hysterically. The other part wants to sob, or run, or melt into the floor like one of those cartoon cats who survive only by defying the laws of physics.

The banging starts again – hammering, persistent, echoing through the flat so it sounds like it's coming from everywhere, from inside the walls and under the floor. I dart into the living room, moving automatically, looking for escape, but there's nothing – no back door, no fire escape, no window that a human being could squeeze through without plummeting three storeys to their death, or at least without inflicting serious injury. My eyes flick to the Juliet balcony in the bedroom, but the metal railing doesn't offer an escape route, locked behind double glass. I'm caged.

I return to the living room, ignoring the hammering and the repeated requests for me to open up.

This isn't the time for logic, but I try to reason with myself. Maybe it's a mistake. Maybe it's a routine check, a noise complaint, a neighbour dispute. Maybe they want to ask about someone else in the building.

Every fibre in my body wants to run, but there's nowhere to run to. If I don't answer, they'll get in. If I do answer, it's over. I force myself to recall every step of the original plan, every what-if, every backup and failsafe I told myself I had. Turns out, I had exactly zero.

I make myself walk to the front door and try to steady my breathing. My legs are shaking so badly it feels like my bones might slip out and clatter on to the floor.

They bang again, louder than before.

I jump.

Then I unlock the door and open it.

Chapter Thirty-Three

JADE

FIVE MONTHS LATER

I've always wondered about prisons. If the TV shows are right, and the walls sweat, and the food makes your teeth melt, and the guards are all monsters, and the inmates are all murderous. The only certainty, from the second the cell door breathes closed behind you, is that you're not going anywhere but inwards, down through your own layers of fat and guilt and memories. I've had plenty of time to imagine my first moments behind bars, and still, I got everything wrong.

HMP Grangefield, a women's prison in Hampshire, is neither old nor threatening. It has the ambience of an airport, with fluorescent lighting that makes everyone look like processed ham, and lino floors that squeak. There's no clang as I walk in, just a succession of quietly operated security doors and the scent of industrial laundry detergent, sharp enough to sting my eyes. The first woman I meet – Andrea – turns out the contents of my bag and pockets with the same indifference she might use for unstacking supermarket shelves.

It's over before I know it. My belongings are documented, bagged, and zipped away. I'm left with a pair of joggers, my bra, and an ugly blue top that looks like a nurse's uniform from the 1980s. I expected the strip search, but not the cold matter-of-factness of a woman who's seen it all a thousand times over. Andrea is efficient, even gentle, her hands practised, her voice low as she explains each step with a patience I didn't know government employees possessed. 'Raise your arms. Turn around. Open your mouth. Thank you, love.' There are no jokes, no tension, just the brisk detachment of someone who knows that, by the end of the week, I'll be little more than another name scribbled on the whiteboard.

After the search, they send me to 'Medical', which is a short corridor with four doors and a poster about hepatitis. The doctor is a Nigerian woman with a gold cross at her neck and no time for pleasantries. She asks about my mental health, my periods, my history of self-harm. I lie to her as smoothly as I lied at the police station, but she takes my blood pressure twice and tells me my heart is 'racing a little'.

'That's normal,' she adds, scribbling a note I can't read. The nurse – pink-haired, younger – offers me a cup of watery tea and half a bourbon biscuit. She watches me eat it, eyes narrowed, like she's waiting for me to spit it out.

My stomach feels queasy, but they insist I have a sandwich and a cup of 'juice', which tastes of undiluted sugar and some synthetic fruit. I eat and drink with the same impulse that makes people shovel food inside them at funerals.

The nurse informs me that I'm allowed to speak to one of their peer workers from *Listeners*, a branch of the Samaritans. I take them up on the offer, not because I want to talk to anyone about anything, but because it's delaying the stomach-churning moment when I'll be taken to my cell.

The Listener is a heavyset woman in her mid-forties, tattoos lacing her arms. She explains that she's done nearly two decades inside, mostly for 'problems with men and money' – whatever that means – and according to her, the Samaritans trained her to keep people like me from stringing themselves up in the first seventy-two hours.

I don't know how to respond to that, so I don't.

'People assume it's the violence that's the worst,' she continues. 'Truth is, it's the loneliness. Gets in your bones.'

I nod and try not to think about my bones, or about Bella's bones – I don't even know where they are.

When the police showed up at Bella's apartment on New Year's Day, I was sure they had come for *me*, for *Jade*. I was convinced they were there to arrest me for my twin's murder. But that wasn't the case at all.

I've been convicted of tax fraud. Or rather, Bella has. So now I'm in bloody jail for something I didn't do. Looks like my twin wasn't the perfect angel I thought she was.

It's landed me with a conundrum. I could simply admit that I'm not Bella and that I didn't do what they've accused me of, but that would open up a whole new can of worms and could possibly incriminate me for her murder. And I obviously can't risk that. So I'm having to suck it up and keep pretending to be her.

The Listener looks me up and down and sniffs. She advises me to keep to myself, at least at first. 'Don't borrow anything, don't offer unsolicited advice, don't talk about your case, and definitely do not tell anyone you've been done for fraud.'

I wonder what she'd think if she knew about my real crime. My heart pounds as she continues talking. I thought this meeting was supposed to make me feel better, not worse.

I discovered from my lawyer that, between March and October last year, Bella submitted a string of false invoices and fraudulently reclaimed over £200,000. I had to go to Crown Court, where I was sentenced to two years and three months for VAT fraud. Obviously, I knew nothing about any of it, so there wasn't much I could say in my defence. To be honest, I barely understood much of what was going on, and my lawyer was shit. I thought Bella's parents would have paid for someone top of the line, but they just left me to my own devices. Never even got in touch to see how I was doing. I guess they were disappointed in the mess their daughter had made of their once-thriving empire.

The woman is still talking, and I'm trying to focus on all the advice, but my mind keeps wandering. 'Keep your cell door shut whenever possible, and if anything happens – anything at all – don't report it, or you'll risk being labelled a grass. Above all, stay humble, know your place.'

I don't know why they're called 'Listeners' – all she's doing is talking. She clearly hasn't finished her training.

After our chat, a thin, hyperactive officer leads me to my house block. She points out the showers, the tiny library ('Don't expect Booker Prize winners, but at least it's warm and quiet in there'), and the communal room with a dartboard that has no darts, and a few battered copies of trashy magazines, each with the faces of disintegrating soap stars on the cover. The room smells like instant coffee, bleach, and feet. I feel my jaw clench involuntarily, the way it used to when Mum would start on at me about not making up my sofa bed.

I think back longingly to Bella's beautiful flat and my one perfect, blissful day there. I later discovered it had a sale agreed before I even arrived on the scene, and I was forced to vacate it after a couple of weeks. I spent most of that time selling off Bella's designer gear as she had no money in her bank account and owed thousands on her credit card. That money gave me enough to stay in a B&B until my court date.

A peer worker with a name badge reading 'KIRSTY' is waiting for me at the main block. Kirsty has anxious hands but a kind smile. 'First night is always the worst,' she says. 'After that, you kind of . . . flatten out.'

I grit my teeth. I don't want to flatten out. I want to scream, to burn the building down, to maybe even swap my fate with the dead girl everyone thinks I am. But instead, I trail after Kirsty, learning about the timings for showers, the rules about kettles ('No boiling anything but water – don't ask'), and the unofficial hierarchy that governs the house block. Apparently, everything can be traded, from cigarettes to cheese triangles, but only if you know how to keep the IOUs straight.

Tomorrow, I'll begin the induction process. This includes meeting with various agencies to assess my needs and going through an orientation to prepare me further for life in prison. Following this, I'll commence a well-being week. I give a grim laugh at the thought of anything in here being labelled 'well-being'.

I spend my first night on a mattress about the width of a yoga mat, and there's a brownish-yellow stain on the ceiling, a far cry from Bella's bedroom with its ornate ceiling rose and crystal chandelier. I stare at the stain until my eyes water, until my thoughts swirl back to the first moments I learned about Bella's death, the endless sequence of panicked, improvisational moves I made to keep up the pretence that she was still alive and that I was her. If I close my eyes, I can picture the plasticine sheen of her face in the Polaroid that Corolla Man sent me as proof. It would be a lie to say I didn't feel excitement in that moment, but the excitement was tangled up in a dark kind of horror, one I couldn't name.

How have I swapped my freedom for this? How did I not see what was happening? How did I believe that Bella was living this charmed life? Even before I came on the scene, her business was failing, and she was on the verge of bankruptcy, desperately trying to turn things around.

I thought she was living the high life without a care in the world, but in reality, she was going to investor meetings, schmoozing with clients, and meeting with her accountant and solicitor, trying to save her business and herself from going to jail. She was hiding the truth from everyone. Trying to fake the perfect life. Burying her head in the sand, rather than facing up to her mistakes.

The ironic thing is that my innocuous tip-off to HMRC was probably the nail in her coffin. I thought it would be just an annoyance, an irritation to add to the string of other irritations I lined up for her. I never could have imagined that it would lead to Bella being convicted and sentenced. To *me* being convicted and sentenced.

The whole thing has backfired, and I'm on the hook for all of it. Mum thinks I've gone travelling abroad and has no idea I'm in prison as 'Bella'. I can't contact her because I don't want to risk anyone discovering what I've done. As it stands, there's a possibility I could be released after a year, but if the truth got out that I'm actually Jade, I could be convicted of murder. And then I might never leave this place. Or I might get sent somewhere worse. My pulse thuds in my wrists at the thought, a constant reminder that the only thing between me and a murder conviction is my own ability to perform. I've always been a decent actor, but being in here will test me.

It looks like Bella's parents are worse than my mum. I still can't believe they never showed up to court, never visited. Neither did Bella's so-called best friend, Tori. Or Reece – so much for us being soulmates. Like rats leaving a sinking ship.

I think when I get out of prison, I'll go back to my real identity. Live as Jade again. That way, I'll have a clean record, and at least I'll have Mum. She'll be happy to see me 'back from my travels'. Maybe I'll go travelling for real this time. Or try to get accepted on to a college course for something I actually enjoy. No idea what that might be, but at least I've got some time to figure that out. Apparently, tomorrow I'm having an assessment to determine my educational needs. Maybe I'll study while I'm in here. Then, when I get out, I can get some proper qualifications and really make a go of my life.

I try not to think about my twin. I didn't think getting rid of her would affect me, but I have nightmares about it. Keep seeing that gruesome proof-of-death photo in my head. I don't think I'll ever be able to shake it. Especially as it looked just like me. The reality is, I'll always be haunted by her. She's the ghost in my bloodstream, the itch in my scalp, the voice in my head saying, 'You'll never be free.' I try to block her out, but she always finds a way back in.

Even now, I can't tell if I regret it or not. I don't know if I'm sorry, or just sorry I got caught. Maybe that's the same thing.

Epilogue

Sitting in a beach bar, sipping cocktails, it feels as though we're on holiday.

But we're not.

This is our life now.

My father orders drinks in Spanish so heavily accented that the bartender grins, instantly forgiving. We lounge like tourists, sunglasses and all, but we're not on holiday. The truth is, this is now home. And this beach bar is the South American version of our favourite restaurant back in Lymington. It's Portofino 'Exile Edition', with rum in place of rosé, and blinding sunlight to bleach away the memories.

One of the older British ladies, who we see most days, gives us a cheery wave from her table under the cabana. Mum and I wave back, and Dad gives her a friendly nod. The other 'expats' have become a tribe, gathering at the water's edge most afternoons, sharing crab legs and local gossip. Others are quieter. The girl with the sunglasses – I don't know her real name, but everyone calls her Montreal – told me, 'We're all ghosts here, so we don't tell ghost stories.' I nodded as if I understood. But I was still too new, too recently dead, to let the old stories go.

We're all running from something – disappointments, bad divorces, criminal charges. They're all here, and now, so are we.

It was a gift from heaven when Jade decided to steal my life. I used her grisly plan as a way to escape and start again abroad. And now I'm in a beach bar in Belize with my parents. We all have new identities and new, relaxed lives. My parents liquidated all their assets, and we're living simply here by the beach.

There's a strange kind of peace to being in hiding. Maybe it's that you're constantly surrounded by the threat of discovery, so every moment you're not discovered feels like a small, secret victory. Maybe it's the drink, or the endless palette of turquoise and ochre outside the window, or the way the air blows in off the ocean with a lulling, amnesiac quality. Maybe this is what it means to acclimatise. Or maybe it's just the first wave of delusion, as all the things you've fled from — the people, the mistakes — crash over you and then, for a time, roll away.

'How are you doing, Munchkin?' Dad asks, his gaze softening across the sun-worn table.

'Good,' I reply automatically with a nod, despite the ever-present guilt tugging at my stomach.

Mum, sitting next to me, rubs my shoulder. 'Are you sure? You look like you're brooding.'

She's not wrong, but I don't want to delve too deeply into how I'm feeling. The past few months have been such a whirlwind of shocks and revelations. I think — I hope — we're finally acclimatising. But I'm not sure if it all feels quite real yet. 'Not brooding,' I answer. 'Just . . . zoned out for a bit.'

I catch my parents glancing at one another. Not quite worried, but not quite happy either.

'As long as that's all it is,' Mum says. 'You know you can talk to us, right?'

I give a small laugh and an eye-roll. 'Yes, Mum. I think after all we've been through, I definitely know I can talk to you.'

The first week here was a honeymoon of sorts — afternoons spent clinking glasses with my parents at the driftwood bar, letting the slow-footed bartender ply us with his special 'jungle punch', a secret recipe guarded with the kind of earnestness usually reserved for war crimes. My mother giggled after her second glass and swore it must be the altitude, which didn't make any sense at sea level. My father, whose sunny optimism has always been the engine of our family, insisted he use only his mangled Spanglish to order, collecting linguistic bloopers like seashells. The official language of Belize is English, but we discovered that most of the locals either speak Spanish or Creole, so we've all been slowly trying to master Spanish.

'You're not thinking about . . .' – Mum lowers her voice a fraction – 'her, are you?'

I hesitate for a moment. 'No. Well, a bit. It's hard not to.'

'You can't feel bad about it,' Dad says, a hint of gruffness in his voice.

'I don't,' I retort. 'Although she is locked up for my crime.'

Mum shoots Dad another look before turning back to me. 'What she did to you was a million times worse, Bee.'

'What she tried to do,' I correct.

Mum nods, lips pressed tight. 'It's a miracle you discovered her before it was too late. I can't even imagine . . .' She swallows.

'A miracle and a little bit of luck,' my father continues, and for a moment the table falls quiet. 'In any case,' Dad eventually puts in, 'she'll be out in a couple of years, maybe less, so no need to feel too guilty.'

'She should be in there for life,' Mum adds. 'Thankfully, she won't have any business or home to come back to, the evil little madam.'

It's all been sold – every asset, every piece of property. We cleared out all our bank accounts weeks before Jade took possession of my name. My parents were meticulous, even ruthless, in shedding our old lives. There was a kind of cold-blooded efficiency to it that I admired, even as it scared me a little.

I first became aware of Jade's scheme last year, when I suspected that someone had broken into my apartment after a few items went missing. I thought I might be losing my mind, especially when my neighbour Marisol was insistent that we'd made plans to meet up – something I had no recollection of doing. Things were definitely off. So I installed cheap hidden security cameras and was shocked to see someone who looked just like me, entering my flat and rifling through my stuff. Shoving items into a backpack and leaving. The whole thing gave me the creeps.

I told my parents about it, and they gave me the shocking news that I'm a twin. To say I was blindsided is an understatement. I looked at them, waiting for the punchline, but they were deadly serious, eyes fixed on their shoes. Mum was the one to explain that she, too, was a twin. That she wasn't even my birth mother. That my biological mother was her sister – a woman named Nicola Morgan.

I felt like I was in some fever dream. It sounded like a joke. Or like something you'd read about in one of those magazines you see in doctors' surgeries.

After hearing Mum's confession, it began to sink in that she wasn't joking. That this was the truth. A secret they'd been hiding from me. I thought I would never be able to forgive my parents. Even though they begged me to see that they'd only kept it hidden to protect me. I spat back that their protection hadn't exactly worked out too well.

'You can't feel bad for her, Bee.' Mum sips her cocktail now, her eyebrows dipping in the middle. 'You need to put it all behind you. We need to move on. It's the only way.' She lowers her voice again. 'That girl . . . she tried to have you killed.'

'Your mother's right. We need to forget the past and concentrate on trying to enjoy our new lives.' Dad raises his empty glass at me, just as the waiter returns with fresh drinks. 'Look around, Munchkin. This is paradise.'

I shift in my seat and try to relax. 'I know all that. And I agree with you about Jade. She isn't a good person. But . . . she's still my sister. A sister I never knew.'

'Maybe that's a good thing,' Mum says too briskly. 'Given what she's like.'

I know what she says is true, but part of me wonders, if we'd been allowed to grow up together, maybe things would have turned out differently – better.

Mum's gaze narrows. 'Seeing as we're talking about things, is there anything else that's worrying you?'

I shrug, not sure if I have the mental energy to bring up everything that's on my mind.

'Bee, you can talk to us.' Her eyes soften and she gives me an encouraging smile that I can't ignore.

'Well,' I blurt out. 'I also . . . I can't stop thinking about how I botched things so badly at Newbury's. You spent years building up a successful company, and I wrecked it.' My voice catches. 'I was trying not to cause you any stress, but I ended up making things ten times worse.'

After my parents' revelation about my twin, I decided that since we were confessing things, now would be a good time to tell them about my own precarious situation in the business. They couldn't exactly get angry with me. And, anyway, I was at the end of the road. I had no other place to turn. I worried about the strain it might put on Dad's heart, but felt I had no choice, because the truth was about to come out anyway.

I admitted that the business was in trouble. That I was in trouble. That a year after I took over, I'd made a bad business decision that had started to sink the company. Instead of sticking to property sales and rentals, I'd decided to branch out into property development and invest in a small block of flats with the idea of refurbishing and reselling each unit. But the whole project had run wildly over budget, and they were slow to sell. I'd ended up making a loss that Newbury's could barely sustain. From that time onwards, my life had become pure stress. I'd tried to fix things. I'd borrowed money, tried to get investors, even sweet-talked a magazine editor friend into running a puff piece about how successful Newbury's was becoming under my ownership. But it was all fruitless.

My parents were dismayed to hear that I hadn't been coping. They thought they were gifting me a life, when the truth was they had gifted me a disaster waiting to happen.

Mum shed quiet tears back then. It was the first time I'd ever seen her cry. She told me she'd always suspected something was wrong. She'd seen the shadow in my eyes when I thought nobody was looking. She knew stress, she said. After all, she'd lived with her own secrets, too.

'I guess I just don't have the same aptitude for business as you guys,' I add now.

'Rubbish,' Dad replies. 'You were just too young and too inexperienced, that's all. We never should have landed you with the responsibility, darling.' He taps his chest. 'It's all this guy's fault. If I didn't have this dicky heart . . .' His voice trails off as he blinks and clears his throat.

Mum puts a hand on his knee. 'It's no one's fault. And anyway, look around . . .' She sweeps her arm out to indicate our idyllic surroundings. 'It's not all bad. Look where we ended up.'

I briefly follow her line of sight, taking in the palm trees and endless beach, before turning back to them with a sigh. 'It's nice of you to try to reassure me, but I know I cocked things up. I buried my head in the sand and let things spiral. I honestly don't know how I could have let it get so bad.'

After my failed refurb project, there was a slump in the property market that I hadn't been able to navigate. I didn't manage the company's finances well, and I may have fudged a few invoices in order to avoid a hefty tax bill. And then I told my parents the worst part – that, according to my accountant, due to the number of invoices I faked, I was probably looking at a prison sentence for tax fraud.

'You did let things run away from you, Bee,' Mum says. 'But it's in the past. I'm sure you've learned from it. We've all made mistakes.'

'Yeah, but mine were pretty big ones.'

With the dual revelations that I might be arrested, and that my twin was stalking me, our lives shifted into fast-forward. My parents hired a private investigator who delivered a sickening report that Jade had paid someone to kill me.

After hearing this, my parents hatched a plan to frame her. I recoiled at first, hesitant to be a part of it. But Dad told me that he would do anything to protect me. To protect his family. Despite Jade being my sister and his daughter, my twin sounded like a dangerous, unhinged person.

We convinced the PI to make contact with the killer, and we paid him – probably far more than Jade had – to fake the hit. Unable to risk a digital image in case she spotted it, we staged a real photograph of me made up to look dead – make-up, prosthetics, my lifeless body sprawled on the cold pavement. It was the most surreal moment of my life. Then we vanished overseas so that Jade would never discover I hadn't been murdered. The hitman was happy, as he was paid twice without actually having to kill anyone at all.

My parents sold everything as quietly as possible, leaving behind a whispered rumour that they couldn't stand the disappointment of their daughter ruining the business they'd spent years creating, or the shame of her ending up in jail. Even though they keep reassuring me that nothing could be further from the truth, I still feel sick at the thought of my mistakes.

Dad sits forward in his chair, eyes bright and unguarded. 'Look, Bella. We're here, we're safe, and we're together – our little family. That's all that matters, isn't it?'

Mum nods, eyes glistening in the dying light. 'We love you, Bee.'

I reach for their hands. 'I'm sorry,' I whisper. 'And thank you.'

After a moment, I gaze out at the darkening ocean, their words echoing in my mind, trying to believe that this is all for the best. But although we're here in paradise, safe and undiscovered, I never stop scanning the internet for news of Jade, never stop imagining the million *ways it could still unravel. It's exhausting, this vigilance, even though I feel like it's keeping me safe. That, and my parents. Back then, for the first time in my life, I saw my self-assured father sweat. It made me realise how much they love me. What they're willing to do to protect me. It allowed me to forgive them for keeping Jade a secret in the first place.*

Sometimes, after too much rum, I think about Jade's life in prison. I picture her, grey and sullen, glaring at the guards through the glass, plotting revenge with the unblinking patience of a python. In these imaginings, she always manages to find a way out. Sometimes she escapes and makes her way here, seeking me out with a cold, righteous fury. Other times, she sends the same hitman to do her bidding. And this time, he succeeds.

But mostly I try not to think about her at all. It's just that some days, like today, the fears and memories can't help spilling out.

My new identity is officially 'Lila Moore', at least according to the counterfeit passport I keep under my pillow, but my parents still call me 'Bee' and 'Munchkin' when we're alone, the old life stuck to us like barnacles. Despite my parents' revelation that my birth mother is Jade's mum, Nicola Morgan, I knew that I would never consider her in any way to be my mother. I rolled the name around on my tongue and instantly dismissed it. Penni is my mum, and that is that.

The three of us spend our days adjusting. The ocean is always there, endless blue like in the postcards, but never the same twice. Some mornings, the tide pulls out so far you can walk the sandbar nearly to the horizon, and the air is thick with the smell of drying seaweed and the frantic activity of tiny creatures scrambling to get back before the sun bakes them alive. My mother says it's a metaphor; I think it's just nature.

There's a rhythm to this life. Small rituals — morning swims at the deserted end of the beach, where the sand is coarse and my only witnesses are the sandpipers. Black coffee at the little café by the canoe rental, where the Wi-Fi barely works but the owner plays old Beatles records on a battered stereo. And, most of all, the long, slow sunset cocktails where the evening stretches out forever.

I watch my parents try to recalibrate their relationship. They hold hands now, something I never saw in England, as if public affection is more acceptable in warmer climates. My mother laughs more, but sometimes I catch her watching the horizon with a tight, worried look. My father has grown softer, his previously sharp edges worn down by the constant sun and lack of routine.

Tonight, the sky is a furious orange, clouds rimmed in gold, and all around us, people are laughing, not knowing or caring who anyone used to be. The drinks burn sweet, the fish is smoky and charred and, for a few magic hours, paradise is real. Sand in my hair, lime on my tongue, I lean back in my chair, and I almost believe it.

ACKNOWLEDGEMENTS

A big, warm thank you to my lovely editor, Sammia Hamer. It's always an absolute pleasure working with you. Huge appreciation once again to my developmental editor, Hannah Bond, for being such a genius and an absolute joy to work with. Thank you to Eoin Purcell, Rebecca Hills, Nicole Wagner, and the fantastic team at Amazon Publishing for getting my stories out there. I'm so grateful to you all.

Hats off to Sadie for nailing the copy-edits, and to Gemma Wain for proofreading like a pro and sorting out my messy timeline! Thank you to The Brewster Project for creating another standout cover. Thanks also to Jonathan Pennock and the team at Brilliance Publishing for producing such wonderful audiobooks.

To my wonderful readers, bloggers, reviewers, sharers, recommenders, and posters – you're the wind beneath my bookish wings, and I'd be lost without you! Special shout-out to Mark Fearn at Book Mark! for always making me snort-laugh.

Lastly, a giant bear hug to my friends and family for your unwavering love and support, especially Pete – I couldn't do this without you!

A LETTER FROM THE AUTHOR

I just want to say a huge thank you for reading my latest psychological thriller, *The Other Twin*. Writing it was a mixture of intense stress and enormous fun, so I do hope you enjoyed it!

If you'd like to keep up to date with my latest releases, you can head to my website and sign up to my newsletter, and I'll let you know when I have a new novel coming out.

If you enjoyed *The Other Twin*, I'd be really grateful if you'd be kind enough to post a review online or tell your friends about it. A good review absolutely makes my day!

Shalini xx

ABOUT THE AUTHOR

© Shalini Boland 2018

Shalini Boland is the Amazon and *USA Today* bestselling author of over twenty psychological thrillers. To date, she's sold over three million copies of her books.

Shalini lives by the sea in Dorset, England, with her husband, two children and their increasingly demanding dog, Queen Jess. Before kids, she was signed to Universal Music Publishing as a singer/songwriter, but now she spends her days writing (in between restocking the fridge and dealing with endless baskets of laundry).

She is also the author of two bestselling sci-fi and fantasy series as well as a WWII evacuee adventure with a time-travel twist.

When she's not reading, writing or stomping along the beach, you can reach her via Facebook at www.facebook.com/ShaliniBolandAuthor, on TikTok @shaliniboland, on Bluesky @shaliniboland.bsky.social, on X @ShaliniBoland, on Instagram @shaboland, or via her website: www.shaliniboland.com.

Visit Shalini's website to sign up to her newsletter.

Follow the Author on Amazon

If you enjoyed this book, follow Shalini Boland on Amazon to be notified when the author releases a new book!
To do this, please follow these instructions:

Desktop:

1) Search for the author's name on Amazon or in the Amazon App.
2) Click on the author's name to arrive on their Amazon page.
3) Click the 'Follow' button.

Mobile and Tablet:

1) Search for the author's name on Amazon or in the Amazon App.
2) Click on one of the author's books.
3) Click on the author's name to arrive on their Amazon page.
4) Click the 'Follow' button.

Kindle eReader and Kindle App:

If you enjoyed this book on a Kindle eReader or in the Kindle App, you will find the author 'Follow' button after the last page.